Praise for
VEIL OF ROSES

"Evocative, poignant, and truly lovely. Laura Fitzgerald
gives us a glimpse of a culture that's terrifyingly different—
and yet heartbreakingly the same as our own. *Veil of Roses*
is going on my keeper shelf."
—Alesia Holliday, author of *Seven Ways*
to Lose Your Lover

"After picking up *Veil of Roses,* I did everything
one-handed for two days, I was so unwilling to put it down.
Charming and heartbreaking and hopeful and funny, this is
the rare book that completely transports the reader.
Laura Fitzgerald is an amazing talent."
—Lani Diane Rich, author of *The Comeback Kiss*

"Poignant and warm, *Veil of Roses* is a story about having
hope, finding love and embracing freedom. I loved it."
—Whitney Gaskell, author of *Testing Kate*

"Romantic fish-out-of-water debut with a feminist
undertone."—*Kirkus Reviews*

Veil of Roses

Laura Fitzgerald

BANTAM BOOKS

VEIL OF ROSES
A Bantam Book / January 2007

Published by Bantam Dell
A Division of Random House, Inc.
New York, New York

This is a work of fiction. Names, characters, places, and incidents
either are the product of the author's imagination or are used
fictitiously. Any resemblance to actual persons, living or dead,
events, or locales is entirely coincidental.

Book design by Karin Batten

Bantam Books and the rooster colophon are registered
trademarks of Random House, Inc.

Library of Congress Cataloging-in-Publication Data
Fitzgerald, Laura, 1967–
Veil of roses /Laura Fitzgerald.
p.   cm.
ISBN-13: 978-0-553-38388-1 (trade pbk.)
1. Iranians—United States—Fiction.   2. Self-actualization
(Psychology)—Fiction.   3. Women—Fiction.   I. Title.
PS3606.I88V45 2007
813'.6—dc22
2006023617

Printed in the United States of America
Published simultaneously in Canada

www.bantamdell.com

BVG   20 19

This book is dedicated to
the women of Iran.

And to Farhad.
Duset daram, Farhad Joon.
And your feets, too!

Acknowledgments

My first thanks goes to the Bantam Dell Publishing Group, in particular: Danielle Perez, Micahlyn Whitt, Nita Taublib, and Patricia Ballantyne. I would also like to thank Wendy McCurdy and Erica Orden for their early support of the book. This story is so much richer for the involvement of so many at Bantam.

I am appreciative to Lani Diane Rich, a great friend and writer, whose enthusiasm and support for my writing has been steadfast. She went first, paved the way for me, and continues to share her learnings. I suspect I'll never meet a writer as generous as Lani.

Huge thanks go to Stephanie Kip Rostan, my agent at the Levine Greenberg Literary Agency, not only for finding this book the perfect home, but for providing her big-picture perspective and always direct editorial feedback. My gratitude also goes to Beth Fisher, Melissa Rowland, and Monika Verma.

Heartfelt thanks: to Meg Files and my Wednesday-night writing classmates, especially Jason Shults; to Michelle, for the sometimes-fresh coffee and always wonderful brainstorming sessions; to both my close and extended family, who expressed only enthusiasm for this book; to Sherry & Todd, Alex & Nanette, Mike & Ilene, Lisa in Tosa, Terri in Boston, and Susan in Hilo—great friends, all. Your confidence in me means so much. And finally, thanks to the members of my own homeland—Farhad, Carly, and Luke. (Carly, I hope this book proves to you for once and for all that your mom *really is* a writer, not a wronger!)

VEIL
OF
ROSES

1

As I walk past the playground on my way to downtown Tucson, I overhear two girls teasing a third: *Jake and Ella sitting in a tree. K-I-S-S-I-N-G. First comes love, then comes marriage, then comes a baby in a baby carriage!*

Curious, I stop mid-stride and turn my attention to Ella, the redheaded girl getting teased. She looks forward to falling in love; I can see it by the coyness in the smile on her freckled nine-year-old face. I shake my head in wonder, in open-mouthed awe. I think, as I so often do: *This would never happen in Iran.*

None of it. Nine-year-old girls in Iran do not shout gleefully on playgrounds, in public view of passersby. They do not draw attention to themselves; they do not go to school with boys. They do not swing their long red hair and expect with Ella's certainty that romantic love is in their future. And they do not, not, *not* sing of sitting in trees with boys, kissing, and producing babies. In the Islamic Republic of Iran, there is nothing innocent about a moment such as this.

And so I quickly lift the Pentax K1000 that hangs from my neck and snap a series of pictures. This is what I hope to capture with my long-range lens: Front teeth only half grown in. Ponytails. Bony knees. Plaid skirts, short plaid skirts. That neon-pink Band-Aid on Ella's bare arm. I blur out the boys in the background and keep my focus only on these girls and the way their white socks fold down to their ankles. The easiness of their smiles. They are so unburdened, these girls, so fortunate as to take their good fortune for granted.

Ella sees me taking pictures and nudges the others, so I lower my camera, wave to them, and give them my biggest, best pretty-lady smile, one I know from experience causes people to smile back. And sure enough, they do. I wave one last time and then I walk on. I am changed already, from just this little moment. These fearless girls have entranced me, and I know that when I study my photographs of these recess girls, I will look for clues as to what sort of women they will become.

I hope they find romantic love. And passionate kisses, and men who look at them with eyes that see all the way into their souls. Then I know they will be happy, and I know they will be whole.

First comes love, then comes marriage. A childhood chant, a cultural expectation. Americans believe in falling in love with every fiber of their being. They believe it is their birthright; certainly, that it is a prerequisite for marriage. This is not so where I was raised. In the Islamic Republic of Iran, marriages are often still negotiated between families with a somewhat businesslike quality. In most modern families, girls have some say in the matter. They can discourage suitors, or, as I did, delay marriage by seeking a university degree.

It isn't that Iranian men necessarily make bad husbands. Like my dear father, many are kind and gentle and interested in their wives as people, not just bearers of their children. Then again, some are not. There are family teas, gift-givings, and dinners, but a woman often spends no time alone with her fiancé before her wedding. So it is, as one might say in America, a crapshoot. A woman goes into her husband's family in a white gown and she leaves it only in a white shroud, in death.

That is our culture.

And that is our future, inescapable for most girls.

Inescapable, it had begun to seem, even for me.

On the occasion of my twenty-seventh birthday, my parents hosted a celebration dinner for me in their fine north Tehran apartment. We typically do not celebrate birthdays in a large fashion, but it had been a troublesome time for me and they hoped to bring me happiness. In only my fourth year of teaching, I'd recently resigned my position, against the advice of my parents. And this after I'd dreamed so long of being a teacher, a teacher of young girls. Increasingly since I'd begun, I suffered stabbing headaches, murderous stomachaches. My constitution simply wasn't strong enough to bear the demands of being a teacher of young girls in a religious regime.

Once I resigned, my physical ailments diminished, but so did my world. I rarely left home; the streets were hostile and I had no destination, no dreams, to carry me forward. Not yet twenty-seven, I felt the weariness of someone who'd lived one hundred joyless years. I fell into a horrible depression.

My dear parents must have suspected my desperation, for they gathered together all the people I loved for a grand birthday celebration, all the people they knew could make me laugh. There were Minu and Leila, my dear friends from university with whom I'd giggled my way through, spending hours at Leila's house dancing to bootleg videos of Siavesh concerts. There were Mehrshad and Roxanna, my father's brother and his wife; and, most important, Ali and Homa Karmoni, whose friendship with my parents was unquestionably the stroke of grace that made their lives in Iran bearable. The roots of their friendship ran long and deep. *Ali Agha* hired my father as an engineer way back when not many would consider hiring him because of his Western ways, and *Ali Agha* had guarded my father's job ever since. Besides that, we vacationed with them and celebrated holidays with them and treated them as if they were our own family.

They had one adored son, Reza, twelve years older than me. He'd been living in London for a long time, although *Homa Khanoum* kept me apprised of his doings.

"You know, *Agha Reza* returns from London next month," she announced on this night as we gathered around a *sofreh* in our dining room and ate a celebration dinner of lamb kebab and saffron rice. "He has accepted a job at the Free University and is ready to settle down and be married. A professor, you know."

I felt Minu and Leila's eyes on me, but I averted my gaze from them and smiled politely at *Homa Khanoum*. I tried to hide my heavy heart, tried to suppress the instant realization that this, then, is how it would happen. I no longer had to wonder. I was cocooned in my father's house with no job and no other marriage prospects. My parents loved *Agha Reza* as if he were their own son.

This, then, is how it would happen. I would go into their house in a white gown, as Reza's wife, and I would leave it only in a white shroud. And in between, my world would remain so small.

So painfully, so suffocatingly . . . small.

Shortly before dawn, the party ended. The women rubbed off their makeup, cloaked their beautiful party clothes under their manteaux, and tucked their coiffed hair under their headscarves. My mother, my father, and I kissed each guest upon both cheeks. We warned them, *Be careful, watch for the roadblocks, and remember, please please remember, if stopped by the* bassidjis *do not say where it was you drank the home-made beer. And do you think perhaps you should spend the night?* But no, no. It was time to brave their way from the safeness of our home into the dark Tehran night, out onto the public streets, where bad things could happen and often did.

When finally they were out the door, my father pushed it closed with both hands and leaned his forehead against it for a long moment.

"Baba?" I asked. "Is something wrong?"

He instantly turned to me. "I remember when I turned twenty-seven," he said with a half smile. "My world was filled with much happiness and hope for the future. Do you remember, Azar, the year we turned twenty-seven?"

"Of course," my mother answered. She stood off to the side and shifted nervously. "Of course."

This would have been when they lived in America, I knew. My father studied as a graduate student at the University of California at Berkeley in the 1970s. In a decision he's regretted for the rest of his days, he brought his family back to Iran for an extended visit during the tumultuous days immediately after the Shah was deposed and Ayatollah Khomeini returned from exile. We got stuck during the clampdown that followed, and my father has never been able to secure for himself permission to leave the country. He, an educated man who's seen a successful democracy in action, who believes deeply in the doctrine of separation between church and state, is destined to live out his years in a repressive religious regime. There are many men like my father in Iran. I lived in America from the time I was an infant until shortly after my second birthday. I remember none of it, of course. All I have are stories handed down by my parents and my sister, Maryam, who is eight years my elder.

"Your mother and I have a present for you, *Tami Joon*." My father loves giving presents. It must have been hard for him to delay giving it to me until after the party. He would have been thinking of it all night long.

"What is it?" I returned his smile.

He nodded at my mother, and she disappeared into their bedroom to retrieve the gift. My father clapped his hands together and blew on them as if he were outdoors in front of our house on a chilly Tehran morning, scraping frost off the windshield and waiting for the engine to warm up so he could drive to his job as a transportation engineer for the city. But he was not outside. He was inside, and our home was toasty warm, and my stomach fluttered with the sudden suspicion that this would be no idle gift.

My mother returned a moment later with a plain white box of about twelve square inches. She handed it to my father and took her place next to him. She wrung her hands together and bit her bottom lip and looked at me in a way I shall never forget. It was a look of pride and excitement and fear all rolled into one.

"Here, open it." My father thrust the box at me.

I stepped forward and accepted it with shaky hands. I lifted the lid and returned it to my mother's outstretched hand. I looked warily at the top layer of tissue paper before peeling it out of the way.

"Is this my . . . ?" I caught myself. Of course it could not be the same; that gift was tucked away in my bureau, underneath a stack of silk *hejab*. That gift had not been mentioned in years, and I had thought it was all but forgotten.

I lifted the blue porcelain perfume bottle from the box. I looked quizzically at my father. He nodded. *Yes, Tamila. It's what you think.*

My eyes filled with tears as I set the box on the foyer table and twisted the lid off the perfume bottle so I could smell it again. So I could see it again. So I could remember the first time I had received this very same gift.

It had been on my fifth birthday. My father, so much younger then, pulled me into his lap and handed me this same rounded perfume bottle. It was my mother's, the one that always sat upon the tray on her dressing table. I loved it. I especially loved squeezing the little spritzer on those special occasions when she allowed me to spray rosewater on the soft undersides of her wrists, which she would rub together and hold up for my little nose's approval. I thought it was a fine gift. A wonderful, grown-up gift for a girl who adored her mother like I did mine.

But when I raised the perfume bottle to my nose and inhaled, I wrinkled my child's nose in confusion and felt my smile leave my face. It was not like my father, my beloved *Baba Joon,* to make a mean joke, but after carefully twisting off the spritzer and discovering it contained only sand, I had to press my lips together and will myself not to show disrespect by letting tears spill from my eyes.

My father pulled me close and kissed my forehead. "My beautiful Tamila, this is not just any sand." He took my hand and stroked the back of it with his thumb, his lullaby to me.

"This," he said reverently, "is sand from *America*. I brought it back with my own hands to give to my beautiful *Tamila Joon* on her fifth birthday, so she can keep it safe and know that when she is older, she has a special job to do. She is to take this sand and return it to where it belongs. She is to return it to *America*."

My mother's gentle voice drew me out of my reverie. "Tami."

I looked to her, met her gaze. "There's more in the box," she prompted me, and handed it back. She no longer bit her lip. She no longer wrung her hands. Instead, she looked at me with a steadiness I rarely see in her. I felt my hope rising, and this frightened me, for in Iran hope is seldom fulfilled and nearly always suffocated. It is a dangerous thing, for an Iranian girl to allow herself to hope.

My father was unable to contain his impatience. "Take it out," he ordered, stepping closer as if to force me if I hesitated any longer.

I braced myself and peeled back the next layer of tissue paper. I gasped. *Was it really, could it be, yes, it was!* I gaped at my father. He broke into a broad, proud grin.

In the bottom of the box was a passport.

For me.

A passport for me! There was also a one-way airplane ticket out of Iran to Turkey, and from there I was to obtain a visa and ticket to the country of my parents' dreams.

He'd done it.

My father was saving me.

He was sending me to America.

"How did you . . . ?" I began to ask in wonder, but my

father waved my question away. He'd done it. That's all I needed to know.

"But what about...?" I looked searchingly into my father's eyes. *What about* Agha Reza, I wanted to ask. *What about him and the marriage proposal that seems to be coming?* But I stopped myself. There was nothing of *Agha Reza* in his eyes.

"Thank you, *Baba Joon.* Oh, thank you so much!" I threw my arms around him.

"Shh, shh." He quieted my sobs, rocked me back and forth. "This is your chance. You go to America and make us proud."

I stepped back, nodded at him, made sure he saw the resolve in my eyes. I would. I would do everything in my power to make them proud of me. I turned then to my mother, and we pulled each other close.

"I'll miss you so much, *Maman Joon.*"

"I love you, *Tami Joon,*" she whispered in my ear. "I love you so, so much. And know that it's a beautiful, beautiful world out there." She choked on her words and did not speak again until she had regained her steadiness. She pulled back from my embrace to grip my forearms, to capture my gaze. "Go and wake up your luck," she commanded me. "Promise me you will."

I looked back at her, and for a moment, this is what I saw: America. Her America. My mother, my mother's younger self, firmly rooted in California's rich soil.

Long ago, she gave me some pictures from our time in America. I consider them my most treasured possessions.

There is one of me eating French fries at McDonald's, sitting on my father's lap. There is one of me being pushed from behind on a baby swing by Maryam at the children's playground at Golden Gate Park. There is one of me naked in the Pacific Ocean, running from the cold waves and squealing in delight.

There is another from that day at the ocean.

In this one, I am wearing a pink one-piece swimsuit with a big yellow daisy in the middle. My mother holds me. My legs are wrapped around her waist, and my head rests on her shoulder. A wave washes over her feet. She looks straight into the eye of the camera. My mother's skin is tanned, her long hair windblown. She knows nothing yet of segregated beaches and confiscated passports and shrouding oneself from the sun's warmth and men's eyes. All she knows is the beauty of this day. She wears cutoff denim shorts and a pink bikini top. She wears big gold hoop earrings and bright red lipstick. Red nail polish, too. Remarkably beautiful, she looks so happy. So happy and so free.

This is not the mother I know. The mother I know has always worn *hejab,* has always covered herself in the regime's mandated head covering. She has always ducked her head and averted her eyes when passing men in the street. I do not remember the carefree, unburdened mother in the picture at all, but I miss her every day of my life, even so. The mother I know has always been sad.

The sun. The waves. The sound of the ocean. The sexy confidence of a bikini top and cutoff shorts highlighting the strong-muscled legs of an able woman. Bare feet. The wind dancing through her hair. She remembers it all. And she wants it for me. I am her dream deferred.

"I promise, *Maman Joon,*" I whisper back. "I promise I will go and wake up my luck."

And then I grasp her to me and I cling to her because I miss her so much already, my sad mother who smells of rose-water. I try to memorize this moment, this embrace. I will need to carry it in my heart forever. I will need to be brave, for her.

For I am not coming back.

• • •

Three weeks later, that little perfume bottle filled with sand from the shores of San Francisco Bay is packed safely in my luggage. I am on an airplane, leaving my homeland behind. When the pilot announces we have left Iranian airspace, a cheer breaks out. Women on the flight unbuckle their seat belts and stand. They look around. They yank off their head-scarves and run their fingers through their hair. They have left Iran, and the future is theirs, to make of it what they will. I remain quietly in my seat and watch them. I think of my mother. My chest is so tight I cannot breathe.

I watch the flight attendants serve peanuts and offer drinks, now that we've left the boundary of our country, where alcohol is illegal. One approaches me. He smiles and asks if I would like a glass of wine. This startles me, the fact that he is looking at me as if there is nothing wrong with an unrelated man and woman looking each other in the eye and chatting casually. In public, no less. And, of course, there *is* nothing wrong with it. It just doesn't happen where I am from.

And so I take a deep breath. I reach up and fiddle with the knot under my chin, and then I pull off my *hejab*. I press it into my lap, as far away from me as possible.

He nods at me in approval. In affirmation of what I have done. I look right in his friendly tea-brown eyes. Strange as it feels, I do not look away.

"Yes, please." I nod back.

I want the peanuts. I want the wine. I want to look into the eyes of a man and feel no shame.

My name is Tamila Soroush.

And I want it all.

2

It is twenty-four hours since I left Iran, since I clutched my parents to me at Mehrabad Airport and we wept our good-byes. After three plane changes on three different continents, I am now ten minutes from Tucson, Arizona, where I am to depart the plane and meet Maryam.

And it is clear to me that the plane is going to crash.

It drops suddenly. Little bells ding politely but insistently, and the airplane attendants scurry to buckle themselves in. Their faces look nonchalant, but I know they are trained to put their faces this way in times of crisis. A man's voice comes on over the loudspeaker. His English is fast and garbled, and although I have studied English all my years in school and my father spoke practically nothing but fast and garbled English to me for the past three weeks in preparation for my journey, the pilot's words are too run together for me to make out what he's saying. Perhaps he's telling everyone to say their final prayers. I grip my hands on the armrests and begin a soft chant to myself: *"Baad chanse ma, Baad chanse ma."*

"Excuse me," the woman next to me says, slowly and with careful enunciation. She has joined this flight from Phoenix. "Is that Arabic you're speaking?" She wears a black T-shirt that says *Power Corrupts* in bold silver letters. She would receive forty lashes on her back for wearing this shirt in Iran. Forty lashes at the very least.

I shake my head. "It's Farsi."

"I thought so. I lived with a Persian guy for a while. Was that a prayer you were saying?"

I give her a rueful smile. The plane is clearly not going to crash. We'd just hit an air pocket. "I was a little frightened from the . . . mmm . . . how do you say, *turbulence*. I was saying how my bad luck follows me all the way around the world." I watch her to see if she is able to understand me or if I'll need to repeat myself. I really don't know how good my English is, and I feel myself blush. It could be just awful.

But perhaps not, because she gets an excited look in her eyes and turns more fully to me. "You're *just* coming from Iran?"

I nod.

"That's awesome! Do you have family here?"

I nod again. "My sister lives here with her husband."

Maryam has lived in the United States for almost fifteen years, ever since she married an orthopedic surgeon named Ardishir. On his yearly visits to Tehran to see his mother, he began courting my sister. My parents were proud he was a surgeon. That means a lot in my culture. But he was only a resident of the United States, not a citizen. That was not good enough. My parents would not permit the marriage until he obtained his U.S. citizenship, for then he could take my sister back with him to America and sponsor her for citizenship.

"How long are you staying?" Her smile is so friendly, I do not mind all the questions. Everyone in America smiles big and talks a lot. I have seen this in the movies.

"I am moving here."

"Really? How did you manage that?"

My heart pounds. I feel myself blush. I tuck my hair behind my ears. I feel like I am lying. But it is true. I *am* moving here.

"I am getting married," I say, as confidently as I can. I smile, knowing happiness is expected with such a statement.

"Congratulations! Did you meet him back in Iran, then?"

I shake my head, swallow hard. "I have not met him yet."

"Oh," my seatmate says. Her broad smile falters and her eyes darken. "An arranged marriage?"

"Yes," I say. "In my culture, it is not so unusual."

"How do you feel about that?"

How do I feel about that? What, I want to ask, does that have to do with anything? I am here on a three-month visa. The sole purpose of my trip is to find a way to stay, and that means I must find a husband who will sponsor my application for residency. The choice is marriage here or marriage there, and for me this is an easy choice. Being married is a small price to pay if it means I can stay in the Land of Opportunity and raise my children, my daughters, in the freedom that would be denied them in Iran.

"Americans only get married if they are in love," I tell my seatmate. "But in my culture, we try to choose someone we can grow to love over time."

"Wow, I can't imagine that." She shakes her head, but suddenly laughs. "But then again, I've been divorced twice already and I'm not even forty. Who's to say yours isn't the better way?"

My eyes get big. I cannot help it. Divorced, twice! She must be the black sheep of her family, to have behaved so badly that not one but two men divorced her. This is why she is so chatty. This is why she talks to strangers on airplanes. Everyone else probably shuns her.

She grins at my shock. "But I'll tell you what. That Persian boyfriend I lived with for a while? He was better in bed than both my husbands put together. He was *fan-tastic*. Maybe that's a cultural thing, too." She shakes her head at the memory. "*Mmmm-hmmm*, the things he could do with his tongue."

The plane jerks to the ground. The rough landing prevents me from having to respond. I am stunned and horribly embarrassed by what she has said. I make myself busy gathering my things as the airplane taxis to the gate.

"Can you find your way out okay?" she asks.

"Yes, yes," I assure her, not wanting my sister to see me with such a *badjen*, a disreputable woman. "Thank you very much for your kindness."

"Take care, then," she says, unbuckling her seat belt and pulling herself up before the plane has even come to a full stop. She grabs her backpack and heads to the front of the plane. I watch her walk away. She is the first American woman that I've spoken to at any length. I know I will remember her forever. She was friendly, and she was crazy.

And I can't even begin to imagine what her Persian boyfriend did with his tongue that made her so happy.

Although it has been fifteen years since I have last seen Maryam, my terror at seeing her again causes me to linger, so that I am the last one off the airplane. And when I do depart the plane, I hear her high, happy voice before I see her.

"Tami! Tami!" she shrieks. "Oh, oh! Over here, *Tami Joon!*"

I turn my head toward the voice, and my heart melts as a blur I understand to be Maryam grabs me and kisses me on both cheeks before enfolding me in her arms. Pressed against me, Maryam curls my hair around her fingers. I'd forgotten how she used to do that when we were children in the bedroom we shared for many years. That's how she used to wake me up in the mornings, by weaving her fingers through my hair and singing to me. I laugh with relief and start to cry and hug her back very tightly.

"Shhh," she says softly, smoothing my hair. "Don't cry. We don't want your eyes all puffy and red."

When she steps back and takes my face within her hands, when she gives me another kiss upon both cheeks, I gasp. "You are so beautiful! How did this happen?!"

Her black eyes sparkle, delighted. "Everyone is beautiful in America, *Tami Joon.*"

It is all I can do not to gape at her. Maryam has always had appealing features, but she has a beauty I have not seen before. She has lost her baby fat and toned her muscles and grown her hair long. It falls halfway down her back in perfect, shiny waves. She wears gold, gold, and more gold—earrings, a necklace, two bracelets. In Iran, gold jewelry is how women show off, revealed at parties after coming inside and shedding the headscarf—*hejab*—and manteau we must wear when outdoors to keep the low-class *bassidji* goons from harassing us.

Here, Maryam openly wears her gold. Her face has laugh lines where before was only smoothness. She wears bright pink lipstick, gold eye shadow. Copied from a magazine model, most likely. That's how she practiced back home. Most different is her chest—this is not the same chest she had when she left Iran.

"Oy, Maryam! What is this? Did you take some special vitamins to make yourself grow in all the right places?" She is my sister; I can ask her.

She laughs, delighted by my naïveté. "They're not *real*, Tami. I enhanced them last year. They call it a boob job." She giggles at the words. A *boob job*, this is unheard of where I am from. It would serve no purpose. Nose jobs, sure. They are all the rage, for noses are the one operable, changeable, *fixable* feature of ours that men actually see. The rest of us remains cloaked anytime we are in public.

I question whether Ardishir approved of Maryam's boob job.

"Approved?" She laughs harder. "Who do you think paid for it?"

I realize now, while looking at her new boobs, that while I may have come halfway around the world, what I have truly done is enter a whole new universe.

"Did it hurt?"

"Not so much." She shrugs. "It's what women do here, especially if their husbands have some money. If they are married to doctors or rich men who own businesses, for instance."

She puts her arm around my shoulder and turns me away from the gate. Toward the exit, toward my future. "Don't worry, if we have a hard time finding you a husband, we'll get you one, too. I'm sure Ardishir will pay for it."

This idea horrifies me.

"I do not want Ardishir buying me new boobs!" This is not something my parents told me about, the need for new boobs.

"You'll do whatever it takes, Tami," she laughs. But when she sees that I am near tears, Maryam pulls me toward her and reassures me with a hug. Then she stands back and strokes my cheek. She adds, quietly, "I don't ever want my sister to be so far away again. So we'll do what it takes, right?"

I swallow and nod. "Right. You're right, of course."

Maryam holds up a bag from Macy's. She is a manager there; my father tells this to everyone he knows. "I brought you some things to change into. There's about thirty people waiting for us back at the house."

"*Here?* You want me to change my clothes *here,* in a public toilet?" I think back to all the times I was forbidden from using the filthy ones back home.

She nods. "Just try not to touch anything."

I have been traveling for one whole day and two whole nights, and I haven't slept for more than three hours in a row. I do not want to enter a public toilet, on this, my first night in America. And I do not want a party. "Ay, Maryam," I groan. "I am so tired. I don't know if I'll be able to keep my eyes open at this party."

"I'm sorry," she says. "But we expected you much earlier. I couldn't call everyone and cancel. It would have been rude. Besides, there's a dentist who will be there whose family we know. He lives in California and has to go back tomorrow. His mother says he is ready to be married."

A pushy Persian, that's my sister. She has always been this way, and I do not have the energy on this night to argue. She promised to my parents that she would find me a good Iranian husband with American citizenship, and she will keep this promise. Starting this very night.

I remind myself to be grateful. She is my sister, and her intentions are good. So I let her slip a form-fitting red dress with a deep V-neck over me. I let her put so much makeup on me that I barely recognize myself in the mirror. I let her spray something in my hair that she says will make it curlier and bouncier. I let her put my feet into open-toed sandals with three-inch heels. I let her polish my toenails. This alone makes me smile, to see my toes so colorful and happy. Everything else terrifies me. Excites me? Yes, I admit that. After a lifetime of living under a cloak, I am ready to dress up all fancy. Just on my own terms, not those of my sister.

And after a lifetime spent trying not to be noticed in the streets, it feels very dangerous to have strangers stare at me. And yet stare they do.

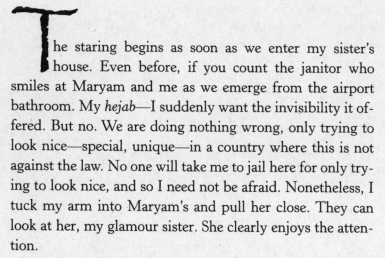

3

The staring begins as soon as we enter my sister's house. Even before, if you count the janitor who smiles at Maryam and me as we emerge from the airport bathroom. My *hejab*—I suddenly want the invisibility it offered. But no. We are doing nothing wrong, only trying to look nice—special, unique—in a country where this is not against the law. No one will take me to jail here for only trying to look nice, and so I need not be afraid. Nonetheless, I tuck my arm into Maryam's and pull her close. They can look at her, my glamour sister. She clearly enjoys the attention.

After we gather my luggage and step outside to the parking lot, I take my first fresh breath of air in what feels like forever. I look up at the sky in wonder. Even the stars are different here. They are brighter and in formations I do not recognize. I should have expected this, but I am startled to realize that even the heavens here are not the same. I have to take a slow, deep breath to adjust.

"It's very different, isn't it?" Maryam's voice is gentle.

I nod, for my throat is too tight from homesickness to answer. I should have sketched the stars above our home in Tehran. I must ask my mother to draw me a picture, and in return I shall draw her one of my sky here. At least we will always look at the same moon, *Maman Joon* and me. This is how I soothe myself. I breathe in the cool desert air. It is good, all good. The air in Tehran is bad to breathe. It is thick with pollution and dust. Here, it is crisp, as if we were high in the Alborz Mountains.

"Wait until morning when it's light out," Maryam tells me. "Remember those old John Wayne westerns *Baba Joon* always watched when we were little?"

I nod.

"Well, they were all filmed right here in this area, and it looks just like it does in the old westerns. You won't find cactus like this anywhere else in the world. And the sky. You'll never see a sky so blue. There are no clouds here, Tami."

"You like it, then?" I murmur.

"I love it," she tells me. "Iran is no place for women. America, it is for everyone."

I look ahead of me into the darkness and try to imagine the daylight. "The land of the free," I whisper, hearing in my words the echo of my father's voice.

"And the home of the brave," Maryam adds while she squeezes me to her. "You are my brave little sister, to come all this way alone."

"You came all this way," I remind her.

"Yes, but I had Ardishir."

"And I have you."

I know right away which car in the mostly empty parking lot is Maryam's. In Iran, most people drive the same cars they had before the revolution and can only dream of driving a new shiny-gold Mercedes-Benz like Maryam's. It is a *pooldar* car, a status symbol like none other.

While she drives, Maryam chatters away about Tucson, the weather, the neighborhood she lives in, the English conversation class I am enrolled in and which starts next Monday. I try to pay attention to her, I really do, but I am trying to recognize this woman sitting next to me, trying to understand once and for all that this is my sister. My Maryam. That I am with her once again. She was my lifeline back in Iran, the only spot of sunshine in my perpetually overcast household. And she left me. She married Ardishir at the first chance she got, and she did not have the decency to even pretend she would miss Iran.

"Hello, Tami!" she laughs. "You're a million miles away!"

"Do you think you'll ever go back and visit *Maman Joon* and Baba?" I pause and watch her jaw clench. "You should hear how they brag about you! You have made them so very proud. You'll visit one day, won't you?"

Maryam keeps her eyes on the road. "Sure I will," she says softly. "Sure I will, one day."

"I'm sure you're very busy here," I offer when I see how sad she's become.

"Oh, totally! I am so busy! My job is really crazy and I don't think Ardishir could manage on his own for very long. You should see that man try to get around a kitchen!"

We share a laugh. As it fades, she turns and appraises me. "You're really grown up, aren't you?"

"I guess so. Grown up enough to get married, anyway."

She smiles at me sympathetically. "Don't worry. You'll

like being married. It's not at all like it is in Iran." She reaches out to squeeze my hand. "Wouldn't it be wonderful if we found a husband for you on your very first night here! Then *Maman Joon* and Baba would really be proud!"

"What's he like, this man at the party? What's his name?"

"Mohammed Behruzi."

"His family is from where?"

"Tabriz. But they've been here forever."

"You know them how?"

"Ardishir knows his mother from having performed surgery on her knee."

"He is how old?"

"Thirty-eight, I think."

That's old. Not in terms of the age difference in a typical Iranian marriage, but in terms of how much more life than me he's gotten to live before having to think about marriage. He got to go to college, establish a career, perhaps travel to foreign lands. I smother the flame of envy that rises in my chest when I think this thought.

"Here it is," Maryam says as we make our last turn onto a street called Calle Splendida. She slows the car.

"*This* is your house?"

Maryam nods proudly. I am in total awe, total shock. It is very beautiful, very rich. And very open. Spotlights show off the house's design, which Maryam has told me is plantation style. There are balconies and shutters, green grass and a tall wrought-iron fence surrounding the property. But still, anyone can see in. And it is clear there is a party going on. The curtains are not drawn, and I can see men and women mingling. I can hear the sound of Googoosh's voice all the way to the street.

"If the police drove by right now," I ask, my heart racing, "what would they do?"

"Nothing, Tami. There's nothing wrong with this. It's only a party."

· Only a party. How many times I have said this back home. Twice, I attended parties that were raided. Twice, my friends and I were hauled to the police station and harassed for being with men who weren't our husbands and for not being veiled in their presence. Leila even spent two nights in jail. Never mind that we were behind high walls, behind closed doors, and behind drawn curtains.

And this...America. Can it really be so open? Everything feels surreal, most especially the fact that I am here at all. That this house, this open life, is in front of me. That I am soon to walk inside, and it will, for a time, become my home, too.

Maryam parks on the street. I get out and stand on the sidewalk, not taking my eyes off the house, off the obvious celebration inside, for even one instant. She opens the gate, and we step onto the path leading to the house.

"Everyone will be so glad to see you," she tells me. "I know Mohammed will like you. I just *know* it."

The sound of the jet engines that have been roaring in my ears finally begins to fade. All I hear are the sounds of the misters watering the lawn. I hate the thought of going inside to a loud, crazy Persian party.

"Can we wait a minute, please? I just need to get my bearings first." I bend down and unhook one sandal strap, then tentatively reach my bare foot toward the grass. I squeal as the night mist tickles my toes. I think, *So this is what bare feet on wet grass feels like.* Surely, when we lived in Berkeley I would have run about barefoot, so I must have felt this before. But I was too young to have captured the memory.

But coming back from America, Maryam would have remembered. She was very young—still a girl—at the time. *No wonder she left again at the first opportunity.* She remembered, and I did not.

I look at her spotlighted house. I look at the people dancing on the other side of the windows, those festive Persians, with their lack of fear, with their arms in the air, weaving their hands to the beat. All the *might I*'s, the *can I*'s, the *will I be able to*'s—I look at the spotlighted house and I look at the people inside and I know that the answer to all of my half-formed questions, my half-formed desires is *yes,* I might. I can. I will be able to.

"Feels good, doesn't it, *Tami Joon?*" I look over at Maryam. She shows by her smile that she understands what life must have been like for me these past years. The repression, the shrinking world, but mostly the loneliness. I nod through the tears that have filled my eyes.

She knows what I have been through. She knows me.

"Shh, shh, shh," she calms me, and gives me a quick, energetic hug. "Let's go. None of this. Are you ready to meet everyone?"

I take a deep breath and nod.

"Are you scared?"

"A little."

"Just smile a lot, that's all you have to do. Here." She slicks one last layer of lipstick over my lips. "Everybody's really nice. And you look beautiful. Mohammed's going to love you. And if he doesn't, he's a fool."

"Keep your shoes on for a little while," Maryam whispers to me after we slip inside. "Just stand here. I want Mohammed to see you in them."

So I stand there feeling foolish for several minutes. First I am greeted by Ardishir, who comes to me and kisses me on both cheeks. He has always been so kind, has always treated me as a younger sister from the moment he began courting

Maryam. "I see Maryam has worked her magic." He grins. "You look very nice."

"Thank you," I reply. "I am not used to dressing like this in public. It feels very strange."

"You're safe here," he assures me and extends his arm. "Come on in, I'll introduce you around."

He wears only socks on his feet, and I can tell from the rows of shoes neatly lined up in the foyer that everyone else is shoeless, too, as is custom.

"I can't. Maryam says I must wait here for Mohammed so he can see me in my fancy shoes."

Ardishir shakes his head at my sister and smiles. "I'll go find him, then."

Maryam and I continue to stand at the doorway, and I can see from the gold-edged mirror that the other guests are sneaking glimpses of me. I smile and try not to look scared.

At last, Ardishir and Mohammed come to the doorway. I size up Mohammed with my eyes, and I see him give me a quick up-and-down of my face, dress, and feet. He does not look too intently, and neither does he look impressed. When he sticks out his hand for me to shake, I stand still and feel my face redden. This is not considered polite. This is not how it is done in Iran, for him to offer his hand first. As the moment becomes unbearably awkward, Maryam nudges me.

"It's okay, Tami," she says in a light tone and nods toward his hand. I shake it tentatively and want very much to pull away from its frail delicacy. "She's just off the plane, you know," she tells Mohammed. "She's still used to how things are done in Iran."

It looks to me like Mohammed hides a sneer under his polite, apologetic expression as he replies, "She dresses so American that I suppose I thought she'd act like one, too."

I know then that I do not like him. I know I will not marry him, and I know this night will be interminably long.

Finally, I am allowed to take off my shoes and enter the house. It reminds me of an opulent home in Iran, like those belonging to older men who were in positions of importance with the Shah's government. All the walls are white, mostly bare except for the occasional rug displayed. Gold-plated fruit dishes adorn the tables, with grapes and apricots and dates piled high. Persian rugs of high thread counts are draped across every available spot in the ample living room. There is a huge television in the room, larger than any I've seen in my whole life, and Maryam points out that we are watching an Iranian television station beamed in over satellite from Los Angeles, where half a million Iranians live and they call it Tehrangeles.

I am much more interested in the music playing on the stereo. It is Siavesh, *the* biggest music star in Iran for young people, but because his music is banned there, you can only buy it on the black market. I am tempted for a moment to cry when I think back to how many nights Leila and Minu and I watched his bootleg concert video while dreaming of life in America, where girls are permitted to go to concerts and weep with joy and longing for their favorite heartthrobs, who sing to them of love. *Em-rika, good. Very good.* That's how we said it.

And yet here I am, feeling strangely let down. I hadn't expected that America would be so . . . so Iranian.

My sister takes me around to everyone at the party and introduces me. I smile until the muscles in my face hurt. They all ask what I think of America. *It's good. All good,* I assure them. What more *can* I say? I've gone from an empty airport to an empty road in the middle of the night to a house full of Persians who are related to an unfriendly dentist who seems not to approve of me, when all I really want to do is sleep. I know this is not a polite way to think, but it is what I think nonetheless.

"This is Mrs. Behruzi, Mohammed's mother," my sister says as she leads me to a larger-size woman with sharp brown eyes. Mrs. Behruzi reaches for my hand and encircles it with both of hers. "You are a lovely girl," she says. I thank her. "Your parents, they must be proud of you to come so far."

"Yes," I agree. "They want for me a better life than I could have in Iran."

She questions me about my education, about the friends I have left behind, and about the northern Tehran neighborhood where I was raised. I can see she likes me just fine.

"My son would do well to marry a nice girl like you," she tells me. Then she calls to him across the room, "Mohammed!" His smile is fixed as he makes his way over to us.

In a country where women can show none of their curves and must always cover their hair, there is only one way to show sex appeal, and it is all in the eyes. When Mohammed approaches, I lower my head and present myself as shy, almost too shy to make eye contact. But then I raise my eyes to meet his with a slightly teasing tilt of my head and a tiny smile I seem unable to hide. There is, contained within the glance, an undertone of both submission and sexuality. It is a look Iranian mothers have helped their daughters perfect over the last two decades.

Mohammed's eye twitches when he notices what I am doing. His facial muscles are tight.

"Tamila is the nicest girl," his mother tells him. "Talk with her. Get to know her. You two have a seat on the couch. Go ahead." She waves us away.

Sweat explodes under my arms as I walk ahead of

Mohammed to the couch. He seats himself two cushions away. From the corner of my eye, I see that we are the focus of everyone's attention, although they pretend to ignore us.

"So, did you have a nice trip?"

I nod and smile. "Very nice, thank you."

"Good food on the plane?"

"Yes, very good."

"What did my mother tell you about me?" he asks bluntly.

I swallow. "That you are a good son." She has not even said this. I realize she has said absolutely nothing about him.

"Has she told you I live with my girlfriend, who she refuses to meet because she's not Persian?"

Mohammed's eyes are sharp. Not unkind, I notice. Just resolved.

"No." I want to cry, I am so humiliated. "I did not know this. I am sorry for any problems this meeting has caused you."

"It hasn't caused any problems," he assures me. "I know a good Iranian son is supposed to marry a good Persian woman, and bonus points to him if he helps her move to America. But it's not going to happen with me. If I get married, it'll be to Shelly."

My heart sinks. Not for me, but for him to be placed in such a horrible position. "I understand. I am very happy for you to have found someone you care for."

"Thank you." He is more relaxed now that he has made his intentions, or lack of them, clear to me. "Can I get you anything to eat?"

"No, thank you." All I want to do is slink away and cry. What a bad idea this party was.

"Come on," he urges me. "It will make my mother happy

to see us talking together like friends. I will tell her later that I am engaged to Shelly and not to bother with these silly meetings anymore. I'll be right back."

Mrs. Behruzi gives me a broad smile from across the room. She is a nice woman. I would like a mother-in-law like her. I feel disappointed for her, and for letting down Maryam. I mentally calculate: eighty-eight days left to find a husband. I can only hope I will not have eighty-eight more meetings such as this.

Mohammed brings me a plate of fruit and nuts. He hands it to me, sits back down, and begins eating his own. I murmur my thanks and nibble on a dried apricot. At least my nerves have calmed now that the pressure to impress him is off.

"Can I offer you some advice?" he asks.

"Of course." I am eager for any advice that will help me find a husband and stay in America.

"The Iranians most likely to marry you are going to be the traditional, religious ones. So you shouldn't dress like that." He gestures with his eyes to my low-cut crimson dress.

I feel my face redden. "But I am not so religious."

"Obviously," he says. Again, I detect that sneer just beneath his smile.

"I didn't come all this way to wear a chador." Of that I am certain.

He sees he has offended me and he raises his palms in defense. "I'm just saying, it's something to think about. If a Persian guy with citizenship wants an arranged marriage, it's because he can't find someone here who'll go along with his traditional ways. Think about it. If he wants someone modern, he can find that here with an American girl who has none of the hang-ups Persian women do."

"I see." I let the edge come through in my voice. I place

my plate on the coffee table in front of me and stand. "Thank you for your advice. Please excuse me. I must splash some water on my face. I am so very tired from my flight."

I pass Maryam on the way to the bathroom. She tugs at my arm. "Well? How's it going?"

"He's engaged to an American girl, that's how it's going. His mother is acting on her wishes, not his. Maryam, didn't you know this? I feel so foolish!"

She pulls me in and hugs me. "I'm sorry, Tami. I didn't know."

"And he told me I have hang-ups."

"What?" She is incredulous. "No, you don't!"

"Maybe I do," I tell her wearily.

She purses her lips at me. I know how important it is to my sister that I believe myself worthy of finding a husband in the next eighty-eight days. And I do. Rather, I will. And maybe I will even convince myself that I want one. But not tonight.

"I'm having a hard time keeping my eyes open," I tell her. "Would it be all right for me to rest for a minute in my room?" It is past one o'clock here and I am too tired to calculate what time it is in my native time zone. But knowing Persians, the night is still young and this party has hours to go.

"This party is in your honor." Her voice is firm and her smile fixed. "Why don't you freshen up? Then we'll find some more people to talk to. Maybe someone knows of another man who is interested in marriage."

Yet when I look in the bathroom mirror at my rubbery, made-up face, with my curls drooping, I don't want to go back out there. *You shouldn't dress like that.* The dentist's words burn in my ears. *Persian women have hang-ups.* I cannot, will not, face anyone else judging me on my first night in America. This is supposed to be a happy night, a night of hope. I cross my arms and turn away from the mirror. I take in the opulent bathroom around me. I look longingly at the deep claw-foot bathtub against the far wall. I want to lay myself down into it, curl myself into its deep curves. I *have* to, for just one minute or maybe two. Just until I am ready to face them all again. I gather the plush towels from the towel racks and spread them on the bottom of the bathtub.

I hold up my dress to climb in, and then sink to rest my head on a rolled-up towel. I cannot suppress a sigh of relief. *This* is good, very good. I close my eyes; I cannot fight it.

As I fade off, my slumber is invaded by strange, swirly dreams unlike any I have had before. I dream of low-cut dresses and boob jobs and sneering dentists.

Those are the bad parts of my dream. I also dream of tongues, of men and their tongues. And those parts of my dream are not so bad. But they are very confusing to me.

4

The dentist is the one who finds me in the bathtub. After I am gone awhile, my sister tries the bathroom door, only to find it locked from the inside. Sound asleep, I do not hear her pleas to open the door. Mohammed comes up behind her in the hallway, realizes what has happened, and uses a paper clip to pick the lock. He opens it to find me unconscious in the bathtub.

I am drooling. And snoring.

And my panties are showing.

They are Persian panties, mind you—big, white, all-cotton briefs with a little blue bow in front. Matronly, is how Maryam describes them. When they are unable to rouse me, the dentist and Ardishir haul me to a futon in a nearby guest room. The party continues without me until shortly before dawn.

"You need new underwear," Maryam informs me the next day as I sink my head in horror as she tells me what happened. It is after noon, and we are only now beginning our day.

"I just *got* new underwear."

We are at the kitchen table having tea and fruit and *Sholeh-zard*, exquisite rice pudding made with saffron, which was left over from last night's party. Ardishir raises his newspaper to hide his smile.

"You can't wear underwear like that and expect to find a husband," Maryam insists.

"It's not like anyone's going to see my underwear until after I'm married."

"Mohammed did last night," Ardishir points out.

"Mohammed probably thought they were too sexy for me to attract a good husband," I grumble.

"Hardly," scoffs Maryam. "Those are the least sexy panties I've seen."

I tell them what Mohammed said about me, about my chances of finding a man to marry dressed like I was last night.

"He's crazy!" Maryam waves her bright red nail-polished fingers in the air in indignation. "You looked great. Ardishir, don't you think he's crazy?"

"Yes, dear," he says to her over his newspaper and winks at me.

"Mohammed doesn't respect his parents, that was clear," Maryam declares. "He should marry a Persian girl. That's really the best way. The right way."

This I do not agree with. I think he should marry anyone he wants to. But I sip my tea and say nothing. It is no use to argue with Maryam.

"I think we should go shopping today," Maryam announces. "Ardishir, you don't mind, do you? I'll show Tami what an American shopping mall is like and help her pick out some new, um, some new clothes."

Underwear is what she means.

On the way to the mall, I cannot get over how relaxed the drive is. No one honks at us or makes us swerve to the side. No men jump out of their cars and argue with their fists raised. America is so very civilized when it comes to driving. I fear for my life in the traffic of Tehran, and this is true even when my mild-mannered father drives. Behind the wheel, he becomes as crazy as the rest. Every perceived infraction is an affront to his manhood.

Once at the mall, Maryam and I link arms and walk slowly so I can gawk at everything. There is so much glitter, so much shine. So much skin! Some women even display their belly buttons for all to see! When it comes to sex, Iran and America seem to be complete opposites. Here, everything seems designed to make men think of sex. There, everything is meant to suppress it. Here, young girls don't have to be accompanied by a *mahram*, no brother or uncle or father to protect them from being fooled by a smooth-talking boy. Here, boys and girls hold hands and openly kiss each other. In Iran, even married people do not do this in public.

"Maryam," I ask in wonder, "how do these girls expect to find husbands if they act in this way?"

She laughs at my naïveté. "You know how every good Muslim man dreams of being greeted at the gates of heaven by a never-ending supply of virgins?"

I nod.

"Well," she continues, "virginity isn't all it's cracked up to be."

"*Maryam.*" This is *blasphemy* where we are from.

She shrugs. "American men like their women a little more

experienced, that's all I mean. Their version of heaven probably includes a bunch of prostitutes who can show them a
thing or two in the bedroom, not some dead-fish virgin who
makes them do all the work."

Before I can even respond, Maryam catches sight of an
upcoming store. She grabs my arm and pulls me ahead. "It's
coming up! Here it is!"

The store we stop at has nearly naked female mannequins
displayed in the windows wearing skimpy lingerie and sporting sexually suggestive poses. I realize that Maryam must be
right that heaven is different for American men.

"Tami, this is Victoria's Secret." She says it like she is in-
troducing me to an old friend of hers.

I raise my eyebrows in wonder. "It doesn't seem to me like
Victoria has *any* secrets."

"Amazing, isn't it?"

She leads me into the store. I am hugely embarrassed to be
standing where anyone can see us. She at least has a wedding
ring. I cover my mouth with my hand as I look around. I am
shocked.

"Do you wear these things?" I ask her in a whisper.

"Oh, yeah," she says in what I can only describe as a las-
civious manner. "Come on, let's try some on."

When the saleslady approaches, I feel a panic attack coming on, the same sort of terror I felt in Iran when the *bassidjis*
approached me on the street to demand that I tuck the wisps
of my hair into my *hejab.*

"My sister needs some new bras and panties," Maryam
says, as matter-of-factly as if she were asking for bread at the
bakery. "She needs some basic everyday things, and then I'd
like to try on some of your sexier items."

"I don't feel so good," I say to her in a low voice. "Can we
do this another day?"

The saleslady eyes me up and down, mostly up. "You're what, a 34-C?"

I bite my lip and feel the tears welling. I shrug like a child.

"Can you believe it?" Maryam exclaims to the saleslady. "A natural 34-C!"

"A nice chest must run in the family," she compliments. Her name tag says *Bonnie*. I wonder if this is her real name. I wonder what her family thinks of her working in a store like this.

My sister laughs. "Mine were dinky before. Barely a B-cup. I had a boob job last year."

"Maryam!" I glare at her. *What is she doing telling this to a stranger?* I am *sure* my parents did not send us to America to talk to strangers about our boobs.

"She just arrived in the United States yesterday," Maryam explains.

Bonnie points to the rear of the store. "Come on back to the dressing room. I'll measure you and bring you some things to try on."

I look pleadingly at Maryam.

"Go on." She nods toward the dressing room. "I'll find some things I think you might like. She's very shy," she tells Bonnie.

My mother wore a pink bikini. My mother wore a pink bikini. I chant this to myself to boost my courage as Bonnie takes my measurements.

"What's your favorite color?" she asks.

"Blue."

Bonnie frowns.

"Nope. You need hot colors. I'll be back in a sec."

Sec. Sec. I puzzle over that word while I stare at my hair in the mirror. Maryam has used a hot iron to make waves that hang over my shoulders. I tuck it behind my ears and smooth it down against me. Then I shake it loose. I love how free it feels as it falls halfway down my back.

Bonnie returns with twelve bras on a tray, like she is serving tea to me. "Orange is the bestseller this season. It'll look great on you, with your dark skin."

She leaves me in privacy, and once I get accustomed to the strangeness of the situation, I feel like a child who has been left alone in a candy store. They are delicious, all of them. I run my fingers through the silky yellows, the lacy limes, the daisies, and the polka dots. I try them all on, and Bonnie is right. I am made to wear hot colors.

I preen in front of the mirror like a model in the forbidden magazines my girlfriends and I used to pore over, and I wish Minu and Leila were here with me so we could giggle together and so they could try some on, too. I am not shy, like my sister tells people. I am just not used to things and I am without my girlfriends. I was always the bravest of my friends, always the one who wore the brightest-colored headscarves and let the most hair show on the street.

"Make sure to try on the add-a-cup," Maryam calls from the other side of the door. "Maybe then you won't need a boob job."

I cringe at her lack of modesty.

"You don't really want her running around in a D-cup, do you?" I hear Bonnie say quietly to my sister. "With those eyes and that creamy skin, the men are going to be all over her as it is. With an even larger chest you're just looking for trouble."

"True," Maryam replies and calls out to me, "Never mind about the add-a-cup, Tami!"

"We only want attention from *certain* men," I hear her tell Bonnie. "Not the *typical American man*."

At the checkout counter, Bonnie rings up our purchase:

seven bras all of different colors and coordinating thongs and hip-huggers and Brazilian something-or-others. While Maryam is busy spraying some perfume on her wrist, I slip a lacy black add-a-cup bra onto the pile.

Bonnie smiles at me and winks.

I wink back.

5

’ll be fine," I assure Maryam for the hundredth time. "We've driven the route twice. I have your cell phone number, and it's only four kilometers from here."

Maryam is leaving for work. Soon after, I will leave for my first English conversation class. She wants me to take a taxicab. I am determined to walk. It is January and a beautiful seventy degrees. I have been in America for a little over a week now, and this will be my first outing without Maryam as my chaperone. And while I admire the ease with which she moves through her world, I am eager to explore it on my own.

She hands me an index card that has her address and cell phone number at the top. Underneath are these phrases written in both English and Farsi:

1. I am lost. Could you call my sister, please?
2. I do not understand what you are saying. Could you call my sister, please?

3. Leave me alone or I will call the police. Could you call
   my sister, please?

"Just point to whatever the situation calls for," she instructs. "And don't talk to any strange men."

"How will I know if they're strange if I'm not allowed to
talk to them?" I ask this mischievously. This is not the first
time we've had this conversation. Besides, I can't fathom a
situation where the opportunity would come up.

"Don't talk to *any* men."

"What about my classmates?"

"*Tami.*"

I laugh, take her elbow, and lead her to the door. I kiss her
on both cheeks.

"Go," I say, gently pushing her outside. "I'll be fine."

I watch and wave until she has backed out of the garage
and driven off. And then I sigh happily. It is such a rare oc-
currence for me to be alone in a house. In Iran, my mother
seldom ventures outside. And this is Maryam's first day back
at work since I arrived. I'd forgotten how much of a busy-
body she is. Ardishir is her exact opposite. He is quiet and
mild and smiles sympathetically at me when Maryam issues
all her rules. He doesn't impose any of his own.

I turn up Siavesh on the stereo and put my sister out of my
mind almost immediately. I am so excited for this day and
only a little afraid. I am wearing a watch that Maryam gave to
me as a present when I arrived. It is a Mickey Mouse watch
she bought for me at Disneyland. I am also wearing Ardishir's
gift to me, a University of Arizona sweatshirt, which is good
because I will be walking through the campus today to get to
my English class. I am also wearing jeans and new black
boots with two-inch heels.

But more important is what I don't have on: No *hejab*. No

manteau. I'm wearing dangly gold earrings and just a hint of makeup—only mascara, eyeliner, and tinted lip gloss. I let my hair hang long. I take one last look in the mirror and practice my laugh yet again. Americans laugh openmouthed and loud. I still can't bring myself to be loud about it, but I now show off my teeth like Julia Roberts does in the movies.

I leave the house at exactly ten o'clock. This is one hour before Maryam thinks I need to leave, but I am allowing myself some time to take a break and maybe buy for myself a cup of tea.

I can hardly describe how I feel on this, my first outing alone. I can barely keep from crying in excitement. This is *me*, finally. *My* route to school. *My* air to breathe. My life, to make of it what I will.

Maryam's house is east of the university, in a neighborhood called El Encanto Estates. There is very little traffic, no sidewalks, and lots of cactus and desert landscape. Her house is at the end of Calle Splendida, a dead-end street with a roundabout right in front. I hardly ever see anyone outside, and so today I am eager to walk through the university campus on my way to the downtown library, where my English class meets.

I lock the door behind me, lock Maryam's wrought-iron gate behind me, and then set out. I inspect each house and yard as I pass it, deciding which ones I would like to live in someday. Maryam's house is truly the most beautiful, although any of these houses would be fine with me.

I turn out of the neighborhood on Country Club Road, cross Sixth Street, and continue walking to Third Street, which is a bicycle route. I am now in what's called Sam Hughes neighborhood. I pass an elementary school and stop for a moment to watch the boys chase the girls and the girls chase the boys. Chase. It seems to be the most popular game.

The squeals and shrieks and laughter tickle my soul and cause me great happiness.

I have been walking for twenty-five minutes now.

I cross Campbell Avenue, a busy boulevard, and am now officially on the campus of the University of Arizona. It is so open compared to universities in Iran. I marvel at the women, with their tanned skin and white teeth and blond hair and sleeveless tank tops, walking along, talking on their cell phones, and eyeing the men just as much as the men eye them.

I didn't count on my solid two-inch boots hurting so much. They are Naturalizers, and Maryam said they were comfortable. But they are new, and I find that to avoid limping I must stop often to let my feet rest. My enthusiasm for this adventure is fading to dread. I have a long way to go. I finished my twenty-ounce bottle of water ten minutes ago, and I am thirsty again.

I will not call on Maryam to rescue me. I must never even mention it to her or she will not let me walk to class again. Okay. *Okeydokey*, as Ardishir says whenever Maryam asks him to do something around the house. America is all about live and let live. No one has minded that I've been taking photographs of houses that I like with the camera Ardishir has lent me. I took a picture of a teenage boy with three earrings hanging from his nose. I took a picture of a barefoot black man with no shirt and long braided hair riding a unicycle and playing a flute. No one has approached me to yank my camera from me. No one has yelled at me to hurry along or demanded to know what I was doing. I have been left alone on the streets, unmolested, for what feels like the first time in my life.

If I were braver, I would bend down and unzip my boots. I would pull them off and walk barefoot. I can just imagine the relief! I would wiggle my poor toes. I would pull off my socks as well, because if they get dirty then Maryam would know what I have done.

Maryam.

She would disapprove. She would say it is low-class, beneath our family.

I leave my boots on. I owe her that much, and so much more.

Yet as for my thirst, I know I can solve this problem. Once I leave campus and cross Park Avenue, I find myself at Main Gate Square on University Boulevard. I see the Starbucks ahead. Maryam has pointed this out to me, as perhaps a place I would like to enjoy a drink on my way to class.

I study the stickers on the door to make sure I am obeying all the rules. *No Shirt, No Shoes, No Service.* I am glad for leaving on my boots.

Make This Your Neighborhood Starbucks. Okay, I think. It is good to have neighborhood places. In Iran, we had so many *bazaaris,* shopkeepers who would look out for us, remember how many people are in our family and how much meat to give us, share with us the news of the day, that sort of thing.

I pull open the door and step inside. I clasp the straps of my backpack with each hand and look around. There is an unlit fireplace. Two men play chess, speaking not at all. A table by the window separates two easy chairs. One is occupied by a woman about my age, who curls her legs under her on the chair. She highlights the passages of a text and chews on the highlighter when it is not in use. In the other chair sits a woman of perhaps Korean heritage, chatting quietly into a cell phone. All four of these people have drinks beside them and backpacks at their feet. All must be students. Not one of them looks at me.

I close my eyes and inhale the coffee smell, surrendering to the memories. I am back in Iran, a little girl at my grandmother's house in Esfahan. I am skipping through the citrus trees, hopping from brick to brick in the courtyard. Inside, the angry talk of my aunts and uncles and older cousins is how the revolution is not so good, how maybe it was not so smart to have traded one corrupt leader they knew well for another they did not know so well. They talk of lessons learned: Beware the charismatic man who speaks the words our hearts long to hear, who rails against misdeeds and excess and promises to create a just society without ever explaining he will silence his critics by executing them, at a rate of four or five per day. They talk of who is in jail and who has been tortured and who has disappeared into the mountains, attempting escape. They talk of how much more expensive things are in the marketplace now and how there are no new cars or refrigerators because of all the boycotts against our country. Maryam sits with them, but this talk is not for me. I am young, six maybe. Young enough that wearing *hejab* is not yet required of me, and their words I have heard many times already. It is all anyone talks about anymore.

So I am outside, running in the crisp autumn air, collecting pecans that have fallen from the trees, when my grandmother calls me inside. As I step into her warm kitchen, the smell of coffee overpowers me just like it does now, here at this Starbucks on the other side of the world. Not many people serve coffee in Iran; I know only of my grandmother. And granted, in Iran there is only instant coffee, no percolation machines. But the smell is the same.

When I open my eyes, I am no longer in my grandmother's warm kitchen. I am back in my very own America. The man behind the counter smiles at me like he knows just what I have been thinking. This startles me. I am not used to a man looking so closely at me, seeming to understand me even without words.

I look past him to the colorful menu board written in chalk. But I want only one cup of water and so I must go closer to talk to him. My chest feels tight, scared. This is the first time I have handled a transaction, the first time I am without Maryam, who usually speaks for both of us. The man smiles and watches me the whole time I approach.

I clear my throat. I swallow hard. "Excuse me, please. Could I have some water?" I say it as fast as I can so maybe I don't seem so much like a foreigner.

He holds out a small plastic cup of something that is not water. "Here, try this. It's our new drink. Mango kiwi tea."

I had not planned on buying some tea right now. I thought perhaps after my English class, on my way home, I might buy a cup of tea and write in my journal. I glance at my Mickey Mouse watch. There is time. Mango and kiwi, these are not fruits we have in Iran. I will try it, I decide. I take the cup, then place it on the counter and reach into my backpack for some money. I pull out five dollars and hand it across the counter, trying not to look at this man in the green apron too closely. Instead of at his face, I look at his name tag. *Ike.* This is a short name. Not one I have heard before. *Ike.*

He waves my money away. "No, it's a sample."

I am confused. This is *taarof*, and Maryam told me that Americans do not do *taarof*. In Iran, this is how you pay for something in a store: You try to pay the shopkeeper. The shopkeeper waves the money away and says, "No, no. Really, I couldn't take your money." You insist; he refuses again. You insist again; he refuses yet again and puts his hand over his heart to show you how sincere he is. Only after refusing three times will he accept your money, and when he does, he thanks you over and over again for your generosity. It is a roundabout way to buy some simple groceries, but it makes everyone feel proud of what they are able to give the other person.

So this Starbucks man, this Ike, is doing *taarof*. He must know, then, that I am from Iran. I am disappointed to look so obviously Iranian, and I wonder what aspect of my appearance or behavior has given me away.

I again try to hand him the money. "Please," I say. "You must let me pay for it."

"It's free," he says, a little louder. "Enjoy."

"No, really, I must insist on giving you some money." My smile says that I acknowledge his kindness, but the truth is I have always found the ridiculous politeness of *taarof* tiresome.

"It's a sample," he says earnestly. "A free sample."

That's three refusals. But he forgot to put his hand over his heart and he is looking more insistent than humble. He does not know how to *taarof* very well.

"You're very kind," I say. "Here, please. I must give you something."

"It's FREE."

Tears come to my eyes; I cannot help it. I am stuck. He won't take my money, but I have to go. I do not have much more time to do *taarof* with him.

"Here," I choke out, trying to swallow my panic. "Take it." I should not have come into this store. I should not have insisted on walking to class. I should have let Maryam call a taxicab for me.

He shakes his head and keeps the same goofy smile on his face. I see there is a clear acrylic box on the counter with some money stuffed in it, some coins and dollar bills. I push my five dollars into it, collect my drink, and rush out without saying another word. I want to leave this place quickly, but my feet are in desperate need of a rest. I take a seat on the patio at the only table available, which is right outside the door.

Blech. This is not tea. It is cold and tastes of fruit so sweet, it is as if there are a hundred sugar cubes in it. This must be what Americans drink, though, or the man behind the counter would not have had it ready for his customers. I keep sipping it, hoping it will perhaps come to taste better over time. I rest my feet and watch Ike behind the counter as I take my sips. He takes everyone else's money the first time they hold it out. And every time he has a free moment, he looks outside and smiles at me.

I narrow my eyes at him the next time he looks over and he raises his eyebrows in response. I look at my watch. I have still more than one kilometer to walk, and I must hurry if I am to arrive on time. But as I push back my chair to stand, I see that a police car has lurched to a stop in front of the coffee shop. Two bulky policemen get out. They have guns in their belts.

My insides collapse. I freeze even though my body wants so badly to shake in terror. They walk right by me, so close they could reach out and grab my neck and haul me to their vehicle and make me disappear, and Maryam would know only that I did not return from class, but she would not know where to find me, how to help me. The bigger policeman yanks open the door to the coffee shop and they go right up to Ike. *He called them!* That spiteful man. I did *nothing* to him. I tried to pay, I really did.

My breath comes out in big heaves. This is horrible. I think how I can explain that it is my money in that box and I tried to give it to him even though he kept telling me no, and that it was him, not me, who did not know how to do *taarof* properly. And please, they cannot send me back to Iran for a simple misunderstanding. *Please.*

I push my lips together and blink heavily to keep from crying. I reach into my backpack and fumble for the index card Maryam made for me. I will ask them to call her and she can explain what happened. I will beg them not to take me to jail, but please to call my sister. Ardishir has money if we need to give them some so they leave me alone. It can be arranged, I am sure.

The policemen come back outside, toward me, carrying large cups. The smaller one nudges the larger one as they approach. I cannot move from the fear.

"Ma'am." He nods. "Is everything all right?"

I swallow over the lump in my throat and my breath comes out like I am having trouble breathing, which I am, only I don't want the policemen to know it.

"Ma'am?" he says again.

I make my eyes look up at him and my breath comes harder. I nod and stretch my eyes out so the tears do not collect in the corner of my eyes and run down my face.

"You're sure?"

I nod again. I even manage a small smile.

"Okay, then," he says. "Have a good day."

I do not trust myself to reply. I would probably be so nervous that I could only talk in Farsi and they would think I am crazy and lock me up. I give them another small smile and try to show that I am okay. For I have realized they are talking to me not to arrest me but because they think I need help. I smile and nod, smile and nod, even after they have their backs to me.

Once they have driven off, I can breathe again. I drop my arms onto the table and sink my head into my hands. You can take the girl out of Iran, but you cannot take Iran out of the girl. I know fears that Americans will never know, *Inshallah*.

"Are you okay?" I hear a voice at my table. I raise my head.

It is that Ike. I let out my breath.

"I thought—" I stop. It is too many words to explain, and he will not understand, anyway.

"You thought what?" He looks like he really wants to know.

"I tried to pay, but you wouldn't take my money. I thought—I thought maybe I did something wrong."

He looks at me with curiosity. "Where are you from?"

"Persia," I say, which is the old name for our country. Americans do not think so highly of Iran, I know.

"Persia," he repeats back, amused. "You mean Iran?" He pronounces it right. *Eee-Rahn.*

"Yes."

"You're new to this country?"

"Yes," I say. "I have been here for only one week."

"And you thought I called the cops to have you arrested for not paying for your drink?"

I nod.

"You poor girl," he says with a big smile. He must be very rich, to have such nice teeth. But then again, if he were so rich he would not work behind a counter in a coffee shop. "It was a sample. You know what *free* means, don't you?"

"I guess maybe I don't."

I know by how he narrows his eyes that he has caught the double meaning of my answer. "It's a new drink," he explains, slowing his words for me. "We want our customers to try it so that if they like it, they will buy a bigger cup next time. You don't really think we'd charge money for such a small glass of tea, do you?"

I shrug one shoulder. "In my country, we have some drinks that are very strong and come in small cups."

"Oh, right," he says. "Espresso, I suppose. Well, don't worry. You didn't do anything wrong. And you don't have to be afraid of the police here. They're mostly decent."

"Thank you," I say. "It is very nice of you to explain this to me."

"My pleasure," he says, bowing his head at me like a gentleman. "Did you like the *free sample*?"

"It's very sweet," I say. "I am not used to drinks so sweet. And I am not used to tea being cold. I have only had it hot before."

"Well," he says, shrugging a little, "I should get back inside. If you wait here, I'll go get your five bucks back for you. I *thought* that was quite the generous tip!"

I like his laugh. It makes me laugh, too. I give him my best Julia Roberts smile, the one I practiced in the mirror before leaving home. He looks at me with a feeling I do not recognize. It feels close to affection, but that is not quite right. I realize suddenly that it is a look of attraction. He is attracted to me.

Oops.

"Oh, no," I say, waving him off. "Please, keep it. Your English lesson was very helpful."

He gives me another dazzling smile. "You're sure?"

I nod. "Yes, very sure."

"Okay, then." He raises his hand in a small wave and backs away, still smiling. "I get off at three o'clock. If you're still here, I'd be happy to help you practice your English."

I remember Maryam's admonition: *Don't talk to any men.*

"Oh, thank you. But I couldn't."

"It'd be my pleasure."

"I have an English class I must get to." I glance at my

watch to show him I must hurry. "But thank you just the same."

"Anytime," he says. "On the days that I work, I always get off at three, and I usually sit outside and have a cup of coffee before leaving. We could practice then sometime. If you want."

"That's very generous of you to make such an offer."

"I mean it. It'd be fun."

He gives one last little wave to me and goes back inside behind the counter. He busies himself by cleaning a coffee grinder and I slip away while his back is to me.

I smile the whole way to English class and my feet do not hurt one bit. I feel almost as if I am walking on air.

6

My English class meets in the basement of the main public library in downtown Tucson. Some-day I will arrive very early and linger in this library. I want to learn what is written about Iran. I want to see for myself that American writers are allowed to criticize their own govern-ment without fear of imprisonment. But today I arrive only five minutes early and find a man with a stringy-haired pony-tail waiting for me outside the classroom.

"Are you Tamila?" I can tell by how his eyes crinkle when he smiles that he is very kind.

I nod and smile back, grateful to find that my heart experiences none of the flutters it did when I spoke to Ike.

"I'm Danny." He bows his head slightly but does not offer his hand. I appreciate this. Shaking hands with men is still so strange for me. "I'm your instructor. I could tell from your name that you're Persian, aren't you?"

I nod.

"I lived in Turkey for two years, back in the late '80s." He looks proud of this fact, so I smile at him. "You're the only new student we have this session. Why don't you come on in and take a seat wherever you feel comfortable?"

I walk ahead of him into the classroom. There is a long table with chairs around it, and four other students are already seated and chat easily with one another. I select a chair next to an old woman who looks like she is from a Baltic state, somewhere very cold. She is tiny in her height but large in her bones. She leans over and pats my hand. "Good girl, good girl" is how she greets me.

"Thank you." I smile at her, grateful for her friendliness.

"*Prosze bardzo*. You are a-velcome." She smiles back. I like that she has a gold cap over her front tooth. It shows her character.

"You know good girl she is?" questions an old man sitting in front of the old woman. "Maybe she no good girl." He is missing a tooth on one side of his mouth. He sucks air in through the space and then laughs at his own joke. Old men must be the same everywhere, I think. They laugh harder than anyone else in the room at their own jokes.

"I take this good girl on a trip to Lake Havasu City with me," Josef announces with a wink to me. "*Only* this good girl."

I draw back, unsure how to respond.

The old lady scolds him in a language I can't determine. He argues back in yet another language, also Slavic but different from hers. I feel like I have somehow caused this rift but can't possibly imagine what I could have done to prevent it.

"Don't mind them," says a man about ten years my senior who sits across from me. "This is how they tease each other."

"What did he mean about taking me to another city?" I ask. I cannot go on a trip with this man!

"He was just trying to get a rise out of Agata. They're smitten," the man explains, extending his hand to me. "I am Edgard, and I am from Peru. We have all been together for two classes by now. At the end of each session, Josef takes the class on a trip. Last time, it was to Disneyland. The time before, the Grand Canyon. Next time, it will be Lake Havasu City. He's renting a houseboat for us to stay on."

"He's very rich?" I whisper.

Edgard shrugs. He leans toward me and lowers his voice. "I think he hoarded money all his life. Then when his wife died a few years back, he realized he should have used his money to have fun with her when he could have. So, he just does things like this now. He doesn't have family left, so he says he has adopted us."

"That's very sweet. Your English, it is very good," I tell him.

"Thank you." He bows his head. "We were required to speak English in medical school."

"You're a doctor?"

"There, I was. Here, for now, I wash dishes in a restaurant." He smiles like this is not so bad.

"How long have you been in United States?"

"In *the* United States," he corrects me. We don't use definite articles like *the* in Iran and it is something I often forget. "Six months. I married an American nurse who was in the Peace Corps in my country."

"What is this, Peace Corps?"

Edgard shrugs. "Mostly, it's a bunch of do-gooders who help poor communities around the world. A bunch of hippies with long hair."

Our conversation is interrupted by the sound of a guitar softly strumming. It is Danny, at the front of the table and sitting on its edge.

"He was in the Peace Corps, too," Edgard whispers to me with a wink before leaning back and sitting upright.

"Let's begin, friends. It looks like everyone's here."

"Except Eva," call out the others. They share a laugh.

"Except Eva," Danny agrees, setting his guitar at his side. "We have a new student joining us today. Let's all say hello to Tamila."

"Hello, Tamila," they say in chorus. I feel very glad to be with such a friendly group. Maybe these people will be my friends. Maybe I will make jokes with them soon.

"Hello, it is very nice to meet you," I respond. "Please, call me Tami."

They introduce themselves. The old woman is Agata from Poland. There is Edgard from Peru; Josef from Czechoslovakia; and Nadia from Russia, who is pregnant-large and speaks very softly. She looks sad or shy, I cannot tell which.

"And here is Eva," announces Agata with a flourish, just as the introductions conclude and a light-featured woman enters wearing the shortest skirt I have ever seen. She carries a tray of some type of dessert that smells delicious. Agata turns to me. "Eva is from Germany, and she is *not* good girl."

The class laughs, even Danny and Nadia. Eva grins at me. The grin reminds me of the woman from the airplane, the one who was twice divorced and liked the tongues of Persian men. I will need to be careful around Eva.

"But I make good *stollen,* no?" She passes the tray to Edgard, who takes a helping and passes it along to Josef. I enjoy hearing their appreciative murmurs as they taste her *stollen.*

As the passing of the treat continues, Danny turns his attention back to me. "When we get a new student, we have that person tell us a little bit about themselves and then we take turns asking questions. Only if you're comfortable. Do you feel up for that?"

Up for that. My nerves shake inside my body as I push back my chair and stand. I take a deep breath. I tell them I am twenty-seven years old and I am from Iran and I am visiting my sister and her husband in America. I say I am very pleased to meet you all. I pronounce my words carefully. My nerves relax as I talk because I realize from their encouraging expressions that each of them has had to speak like this in front of the class at some point or other.

"Thank you, Tamila." Danny compliments my diction and gestures for me to sit. "Now, who would like to ask the first question?"

Eva raises her hand very quickly. The whole class laughs. "Not you, Eva," chuckles Danny.

"Darn." Eva snaps her fingers as she says this. *Darn.* I need to find out about that word, too. I write it down in my notebook.

"Nadia, why don't you start?"

Nadia offers me an apologetic smile. My return smile lets her know it is okay, I do not mind. "Do you have husband?" she asks.

"I do not have husband," I reply.

"*A* husband," Edgard corrects. "I do not have *a* husband."

"Sorry," I say.

Danny lifts his eyebrows at Edgard. "Today, we're helping Tamila speak publicly. That is all. We'll not correct mistakes."

"Oh, please do," I say. "I very much want to learn good English."

Danny says there is time for that. It is now Edgard's turn to question me.

"Do you miss your family back home?"

I nod as it hits me, a terrible wave of missing *Maman Joon* and *Baba Joon*. I feel their presence right here with me in the room, waiting to hear my response.

"Very much, I miss my family." I stop to clear my throat from a lump of sadness. I receive smiles of sympathy from everyone. I want to say more, but the smiles tell me I don't have to.

"What job does your father do?" This from Agata. He builds roads, I tell them. He is an engineer educated in America. He builds roads and studies maps, but he himself is not allowed to venture outside his homeland.

"What is I-Ran like? Is it as bad as the news says it is?" This is Josef talking. He pronounces my country *I-Ran*, as in I Ran to the Corner to Buy Some Milk. It sounds harsh and ugly to hear it this way. *Eee-Rahn*, that is how Persians say it. But I do not correct his mistake.

"It is . . ." I do not know how to describe it for them so they will understand. It is crazy drivers. It is open-air markets all over the city selling spices and onions and fish with their heads still on. It is linking arms with your girlfriends and whispering about the good-looking boy you have passed. It is saffron and tea and naps in the heat of the afternoon. It is escaping sometimes to the mountains or the Caspian Sea, where the air is moist and not so repressive.

It is, I want to say, all that I know.

"It is not so good for womens," I tell them instead.

"My turn," Eva announces. There is a sudden electrical charge in the air as everyone turns to her. Her eyes sparkle at me. She leans closer. "What do single women such as yourself do for fun? Do you ever sneak off and meet men?"

I know that she expects me to say no. But it is not true that there is no fun to be had.

"We go to clandestine parties in our friends' homes," I say. "In the street we must wear *hejab,* but in private homes we can wear miniskirts and makeup. Or we go to Internet cafés, and women are on one floor and men are on the other and we meet together in the chat rooms. Or we go to the mountains." I explain how in the mountains, we can let our *hejab* hang down our backs and our hair, too. "We gather in mixed groups in the mountains. It is not so bad as you might think."

"Do your parents know you do this?" Eva asks. Her eyes tell me she is impressed with our daring.

I think of my mother, her wistful eyes. She so wants for me to know some of the freedoms she herself used to have. "Our parents know. They tell us go. Have fun." Even so, I do not go to the mountains very much. I fear the *bassidjis.* Not so much for me—I do not fear one night in jail or two—but for *Maman Joon;* I would not want her to worry.

"Do you have a boyfriend there?" Eva asks.

I shake my head. "No, no boyfriend."

"Forgive such personal questions," Danny says. "But we are all interested in life for you back there. It's so different from what we know. No matter where we're from, we know Iran is very different. Don't feel you have to answer our questions if they're too private or if they upset you in any way." He looks directly at Eva as he says this.

"I do not mind," I say. "I am curious for all your cultures as well. I am eager to know all of you, too."

Nadia looks at me and holds my gaze. She has both hands on her pregnant stomach and rubs it gently. She looks very much like she could use a friend.

"Should we introduce Tamila to an American folk song?"

Danny asks, perhaps to lighten the mood. He reaches for his guitar.

"Do 'This Land Is Your Land,' " Agata suggests.

"The great Woody Guthrie." Danny nods in agreement and strums the tune.

His voice sounds out loud and true, a beacon for the others. Eva and Edgard bob their heads and sing gamely, while Nadia mouths the words and remains silent. The stars of this little performance, though, are clearly Agata and Josef. They claim this land, this country, as theirs, every square centimeter of it. Tears come to my eyes listening to this campy, off-key serenade, as I see how they cover their hearts with their hands. For it makes me realize, yet again, how much has been denied us back home.

For many years, it was illegal for women to sing in public, as it was deemed too provocative. Now they may perform in concert, but for other women only. And yet here we are, in a mixed setting, and none of the men seems lustful and none of the women seems immodest, except for Eva, and I suspect that has nothing to do with the singing. Mostly, they simply seem happy.

It was the Ayatollah Khomeini who forbade us to sing. I see his face now, glaring at me as I admire the others. He glares at me as he did throughout my childhood from high brick walls and the sides of buses and from picture frames in government buildings. His image was everywhere, omnipresent, judging my most secret thoughts. The memory of his voice admonishes me now as he admonished us back then: *There is no joy in Islam.*

I shudder away his terrible words. *This land is your land.* These words are so much better.

It angers me that I must leave my homeland to seek the joy that has been denied me in Iran. For even in the best of circumstances, America, the land for you and me, can never be anything more than a stand-in, a substitute. I want my homeland to be for me.

How *dare* women be forbidden to sing?

I sit up straighter in my chair.

How *dare* they stifle our voices?

I do not know the words to this American song, yet I have picked up the catchy tune. And so I begin to hum, softly, softly, as the others sing on.

Someday, I know, the people of Iran will sing in joy and in chorus once again.

My homeland will one day be for me.

And I will be ready.

7

As I approach the Starbucks on University Avenue after my English class ends, I am intensely aware of the time. Ike said he would be outside at a table at three o'clock. It is now three-thirty, so I expect that I shall pass right by with no notice.

But it is not to be. He sits at a table facing the direction from which I approach. He gives a big wave from a distance and stands to wait for me. At the table with him are two other Starbucks employees, both women. It still astounds me, and makes me envious, to see how men and women can sit together so freely and talk. They have no idea what a luxury this is. Freedom, I am beginning to realize, means not even being aware you're free.

"Hey, Persian Girl!" Ike calls out and waits for me to approach. *Persian Girl.* His loudness makes me cringe with embarrassment, but I smile at him my Julia Roberts smile. I see his head shift back a fraction and he seems to hold his breath for a moment. It is almost like what happens in the movie I have studied so much, *My Best Friend's Wedding*, when Julia Roberts smiles at her best friend and he loses himself. It is almost like Ike is so startled that he cannot think fast enough to smile back.

I do not stop to join them. I continue my walk toward the main gate of campus and don't look back. Inside I laugh, to think that maybe I was flirting back there. I am not sure. I may be making this up in my head, that I affected him in some way. I replay the moment over and over like it really is a scene from the movies, where the man falls in love with the pretty girl who passes by. This is fun to imagine, and it also takes my mind off my feet, which I suspect may be bloody inside my boots, that is how bad they hurt. I try to walk upright without evidence of a limp. And I think I am doing okay, until a few minutes later I hear a *beep-beep,* followed by the sound of a motor scooter pulling to the side of the road near me. I stop and turn in time to watch Ike pull off his helmet.

"Want a lift?"

The idea of this is so absurd, I have to laugh.

"No, thank you," I say. I cannot even imagine what the punishment would be in Iran for riding on the back of a motor scooter with a man who is unrelated to me.

"You look like your feet hurt."

"I have new boots, that's all."

"Do you have much farther to go?"

"Maybe about two kilometers." I try to keep my tone light, but I am afraid the dread comes through in my voice and in my eyes.

This Ike is a perceptive man. He studies my face, looks thoughtful.

"Come on," he says, gesturing with his head. "I'll have you home in no time."

We look at each other, and this is what I am saying with my eyes: I know that's how it's done here. I know men and women can sit at tables together and have coffee. I know they can smile and make small talk and no one will harass them. I know that I could climb on the back of your scooter and my world would not come to an end. I know this. But even so, it is a big step for me, too big a step for me to take right now.

"Come on," he says again. "I dare ya."

I shake my head a little. "I do not know what that means."

He smiles. "It means I challenge you to get on."

"You can't challenge me," I reply, with a little bit of indignation in my voice. "This isn't a game."

"But it is," he says, in a teasing tone.

And all of a sudden, it is. *Will Tami get on the scooter or won't she?* Because of his dare, he wins if I don't get on the scooter. And I win if I do. He is very clever, this Ike.

I think of Maryam. I know what she would say. *Stay away from all men.* Yet I know, too, that I have what is a much bigger game ahead of me: *Will Tami be able to convince a modern Iranian-American man—one who does not forbid joy—that she is worthy of marriage?* To win that game, I must learn to flirt. I must learn to make myself fun to be around. I must learn to convince a man that it is more fun to be with me than without me. He must choose me above all the American girls. To win that game, I must first win this one.

And besides, he's cute and it's a new feeling for me, to have a man admire me. If that's what this is.

I glance at my watch. He could drop me off and Maryam would never be the wiser.

"Okay," I say, smiling broader and stepping dangerously close to him. "I accept your challenge."

I give Ike that slightly teasing tilt of my head, the tiny

smile I seem unable to hide. It is the same look I gave the
dentist one week ago.

The look did not work on the dentist at all. If anything, it
repulsed him. But from the sharp intake of his breath and the
momentarily stunned look in his eyes, I can tell it succeeds
with Ike quite well.

At dinner that night, Maryam asks me question after
question. She asks how things looked to me and what confused me and did I meet any nice people at class and what
mistakes did I make. Her eyes gleam as if I am telling an adventure story. And I suppose it is, Tami's Great American
Adventure.

Of course I do not tell Maryam or Ardishir about my ride
on the back of Ike's scooter. But I tell them how very much I
enjoyed walking through the Tucson neighborhoods and
through the university. I tell them about my English class,
about how Danny lived in Turkey and how Agata is from
Poland and Josef is from Czechoslovakia and how they have
a cranky affection for each other like they are an old married
couple. I describe them in detail, how they are both so short
and how Agata is hunched over and how Edgard from Peru
told me that Agata lost both parents in the Holocaust of
World War Two. I tell them how Josef is a widower and that
he takes the class on trips after each session. I tell them about
Eva, who is German and who laughs all the time, who seems
to laugh at life itself. I tell them about Nadia, how she looks
like she maybe could use a friend. I tell them how the class
sang for me. I tell them about my mistake in trying to pay for
a free sample of tea. At this, they laugh very hard. I tell them
of my fear when the police came to the Starbucks and I

thought they were coming to arrest me. I tell them about Ike, and how he came outside to look after my welfare and explained to me what a free sample is and how he offered to help me practice my English.

At this, Maryam's eyes narrow and so I turn my attention to eating my *chelo* kebab.

"I can take you to school tomorrow," Maryam informs me in a slightly hardened voice. I stuff a large spoonful of rice into my mouth. "And I can pick you up afterward, too."

I should not have mentioned the incident with the police. Or anything at all about Ike.

"My boss says that perhaps soon I can change my schedule," she continues in a pleasant voice. "Then I'll be able to drive you to class each day. You shouldn't be walking alone on the streets."

I drop my eyes and concentrate on scooping more yogurt onto my rice. "My teacher has given us an assignment to speak with three strangers every day to practice our English." I keep my voice neutral. "I intended to stop in at several stores each day to ask questions of the shopkeepers on my way to and from school."

"I'll take you to the mall. There are plenty of shopkeepers there."

I reach for my water glass and will myself not to cry. Today was my first day of true freedom all by myself, free even from my sister's admonitions, and I am heartbroken to think it may be my last.

I am thankful when Ardishir speaks up. "It seems like she enjoys walking."

"She doesn't need to be distracting herself with talking to American men," Maryam snaps at him.

I knew it.

Ardishir studies me for a moment, and then asks Maryam, "What would your new work schedule be?"

"Four to ten P.M. Wednesdays through Sundays."

He frowns. "That is no good. That's when I'm home."

"Tami can prepare dinner for you. Can't you, Tami?"

"Of course," I reply, over the lump in my throat. I stare at my plate so they do not see the despair that I am sure is in my eyes.

"I want for us to have dinner together," Ardishir says firmly. "Husband and wife. That is what is right. I want for us to spend our evenings and weekends together like we always have. When you accepted your job, that was part of the arrangement."

"Well, things change," Maryam replies with anger in her voice. I suspect he seldom orders her to do anything.

"Ardishir is right," I say quickly. "I don't want to be a burden to you. I don't want to come between you and your husband."

"You're not coming between us." Maryam glares at Ardishir. "She was almost arrested!"

"No she wasn't."

"Well, she thought she was. That's bad enough. Can you imagine how frightened she must have been?"

"Walking is good for her," Ardishir states.

"I felt very safe today, except for those policemen, and that was my mistake," I tell Maryam. "Please, it's very important for me to learn about America and learn how to handle things on my own. I do not want my husband to have to accompany me everywhere after I'm married. I should learn how to take care of myself."

She sighs.

"It's just—you're so naïve, Tami."

"I know," I agree.

"You need to be careful around men."

"I am," I tell her.

"They take advantage of women alone," she continues. "Especially when they know you're new here and don't understand American customs. They'll try to be alone with you and corrupt you."

I think of my ride on the back of Ike's scooter. I tried to hold on only to his shirt, but when we went up a hill, I tightened my arms around his waist and felt a rush of longing for the moment to stand still. The closeness of a man against my body was a new sensation for me, and it was exquisitely delicious. *If that's corruption, I want more of it.* That's what the not-so-naïve part of myself thinks in response to my sister's warning.

"I'll be careful," I promise.

"Maybe Tami can find an American man to marry," Ardishir says casually. But his tone is a joking one, designed to get a rise out of Maryam, which it does.

"Right! No American is going to marry her just so she can get a green card!"

"That seems unfairly critical," I say. "You do not think even one American man would do such a favor for a female friend of his?"

"No." She is adamant. "They'd only do it because there's something really wrong with them. Or they'd only do it for the sex. Here, people take a long time to date before they get engaged, and then a long time being engaged before they get married."

"I know that," I tell her sullenly. "Do you really think I don't know that? All I'm asking is to walk to school." My voice catches in my throat. It does not seem like this is too much to ask. "I just want to walk to school."

"I know," Maryam soothes, patting my hand. "And that's fine. But you must promise me you won't get yourself into a situation with an American man that could affect your chances of marrying. Word gets out, and if you act in a dishonorable way, like a *badjen,* we won't be able to find you a husband."

"I just want to walk to school," I insist.

"I know," she soothes.

It is time to change the subject.

"Eva brought to class a wonderful dessert called *stollen,*" I say. "Do you think I should make some *Nane Shirini* cookies tomorrow?" I am an expert at making these delicate cookies, which contain orange rind and lemon juice and walnuts, but with the main ingredient of sugar.

"An excellent idea," Ardishir offers, quick as me to change the subject. Ardishir is one who likes to keep the peace. He likes things to be pleasant in his home. "Make some extra for me, please."

"We can bring them to your office," Maryam offers.

Ardishir's office is on the north side of town. Maryam has the day off tomorrow, and she is taking me there to see where he works, and then to Sabino Canyon, which she says is very beautiful and full of cactus that are not seen anywhere else in the world. I am very much looking forward to our outing, although I do not think I will be able to do much hiking in the canyon. Maryam was kind to make for me a foot bath of hot water and rose petals when she arrived home from work and saw my blistered feet, but even now, they still throb unrelentingly.

After dinner, I help Maryam with the dishes and I watch Iranian television out of Los Angeles with them for a little while. But I am very tired and I am feeling something close to sadness, so I excuse myself and announce that I am going upstairs.

I close my bedroom door behind me in relief. The master bedroom is downstairs, which means I have the whole upstairs to myself. I pretend sometimes when I am up here that I live alone, and I relish the quiet. I cannot hear the Iranian television and I cannot hear Maryam. For this, I am so very grateful.

I have developed a nightly ritual for myself since arriving. I have bought what is called a Perpetual Light candle from the grocery store, which from the label I see you are to light and perhaps your hopes will come true. I have created a little altar for myself on my dresser, with the candle and the blue perfume bottle of American sand that my father gave me. I have tucked my favorite picture, the one of my mother in her pink bikini, into a bottom corner of my mirror and I have hung my brightest *hejab* over a top corner of the mirror, having vowed only to use it for decoration and never again for concealing myself from the world. Every night, I light my candle. Every night, I turn on my CD of Googoosh and climb into my bed. While lying in the dark, I watch how the flame from the candle dances, how it dips and weaves all by itself in the night. It dips and weaves and moves in whatever direction it must in order to keep from being extinguished.

Googoosh. Her voice is a gift to the world, a gift of true beauty. She is, without question, the most famous Iranian singer, loved by both women and men. Before the revolution, girls went into beauty shops in Tehran and asked for a Googooshi haircut. She *was* the fashion; she *set* the trends under the Western freedoms the Shah permitted. It is she who introduced our country to the miniskirt, and my mother loved her for it.

Once the revolution came, she, like so many other women, was forbidden from singing in public. I am sure she could have fled her homeland, but for twenty years she remained in her apartment in Tehran like a bird whose wings had been cruelly clipped. Her fame only grew. Bootleg copies of her music flourished, and she became for us a symbol of the bitter choices we all face. Do you stay in your homeland even as it suffocates your spirit, do you love it even if it does not love you back, or do you declare defeat, do you hand over to the thief the keys to your home and say, *Take it, it doesn't matter to me anymore anyway, you have already taken too much and there's nothing here for me now?*

After twenty years, Googoosh's husband secured permission for her to leave Iran. She performed first in Toronto to a crowd of twelve thousand, and we heard back in Iran that her voice, so long suppressed, was never more beautiful. We heard there was not a dry eye in the crowd, hers included. We heard this and we cried, too, and we urged her in our hearts, *Sing, Googoosh, sing. Sing for us. Sing for yourself.*

On this night, I watch the flame from the candle and listen to her voice. I feel her sadness; it washes over me. I saw real freedom today on my walk to and from English class—I saw young boys and girls chase one another on the playground; I saw Agata and Josef make their way toward love. I saw men and women sit together at outside patio tables; I saw university girls bare their skin to the sun. I rode on the back of a man's motor scooter and felt a thrill when my body touched his. My girlfriends in Iran might never have a day like I had today, and this makes me so very sad. As for myself, I want to have days like this again and again and I do not want to fight with Maryam every step of the way.

I will make my parents' dream come true. I will find a husband. I will get married. But I do not want to wait a lifetime in order to find my happiness.

I love Googoosh. But I do not want to be her.

8

I am happy for Ardishir when I learn how he spends his days. His office is in an adobe building with a four-tiered fountain out front. He has three women assistants who answer the phones and file insurance information and make appointments. It is very pleasant; the music he plays in his lobby is not Persian or even classical.

"What is this music?" I ask Maryam. I have not heard this style before.

"I don't know," she replies. "Ardishir takes care of everything for his office." She chats with one of the receptionists and picks up a picture on her desk to admire.

"It's Keb' Mo'," Ardishir says as he greets us out front, kissing us both on our cheeks. "Sort of New Orleans-y."

I remember that Ardishir got his undergraduate degree at Tulane in New Orleans. This was before he knew Maryam. He has told me several stories about how much fun he had living in the college dormitories and then with friends. It sounds like he had many years of fun times before he got married.

Seeing his office is like seeing a whole new person. It is as if he has carved out for himself a piece of the world only for him, designed just how he likes. I feel in myself a sense of envy, that he gets to nurture a whole other self besides the one he is in his home, in his marriage.

"I like your office," I tell him. "I like it very much."

He extends his arm. "Come on, I'll give you the grand tour."

While Maryam stays to chat with the employees, Ardishir shows me the X-ray room, two patient offices, and finally, his personal office. It is decorated with sleek modern furniture. Copenhagen style, he tells me. The walls are painted a rich cream. There are photos on his walls of his patients after surgery, using the limbs and muscles he has repaired for them. I see a picture of a woman waterskiing; another woman rock climbing. Yet another is on a bicycle; while a fourth is running a footrace.

He sets women free. I feel a new admiration for Ardishir, and I am suddenly so thankful for his intervention last night on my behalf, to convince Maryam to let me keep walking to school. *He's trying to set me free, too.*

"I admire the work you do," I tell him. "I admire it very, very much."

"Thank you. Tell me, are your feet still very sore?"

I confess they are. "But please, do not tell Maryam."

"You really like to walk?"

"I love it. It's so different from home. It's how it should be, you know? Clean air, no one bothers me. It will help me, I think, to learn to be unafraid."

His eyes crinkle with kindness. "Takes practice, doesn't it?"

"It's a big change."

When we get back to the lobby, the women have eaten all the *Nane Shirini* cookies that I brought.

"These cookies are delicious!" one of them says. Her size indicates she perhaps enjoys sweets a little too much. Poor Ardishir. This lady ate his share. He will have to wait for dinner tonight to have some.

I smile. "Thank you, you're very kind."

"Really, they're awesome. Have you thought about opening a Middle Eastern bakery?"

"Oh, no," I tell her. *I have to get married,* I think.

But as Maryam drives to Sabino Canyon, I consider her suggestion. If I didn't have to get married right now, if I really had the freedom to choose my life's path, I think maybe I would like to open a school for girls. I would teach them to think for themselves. I would teach them to look inside their hearts to recognize the right way to treat others. Their hearts know what is kind and just, better than any book or government. I would teach them that they are not better than anyone else, but they are not worse, either. They are not worth only half of what a man is worth. They do not need to veil themselves from the world. They are not the cause of all corruption in the world. I would teach them it is okay for girls and boys to be friends. I would teach them it is okay to sing. *Go ahead,* I would urge them. *Go ahead, it will make you happy.*

This is what I would like to do, open a school such as this. But then I remember: My school is not needed in America. It is Iranian girls who need to hear this message. *No, Tami,* I catch myself. *They need more than the message. They need to live in a world where it is all true, every word of it.*

Maryam takes me to what is perhaps the most beautiful place in the world. I have certainly never seen anything like it, so many shades of brown and green, with the sky so purely blue. Sabino Canyon began forming over seven million years ago, and much of the canyon was created due to an earthquake in Mexico that made the rocks crash down. There is a river in this part of the desert and cactus like I have only seen in the old black-and-white western movies.

"There's no place like this in the whole world," Maryam tells me as our tram ride begins its journey through the desert canyon.

"I can't believe how much work must have gone into building this road," I say. The three-kilometer recreational road throughout the canyon is better than ninety percent of the roads in Iran.

We weave up and down hills, around shady bends, past walkers and joggers. I marvel that all around me, women both alone and in groups walk and jog, exercising their bodies and building their muscles. I long to be one of them. I could truly be alone in my thoughts in a place like this. Here, the earth seems big and old and my grievances seem petty. My concerns about marriage and Maryam's rules seem not so major, not so permanent in a place so timeless, that has withstood so many centuries.

Maryam suggests we disembark the tram at the river and have our lunch of the leftover rice and *chelo* kebab and hot tea we have brought in a thermos. We climb down into the sand on the riverbank and claim a log. While I begin spreading out our little picnic, Maryam slips off her shoes and steps into the river.

"Oooh, it's so cold!" she squeals. In a flash, I have a memory of being at the ocean in America with her and my parents. Though still a girl, Maryam seemed so much bigger than I. She was always the one who ran ahead, who put her feet into the ocean first, and squealed in much the same way. And then she'd come back out, take my hand, and lead me to the water's edge. With Maryam, I always felt safe.

"Can you believe we're actually here in *America* together, drinking tea by a river, Maryam?" Happy tears spill from my eyes. There are some sad tears mixed in, too, for how long it has taken for us to be together as sisters again. "Did you ever imagine it would really happen?"

I love the smile she gives me. "Always, *Tami Joon*. I knew my sister and I would be together again one day. And we'll never be apart again."

"We'll never be apart as long as we find a husband for me." That, as always, is the caveat. So far, I've met three potential husbands, but none has worked out.

"Well, the one coming to dinner tonight sounds promising."

"Maybe," I say without much enthusiasm. I carefully pick up dried leaves from the sand and throw them in the river. They float past Maryam, and I watch the stream carry them away from me. Each one gets stuck when it drifts into an area with large rocks jutting out of the water. Each one bumps into a rock and can move no more. Stuck, stuck, stuck. I stare at the leaves, mesmerized. "If I can't find a husband here, I can always marry *Agha Reza*. Did Maman tell you he was coming back?"

"Tami." I look up at my sister. Her lips are pressed firmly together. She walks over to the log and stands at my feet.

"You should not even think about marrying Reza."

"He's not so bad." I shrug.

"Yes, he is, Tami."

Her sharp voice causes me to look at her.

"Does Maman think this, too?" I ask, wondering what it is they have not told me.

Her voices sharpens even more. "Maman doesn't always know *what* to think. If you haven't noticed, she doesn't exactly make the best decisions."

"What are you being so mean for, Maryam? She's gone through a lot in her life, and you should be more respectful of her."

She issues an exasperated sigh and sits next to me.

"Listen," she says, softening her voice. "Ardishir and I talked last night. He pointed out that maybe I have not been too understanding of your situation. You are young and new to America, new to all these freedoms. You want to experience some of the fun things in life before you get married."

I shrug. I am still upset over how she spoke of *Maman Joon*. "It's no big deal."

"Yes, it is. How you feel is a huge deal, Tami. It would make me so sad to know you were unhappy here. There's no reason for it. *I* don't want to be the reason for it."

"It's just . . . I look at the girls around me with such envy. They get to do so much, so many simple things that have been denied me my entire life."

I sweep my arm toward the main road, toward a woman running past us wearing nothing more on top than a sports bra. Her long hair is in a ponytail and tucked through the hole of a baseball cap. I admire her. I want her strength.

"These women have so many choices," I tell Maryam. "They can do *anything*. They get to live life on their own terms, at least for a while, before they get married. And I envy them for that."

She reaches over and squeezes my hand. "Maybe you can make friends with those girls in your class. What were their names?"

"Nadia and Eva."

"Yes. You mentioned that Nadia looks like she could use a friend and that Eva seems like she would be fun. Maybe you could ask them to do some social things, like go to the movies or the mall."

I brighten at the thought. "This would be okay with you?"

"Of course." After a pause, she adds, "They're both married, right?"

"I think so."

"Then, sure. It's fine."

"*Thank you,*" I say, and lean into her for a hug.

"Just—" She stops herself.

"What?"

"Nothing."

"What, Maryam?"

"Just don't get distracted."

She's talking about Ike again, I know it.

"I won't, Maryam."

She squeezes my hand apologetically. "I don't mean to spoil your fun, Tami. But I would hate to see your life ruined because of one mistake. That's all it takes sometimes, *one mistake.*"

I squeeze back. "I am so lucky to have a sister who looks out for me."

We eat our lunch and drink our tea from the thermos, and then we climb the riverbank to wait for the tram. On the whole drive to my English class, my spirits are high as I plan how to invite Eva to do something with me after class one day. I have a feeling that it is with Eva I would have the most fun. She seems so confident, so sure of herself.

"Don't forget," Maryam reminds me as I wish her good-bye. "Haroun is coming to dinner tonight at six."

"Of course I remember," I tell her. "How could I forget? He has called for each of the last three nights to confirm!"

Maryam laughs. "He's eager. That's good. You want me to pick you up after class?"

"Oh, no thank you. I might perhaps see if Eva wants to stop for an ice-cream cone. Do you think it would be appropriate for me to ask her?"

"I don't see why not." Maryam smiles and brushes the wisps of hair from my forehead. "Just try not to be home too late. We want to get you all prettied up for tonight. Wouldn't it be great if we found you a husband so soon? Tami, you could be married by the end of the month!"

"*Maman Joon* and *Baba Joon* would be so happy." Me, not so much.

"They would," she agrees. "You know how much they want for you to stay in America, right?"

"I know."

"You shouldn't even think about going back. You shouldn't even think about marrying Reza. Promise me you won't, okay? You must focus on staying here, on marrying someone *here*."

"I *know*, Maryam."

I climb out of her car. She waits at the curb until I've stepped through the automatic doors of the library. As I turn back, I can't help but notice that my heart feels lighter as I watch her drive away.

9

I find it fortuitous that I am paired with Eva this afternoon for one-on-one discussion to practice our English. Her light blue eyes sparkle with mischief as she pulls her chair near mine and leans in close enough for me to see her cleavage. I sit up tall and realize immediately I was correct in my first impression of her. She is a girl who pushes things into exciting territory.

"So," she says directly, "I want to know *everything* about you. You're so beautiful. Do you have a boyfriend?"

I hesitate to explain my situation. For one, it would take too long and by the way she taps her long red fingernails on my desk, it is obvious she does not have patience. For another, I am afraid it will make me seem not as fun and carefree as her, to be burdened by my need for marriage. Yet she wears a plain gold wedding band, so it is not like she will want to go out looking for boyfriends, anyway.

"You have heard of arranged marriages, yes?"

Her eyes widen, and the way she wrinkles her nose makes me smile.

"That is what we do in my culture," I tell her. "We can't officially have boyfriends. Only fiancés and then husbands."

"Y'all don't even date? You just get *married?*" She says this like it's the stupidest thing she's ever heard, and she chomps on a large piece of gum as she waits for my response.

"Y'all," I repeat, sounding it out. I want to change the subject. "What is this word, *y'all?*"

She sniggers. "My husband's from Texas. They slur all their words together down there like lazy asses. You all. Y'all. Get it?" She blows a bubble slowly and deliberately for effect, like an actress. "But seriously, dating is the fun part! Once you're married, it's all downhill!"

"I hope for me that my marriage will be fun, too."

"Yeah, well, don't hold your breath." Eva tells me she has been married for only one year, to an American soldier she met when he was stationed in Germany. He is on a mission now, and she lives by herself in an apartment downtown while she waits for his return.

"It must be hard to be alone in a new country with your husband gone." I commiserate, yet secretly I am pleased because this means she might have more time to be my friend.

Eva shrugs. "I could live on base with all the other military wives, but they bore me to pieces, most of them. All they talk about are their husbands and how hard it is to be away from them. *Get a life,* I want to tell them. Life's too short to be waiting around for someone all the time."

We chat more about how she has applied for her green card so she can get a job and make some money of her own. I have many questions for her, like has the government interviewed her yet to make sure her marriage is for real, and did they ask questions such as what is each other's favorite color and what the other one likes the best to eat. Eva laughs. She tells me they studied those things, but all the interviewer asked them was how they met. Which was at a dance club in Dresden and they were both very drunk.

"Did you tell the interviewer this?" I am shocked as much by her openness as by her drunkenness.

She laughs at my shock.

"*Of course not.* I was just telling *you.* Man, y'all are so wide-eyed about everything that I'm tempted to make it my personal responsibility to corrupt you."

I am delighted by her statement and cannot hide a broad grin. "I would very much enjoy being your friend and spending time with you. But as for corrupting me, well, I am not so sure that's possible."

"I'll take that as a challenge."

"Please, do not take it as a challenge," I say, wondering what it is with these challenges people keep issuing to me—first Ike, now Eva. It must be a popular thing to do in America. "But you could take it as an invitation to do something together sometime."

"Have you ever gotten drunk?" Eva asks.

I shake my head. "I have drunk homemade beer sometimes. And there are parties with alcohol, definitely. But I didn't go out much."

"So you *can* drink."

"Well, alcohol, it is not legal in Iran."

She grins. "Good thing we aren't in Iran, then, isn't it? Have you ever gone out dancing at a club?"

"That, too, is illegal."

"What, dancing or going to clubs?"

"Both, I imagine."

"Man, you guys are repressed."

"Why do you keep calling me *man?*"

She laughs. "Slang. Thought you should get to know it. Another popular thing to do is say, *Girlfriend.*" She says this in a funny tone. "Like, *Ooh, Girlfriend, check out that fine dude.*"

I burst out laughing. "I didn't understand a word of that."

"*Fine dude* means a sexy man."

I refrain from asking what makes a man sexy. Her explanation might very well make me blush. And besides, I have an idea. He would have eyes as blue as the Caspian Sea. He would have hair blond from the sun. He would be a gentleman. He would be, I realize, someone remarkably like Ike.

"And *check out.* What does this mean?"

Eva raises her eyebrows twice at me. "*Check him out.* Look him over."

"I see." I am very amused by this.

"Do you do that in Iran?"

"Check out the fine dudes?" I enunciate carefully and laugh at how silly I sound.

"Yeah."

"Sure," I say. "But all we do is look."

Eva sighs, like that's so sad.

"And talk on the phone," I add, wanting to show the daring side of my generation. "Sometimes we used to go out driving and pass our phone numbers to boys in their cars."

"Mmmmm, sounds thrilling. I suppose you're inexperienced in matters of the heart?"

"That would be correct," I say with a smile.

"How long until you get married?"

"By the beginning of April." I explain my visa situation.

"That's not much time," she says. "But we'll have a bit of fun first, you and I."

"I would very much like that."

She stands. "Excuse me," she calls to our classmates, who are partnered off at various spots around the room. When she has their attention, she continues. "We're going to take Tami to a nightclub. She's never been to one before."

Agata claps in support of the idea. Edgard laughs. Josef sucks air into the missing space where his teeth should be. And Nadia smiles sadly.

"I suggest we take her to Eye Candy," Eva proposes.

"Not appropriate," Danny warns. He explains to me, "It's an adult nightclub. Naked women dancing around onstage."

"Ah, not appropriate." I feel a hot blush. I nod gratefully at Danny and wonder why Eva thinks I would like to see naked women dance.

"Let's take her to The Rustler and teach her how to line dance," Edgard suggests. Agata and Josef nod their agreement. Danny gives me a smile that lets me know it will be okay. I shrug my shoulder at Eva to tell her The Rustler is fine with me.

"Line dancing it is." Eva turns to me. "How about Saturday?"

"This Saturday?" She nods. I should ask my sister. But she was the one who suggested to me that I make friends with Eva, after all. It would be rude to refuse her invitation. But still. "I must ask my sister, to see if we have any plans. Maybe not this Saturday. But for sure, I will go."

Eva plops back down in her chair with a self-satisfied grin. I watch her blow a big bubble with her gum.

Unable to resist, I reach out and pop it.

10

I leave my English class in high spirits and with one goal in mind: to get myself home quickly to prepare for my dinner date with Haroun the engineer. Maryam has given me a bottle of face mask from Origins that has charcoal in it to rid my face of impurities. She has also left for me expensive conditioner for my hair and full use of all her makeup. She has suggested that I take a bath in rosewater and do my face mask right away when I get home. After I do this, she will help me select my clothing and put on my makeup. And she will prepare the food, so that my skin does not smell like onion and garlic, so that it remains appealing to Haroun.

As I walk, I talk to myself in a positive manner. I tell myself this engineer will be very nice. What I know of him is this: His name is Haroun Mehdi. He has been in this country for as long as Ardishir, having come right after fulfilling his military duty in Iran. He is eight or maybe ten years my senior, which is not so old, and good because he will be established in his business. His parents live still in north Tehran.

He will be nice. He will be funny. He will be handsome and engaging and interested in my thoughts. He will be open to me working outside the home. He will encourage me to have friends. He will like Persian and American food and he will think restaurants, both to visit and for takeaway, are excellent means by which to have dinner. Haroun. Haroun and Tami, happy together.

I am so deep in my hoping that it takes me a moment to recognize that the pedestrian signal to cross Fourth Avenue has turned from walk to remain in place. I take one step off the curb and must jump back as a large pickup truck comes at me. The driver yells something through his closed window and I see that I have angered him. I narrow my eyes at him to tell him, *Big deal. No need to be rude.* He drives off, and I feel pleased for standing up for myself.

I am now only a few blocks from the Starbucks where Ike works. My nerves increase as I near the coffee shop and I try my best not to limp as I approach. I cannot accept a ride from him again. To do so would be a betrayal of my agreement with Maryam. I tell myself I will walk by Starbucks fast, without glancing toward the patio.

Yet my plan shatters as I hear his voice call out, "There she is!" I look over to the patio to see him jump up from his chair. Today he sits alone. My heart stops from the shock of him, for in his arms is a large bouquet of red roses. He walks over and holds out the flowers. I cover my heart with both hands, that is how taken aback I am.

"Here," he says. "These are for you."

"But, but . . ." I stutter. "But why?"

His eyes smile at me, those eyes that remind me of the Caspian Sea with waves twinkling in the sunlight.

"I enjoyed meeting you yesterday," he tells me. "I give you these roses as a sign of our new friendship."

"Oh." I feel so light-headed that I am afraid my knees will collapse and I will fall to the ground.

"Are you okay?" Ike asks. "Your face is white as a ghost."

I catch my breath. *A sign of our new friendship.* I can manage my way out of this.

"I, ah, it's just that I, ah, have never been presented with flowers before. I am not quite sure how to respond."

He chuckles. "You respond by saying thank you and accepting them."

Maryam. This is my first thought.

He's so beautiful. This is my second thought.

Careful, Tami. The engineer, Tami. This is my third thought.

"Oh, but I don't think I can accept them." I cannot meet his eyes. I look instead at the window of the coffee shop. Two girls behind the counter who have been staring at us turn quickly away.

"Oh, but you have to," he replies in a playful voice. "It would be rude not to. Plus, everyone inside is watching, and they'll never let me live it down if you refuse them. They'll positively torture me."

"By torture, you mean what?"

"They'll make me feel like a real loser."

"Oh," I say, relieved. Where I am from, it means something very different.

"They've already been teasing me all day, getting me all nervous to give roses to a girl whose name I don't even know."

I cannot help but smile to think I've made him nervous. "Tami," I tell him. "My name is Tami."

"I'm Ike."

"I know," I tell him. "I know this from your name tag."

"Oh, right," he says, glancing down at his name tag. It

says *Ike*, then *Shift Supervisor.* "Well, Tami, will you please help me out here and take these roses off my hands?"

I reach out and he places the bouquet in them. Their sweet fragrance wafts over me and I close my eyes for a brief moment from the beauty of the smell. When I open them again, I see that Ike is very pleased with my response.

"Will you have a cup of coffee with me?" He gestures toward his table. "I promise no mango iced tea today."

I grin. That mango tea was *not* very appealing.

"I cannot," I tell him, making my face to look regretful. "I have to get right home today."

Ike's face falls. But he brightens again almost immediately.

"I'll give you a ride home, then," he offers.

Maryam. The engineer.

"No, no! Thank you very much, but I cannot."

"Oh, come on," he urges. "We're not going to have to go through this every day, now, are we?"

Today, I do not have time for a game. Today, I must make myself ready for Haroun.

"I cannot," I tell him again, kindly. "It is not something my sister would approve of, and I cannot go against her wishes. I'm sorry."

He lets out his breath, foiled by my cultural rules. He stares off into the parking lot for a moment. Then he nods to himself and looks back at me.

"Then I will walk you home," he determines. "Your sister can't possibly be opposed to that."

"Oh, yes, she can."

"Tami," he says firmly.

"Yes?" I respond warily.

"I'm not going to take no for an answer."

I raise my eyebrows at him.

"I couldn't stop thinking about you last night," he continues, his face reddening. I feel mine color as well. "I couldn't believe I let you get away yesterday without getting your phone number, or at least your name. I'm serious. You've got the most amazing smile I've ever seen in my life."

I experience a shortness of breath the likes of which I have never felt before.

"If you hadn't walked by here this afternoon, I was going to come to your house and deliver these flowers in person."

"No, *please,*" I beg him. "That would not be a good idea." I never should have let him drop me off at Maryam's house. I should have insisted that I walk the final few blocks.

Ike shrugs off my plea. "A guy's gotta do what a guy's gotta do. Let's go." He nods his head in the direction of Maryam's house.

"I will go alone," I say firmly.

"I don't think so," he says in a teasingly matter-of-fact voice.

I bite my lip and look down at my Mickey Mouse watch. It is three-thirty. The longer I delay in getting home, the less time I will have to make myself attractive for the engineer.

"If I let you accompany me part of the way, you must let me walk the last few blocks by myself. Do you agree with this?"

"Nope. Door-to-door service." His refusal comes with a smile.

"My sister will not be happy." I feel I must warn him of this.

He grins, not at all bothered. "To know me is to love me. She'll like me soon enough."

"No," I say. "You do not understand. You will not be

meeting her. She will be mad if she sees you from the window. It will cause trouble for me. You must respect my wishes, please."

"This is so *Bend It Like Beckham*."

"So bend it like what?"

"Nothing," he laughs. "Just a movie. Cross-cultural romance-type thing. I'll respect your wishes. I promise." Ike reaches out for my roses and takes them back. We begin to walk, and it is clear that Ike must shorten his pace to match mine.

"Your shoes still hurt?" he asks after a moment.

"A little."

"I could run back and get the scooter. Have you off your feet and home in no time."

I imagine Haroun arriving early and seeing me climb off the back of Ike's scooter, seeing my arms encircling his waist. Seeing me with roses from him.

"Walking is better."

"How come you don't just get walking shoes?"

I sigh. "It's complicated."

Ike gives a short laugh. "I'm pretty smart. Tell me. Let's see if I can follow."

I laugh. I try to think of how best to explain it. "You have heard how in Iran life is restricted for women, yes?"

"Sure." He nods. "I've seen things on the news. You all have to dress like nuns in those black things."

"Chadors," I tell him. "And we do not have to wear them, only people in very religious families wear them all the time. But we must wear other garments to cover ourselves."

"And this has what to do with walking shoes?"

Now he has me giggling.

"Nothing," I admit. "It is only that for me to be on the street in America all by myself dressed like this is a big deal.

My sister already wishes I would take a taxi or accept rides from her. If I make trouble or complain or show that my feets hurt, I will be forbidden to walk anymore. And I do love to walk, even with my feets hurting."

Ike stops and turns to me with a smile. He puts his hand over his heart. "That is *so* sweet, you call them *feets*."

I can tell he is not making fun of me, but I find my face hot nonetheless. "What is the correct way to say it, please?"

"Oh, you are so adorable. You're breaking my heart here, Tami, I swear. *Feets*." He begins to laugh and continues laughing until tears come to his eyes.

People don't laugh like this in Iran. Life is not so funny there. But what I have said is apparently very funny. *"Feets,"* Ike keeps repeating. He bends over and clutches his stomach and laughs and laughs. I watch him until I am infected with his laughter. Soon enough, I am crying from laughter just like him. I wipe my eyes, but he allows his tears to flow freely. Several cars honk as they pass us. This makes Ike laugh harder.

It is a very long time and many half starts before we calm down enough for me to learn that the correct plural of *foot* is *feet*, not *feets*. I know that I will not be making this mistake ever again, at least not without remembering back to this moment.

As we continue our walk, I cannot stop smiling. I used to laugh this hard with my girlfriends sometimes. The littlest thing that happened on the street we found extraordinarily funny and we would have to pull one another into the alleys to hide our loudness from the *bassidjis*. When fun is forbidden, it is all the more treasured. Perhaps that is why I am having so much fun with Ike right now. He is forbidden to me.

"What's it like, having to wear a veil all the time?" he asks, interrupting my thoughts.

I explain that it is not so bad as one might think, that the streets in Tehran are dirty and windy and it offers protection from those elements. That I am so used to it that I still feel strange without one. Not, I am quick to point out, that I miss it. It only feels strange to be without something I have known for so long.

Ike has been watching me as I speak. When I finish, he looks down to the ground. After a moment, he clears his throat.

"To force you to wear a veil is like forcing the sun to hide behind the clouds," he says quietly.

I stop walking. I take a deep breath to steady myself. Ike also stops and slowly turns to me, looking for my reaction. His eyes are so kind and beautiful and searching, *searching for me,* searching for who I am and how I feel about him in return, that I cannot look away and I want him to look at me this way forever, for this moment never to end. *He sees me,* I think. *He really sees me.* This thought tips my emotions into sadness, for I realize that no one has ever *really seen* me before, not even my family or my girlfriends. No one has ever made me feel the way I do at this moment.

Ike sees my sadness. "I'm sorry. Was that too forward of me?"

I wave off his apology. "I am not used to men saying things like this to me."

"Then I was too forward," he declares. "I'm sorry. It won't happen again."

"It was beautiful," I assure him. "It was like poetry. Do you write poetry?"

Now it is Ike who blushes. "I may have come across it on a website or something when I was looking for information on Iranian women. I don't *think* I came up with it myself."

"You researched Iranian women on the Internet?" I am incredulous. And flattered. So very, very flattered.

He nods.

I swallow hard over the lump in my throat. But then I remember it is the engineer who needs to have these feelings for me, not Ike. I stumble over my words. "I, um, I need to get home."

"Are you mad at me?"

"No, of course not."

"You're sure? I didn't offend you?"

"No," I say firmly. "I am sure."

Ike hands the roses back to me. "Shall I compare thee to a summer's day? Thou art more lovely and more temperate...."

I tilt my head. "Yours?"

He laughs. "A guy named Shakespeare."

"I see."

We smile at each other for a moment.

"I *could* write a poem for you," he offers.

I feel my smile grow larger.

"I'd write about your smile," he says in a decisive tone. I close my lips involuntarily, but continue smiling. "And your feets," he tells me. "I'd write about your feets."

I belt out a laugh. "I must go," I tell him regretfully. "Thank you for walking with me. It was very much fun."

"Will you come by the store tomorrow on your way home from class?"

"I do not know if this will be possible." I look at him directly. I want him to know that what I am really saying is no. It is not possible. I cannot spend time with him anymore. I can tell it is too dangerous.

"You wouldn't want me knocking on your door tomorrow, would you?"

"*No.* Please, no."

"Then you stop by and see me so I don't have to stop by and see you."

I shake my head at him. "You're—"

"Incorrigible?" he asks hopefully.

"I'm only here in America for a short while."

His eyes show confusion. "But I thought you'd moved here."

I decide he does not need to know of my situation. "I'm only visiting."

"How long are you here for?"

"A couple of months."

"Oh." His face falls as he processes this new information. But soon enough, the smile is back. "Well, then let's make the most of the time we have."

I am not sure what he means, but I know I cannot be seeing him every day like this. Already, I like him too much.

"I have responsibilities to my family. I do not have time for socializing, only for going to my English class."

He searches my eyes. "Let me walk you home, then. You can tell your sister I'll be your bodyguard."

I laugh. "You're the sort of person she thinks I need protection from."

"Please, Tami." His voice softens. "Just stop by for a few minutes every now and then and say hello."

I cannot tell him yes. Yet I do not want to tell him no.

"I will do my best," I promise.

"Great," he says with a relieved grin. "Then I'll see you tomorrow."

"You *are* incorrigible."

"In a good way," he adds.

11

The house smells of barley stew and unleavened bread, and I make my way toward the kitchen to greet Maryam, but she is not there.

"Maryam?" I call out. I saw her car in the driveway; she must be home. But there is no answer.

I make my way down the hall toward her bedroom and peer in. My heart softens as I see her lying asleep on the bed, with one arm thrown over her forehead, as she has done since childhood. I slip up to the bed and spread the throw quilt over her. She stirs but does not wake, and I decide to let her sleep while I take my bath. I lay the roses next to her, so she will see them upon waking. I will tell her they are for her, in thanks for our lovely day at Sabino Canyon.

I make my bath as hot as I can stand it. I pour in rose oil and I sink into the bubbles and close my eyes. My thoughts go immediately to Ike. I imagine him seeing me now. I wonder what his face would look like to see me this way, wearing no clothing and covered only by bubbles.

Ike.

Haroun.

I smile as I remember the special moment of laughter Ike and I shared. I lift my feet out of the bathwater and admire their new coat of pink nail polish. I wiggle them and make them wave up at me from the other side of the bathtub.

Hello, feets.

"Tami?" my sister calls into the bathroom as she knocks softly on the door. "Can I come in?"

"Of course." I sink my feet back under the water.

Maryam comes into the bathroom and takes a seat on the closed toilet lid.

"Did you bring the roses home?"

"They're for you."

From Ike.

"Well, thank you." I can tell she is touched. "How was English class?"

"Very good. My classmates have invited me to go dancing with them at a country-western bar one night. I said I would. Is this okay with you?"

"Which bar?" I see her trying to hide a frown.

"The Rustler, I think."

Her eyes brighten. "That's owned by a Persian!"

"What?! What does a Persian know about being a cowboy?"

"Persians know it is good to own your own business in America. That is the way to become rich."

"Is this Persian bar owner looking for a wife?" I wonder.

"I don't know," she says thoughtfully. "You should introduce yourself to him when you go."

"I will," I agree.

We discuss once again what the best outfit is for me to wear. Maryam feels strongly that I should wear a black sleeveless dress. I feel just as strongly that I should not.

To force you to wear a veil is like forcing the sun to hide behind the clouds.

"I cannot wear black," I insist to her. "Black is a chador. Black is death, and my new life is just beginning."

It takes some firmness, but ultimately I am outfitted in an elegant long-sleeve blue dress. Underneath, I wear my new add-a-cup bra from Victoria's Secret.

Haroun arrives right on time. By this, I mean *exactly* on time, not one minute before six and not one minute after six.

"He's prompt, that's good," says Maryam. Ardishir nods his agreement. Persians are notoriously late to everything; his punctuality means to me that he has adapted to life in America and wants to make that known. Maryam and Ardishir met Haroun at last year's *Noruz* festivities. Maryam knew at that time that my father was trying to get a visa for me, and so when she learned he was unmarried but established in his engineering practice, she told him about me and he seemed open to meeting me.

Maryam answers the door and welcomes him in. She takes his hand and kisses both cheeks. I approach once their greeting has concluded. Ardishir stays behind me, in the doorway.

"*Salaam,*" we say to each other. Remembering the dentist's approach to me on my first night in America and how badly I handled it, I hold out my hand for Haroun to shake. His grip is suitably firm. He assesses me with kindness in his eyes.

"How are you finding America?"

I assure him it is wonderful, everything I hoped for.

Ardishir comes forward and shakes his hand. After

Haroun removes his shoes, we all take seats in the living room and have a very friendly conversation about the weather, the well-being of our families, and our respective experiences being newcomers to America. Haroun tells several very witty stories, and when he is not looking, Maryam and I exchange glances. *So far, so good* is what we signal to each other. I like how he carries himself. His posture is admirable, and his manner of dress is neat and presentable. Even Ardishir, at the end of a long workday, comes home rumpled. Yet I suspect that Haroun does not. And he is handsome, with noteworthy cheekbones and an easy smile.

It is at the dinner table that things begin to take a strange turn. Rather, it is just before we sit down to dinner. Haroun washes his hands at the kitchen sink for an inordinately long time; it is as if he has several hundred hands to wash rather than only two. Behind his back, Maryam, Ardishir, and I make big eyes at one another, to say, *What is this all about?* But we follow him with quite vigorous cleansing of our own, so as to continue with the good impression.

Maryam and Ardishir sit at each end of the table, and Haroun and I sit across from each other. The vase of Ike's roses obstructs our view of each other until Maryam reaches to move them.

"Beautiful roses," he admires.

Maryam tells him that I purchased them for the centerpiece of such a special dinner. As a smile of gratitude crosses his face, I smile back and wonder how Ike would feel, knowing his roses are being used to impress another suitor of mine.

Maryam's dinner is delicious. Haroun says he is happy to be eating Persian food again, as living alone he mostly eats takeaway food from restaurants. The conversation continues to be lively and engaging. All is going well. After a period of roughly twenty minutes of general conversation, Haroun turns his attention solely to me.

"So you were a teacher in Iran?"

"Mmmmm," I reply, as I am taking a sip of my water when he asks the question.

"What age did you teach?" I can tell this is all polite talk, nothing more. Nothing to be upset about. Yet I feel my stomach muscles tighten.

"I taught eight-year-olds," I say evenly. "Eight- and nine-year-olds."

"What is it you hope to do here in America, Tami? Do you want to teach here as well?" His tone is pleasant, yet unreadable.

"I hope to be married."

"I think she should be a photographer," Ardishir says. "You should see some of the pictures she's taken since she got here. None of those posed, one-two-three-smile-everybody pictures. Hers are quite unique. Artistic. She's really trying to say something."

I look at him with curiosity and appreciation.

"What is it you are trying to capture with your pictures, Tami?" Haroun asks.

Freedom. It comes to me instantly, now that I have been asked. I am trying to capture freedom. Today I photographed: The first bloom of a prickly cholla cactus. An old lady wearing a goofy red hat. A car with pink daisies painted on it. A teenage boy and girl were holding hands on Fourth Avenue; I took a picture of their intertwined hands.

But does Haroun really want to know this? Or does he want to know that I will be there for him, put him first, put his career ahead of my own? There seems to be no sense in silly talk like capturing freedom. What I must capture is a husband.

"Oh, taking pictures is just something I do for fun." I wave the topic away. "What I really hope to do is be married and have children, *Inshallah,* if it pleases my husband. Not right away, but someday."

"Children are important to you?"

"Oh, yes," I tell him earnestly. "It has always been my dream to raise my children in freedom, to give them a life where they know nothing of repression. I think that is the best way for a child to reach his true potential in life, to have no ugly messages put into his head that he later has to struggle to rise above."

I say *he* and *his,* but what I really hope for is a girl. Yet I know better than to tell this to a potential husband, who will surely prefer a boy.

Haroun listens pleasantly to my response, yet when I finish, his eyes snap from me to the corner of the ceiling. He points. "There's a bug! A large bug!" He moves to shield his plate with his hands.

I cringe inwardly, for this is a horrible impression to make and the evening has gone quite well until now.

But upon inspection, there is no bug. No one but Haroun has seen it, anyway. Maryam, Ardishir, and I see nothing. Ardishir even stands and walks toward the corner of the room for a closer view, and then turns quizzically to Haroun.

"Maybe I was mistaken," Haroun apologizes, and with that, the matter is closed. He continues with his dinner as if nothing has happened. I am afraid to look at my sister or brother-in-law for fear of their reaction. Haroun again compliments Maryam on her stew and assures her that, no, it is not too salty. He tells of some interesting weekend trips he has taken to Santa Fe and San Diego. I try to pay attention, but I am confused by what has just happened. I keep glancing to the corner of the ceiling, hoping to catch sight of the horrible bug Haroun thought he saw. But there is nothing, not even a shadow or speck of dirt that might have confused him.

"Are you interested in travel, Tami?" he asks.

"Oh, yes," I tell him. "My English class is going to Lake Havasu City for our final trip, and staying overnight on a houseboat. That sounds so fun."

"Will you be going, too?"

"Ah..." I don't know what to say. "I'm not sure. It depends. Probably not."

Maryam and I exchange glances. She knows as well as I that it depends on whether or not I am married. It is not a decision I alone can make.

"Oh, you should," Haroun tells me eagerly. "Did you know the London Bridge is there?"

"The London Bridge?" Maryam asks. "In Lake Havasu, Arizona?"

"Yes, you know that children's rhyme?" He sings, "*London Bridge is falling down, falling down....* Well, it *was,* and some businessman in America had it taken down brick by brick and reconstructed in Lake Havasu."

"Why on earth would anyone do that?" Ardishir is incredulous. "What a total waste of money."

"It put the place on the map. Now it's a huge tourism—" Haroun suddenly drops his fork and swipes at his shin beneath the table.

"What's wrong?" Maryam asks with urgent concern.

"Something was crawling up my leg." He gives Maryam an accusing look. "Have you sprayed for pests lately?"

"Yes, of course, we're on contract with Truly Nolen," she assures him.

Haroun continues rubbing his shin. "I think it bit me, whatever it was. Felt like a scorpion."

"A scorpion wouldn't come inside," Ardishir tells him. "It was probably only a fly."

"In any case," Maryam says, "I am very sorry it bit you."

"A fly wouldn't bite him," says Ardishir.

"It *wasn't* a fly, I am sure of it. It was much larger and had tentacles."

"You could feel that it had tentacles?" Ardishir sounds doubtful.

"Yes." Haroun looks Ardishir straight in the eye. "Tentacles."

"Do you need some ointment?" I ask him. "Or a washcloth?"

"No, thank you," he says brusquely. "I'll address it when I return home."

My hope for a marriage to him is quickly fading to dread. I have not seen any bugs, inside or out, since arriving at Maryam's house, and I do not believe Haroun has been bitten. I think his imagination tricks him. I take a long drink of water and pour myself some more from the pitcher.

"Your hands are shaking," Haroun points out.

That's because you're weird.

But I smile, as if I am touched that he noticed.

"My sister is perhaps just a bit nervous," Maryam speaks for me.

"Please, we're all friends here."

I smile again, closed-lipped. Perhaps a fly really bit him and perhaps there really *was* a bug in the corner. Perhaps I am misreading the situation because the stakes for me are so high.

"Did you have to see a doctor before leaving Iran?" he questions, still rubbing his leg. "Is that still the law, that you need a medical examination to enter the United States?"

"Yes, I did see a doctor. It's still the law." Out of the corner of my eye, I see Ardishir and Maryam exchange glances.

"Do any degenerative diseases run in your family?" he asks me.

"Tami is very healthy, if that's what you're asking," Maryam says. Her polite tone is strained.

"I'm sure she is," he assures her. "I was asking more about whether anyone in your family required a health attendant or long-term care."

"Tell us more about your travels," Ardishir urges Haroun quickly, seeing how Maryam is angered by the question.

But Haroun now turns to me. "You would not object to getting a complete physical, would you? I would pay for it, of course. And send you to my personal physician."

"Um..."

Ardishir comes to my rescue. "We are perhaps talking too far ahead of ourselves."

"You are correct, I am sorry." Haroun turns to Maryam and his eyes become polite. Less insistent. Less crazy. "How did you prepare this meat? It is delicious."

Maryam describes her cooking process, and we slip back into pleasant, normal getting-to-know-each-other conversation. I tell of the beauty of Sabino Canyon and some of the houses I admire on my route to school. Ardishir tells of a funny woman patient he had this afternoon. Maryam teases about some of the *pooldar* American women who shop at Macy's. Haroun tells a funny story about his neighbor. By the end of the meal, I am back to feeling hopeful about Haroun. A long conversation over tea and sweets does nothing to dispel my hope.

When it comes time for Haroun to leave, Maryam and Ardishir say good-bye and discreetly disappear into the kitchen. I walk him to the door and wait as he slips his shoes back on.

He straightens and smiles at me.

"Thank you for a lovely time, Tami."

"Thank *you*."

"May I call on you again?"

"I would be honored." I give him my Julia Roberts smile, the one that worked so well on Ike, and suddenly his forehead wrinkles. He leans in.

"Open your mouth, please."

I draw back. "Pardon?"

"Let me see your mouth."

This request startles me so much that I do what he asks without thinking. I open wide. He leans in again and studies each tooth individually. When he backs off, he taps me on the nose in what I am sure he thinks is a playful manner. "Not to worry. There are some good corrective smile surgeons in town. Have you thought about seeing one?"

But Ike said my smile is dazzling.

I snap my mouth closed and firmly shake my head. He laughs like I am joking and makes a move to take my hand.

I hesitate.

"You're a shy one, aren't you?" he asks, as if this pleases him.

I'm not shy. You're just strange.

He reaches for my hand again. With dread in my heart, I let him take it.

"I think we'd get on quite companionably, don't you?" he asks. It is all I can do not to pull my hand back. We look at each other for a moment. "I'll call you in the next week or so to make arrangements. Okay?"

"Mmmm." It is all I can say. I am afraid I will scream if I

open my mouth. Thankfully, he takes my response as agreement and moves to step outside.

I close the door quietly behind him and lean my head against it. I begin to bang my head on the door, over and over, harder each time. I am thinking one thing only, chanting one thing only.

He wants to marry me.

He wants to marry me.

May God strike me dead; he wants to marry me.

12

ami?" my sister says quietly, coming up behind me.
I stop banging my head. I take a deep breath and
turn to face her. She looks at me with great compassion.

Ardishir is at her side. He is incredulous. "Did he just inspect your mouth?"

I nod and sniff to keep my nose from running. "Like I am
a horse he is considering to buy."

"Did I hear him right? Did he say he's open to a marriage?" Maryam asks.

I nod with a heavy heart.

"Don't worry," she says kindly.

I avert my gaze.

It is easy for her to say, *Don't worry*. She is lucky to have
found such a decent man as Ardishir. She is not the one who
will have to hunt down imaginary bugs and nurse imaginary
scorpion bites.

"At least he can provide for you a decent home," she consoles.

"She's not going to marry him!" Ardishir explodes. "He's a nut job!"

I sink my eyes into Ardishir. My savior. My lifeline. Yet again, he is rescuing me from Maryam. Or trying to, anyway.

"What makes him crazy?" Maryam demands. "What? Because he got bit from a bug?"

"He didn't get bit," I declare. "It was all in his head."

"And that bug on the ceiling!" Ardishir mimics Haroun, how he snapped his head and bulged his eyes. He laughs as he remembers. I take Ardishir's cue and join in with his laughter. I hope it causes Maryam to see that two reasonable people in the room, Ardishir and me, think Haroun is crazy. And if she is reasonable, she will think so, too.

And of course, I cannot be expected to marry someone who is crazy. *Can I? Or is this, perhaps, the price I must pay?*

"And the way he washed his hands!" Ardishir slaps his hand to his forehead. "I thought he'd be at the sink all night!"

Maryam's eyes are dark and determined. "There is nothing wrong with cleanliness. And perhaps he really did see a bug on the ceiling. Only last week, one climbed out of the bathroom drain. I saw it myself."

"He's cuckoo, Maryam," Ardishir insists. "You don't want your sister marrying someone like him."

Tears come to Maryam's eyes. "I want her to stay in America, *that's* what I want."

"I know," soothes Ardishir. "And she will. We'll find a way."

"She doesn't have all that much time," she snaps at him. Then she turns to me. "Tami, he was not so bad. You must admit, ninety-five percent of the evening was very pleasant."

Ardishir bursts out laughing at her logic. "The remaining five percent was *pretty freaky*, though, wasn't it?"

Maryam shrugs, turns her palms upward. "So what if he does not like bugs? It is not the worst thing in the world, for him to dislike bugs. I do not—"

"No, Maryam," Ardishir interrupts. "You have it wrong. Haroun does not like *imaginary* bugs."

"She would do much worse marrying in Iran. You know what her options are there." Maryam gives him a meaningful look. "So Haroun has issues with bugs. He is mostly okay. He makes a good living, he can provide for her."

I let out a shaky breath. "I am very tired. Let us save our decisions until the morning."

"This is not something even to consider," Ardishir insists.

"Yes it is!" Maryam looks as if she will scratch his eyes out with her long red fingernails.

I am ashamed that I have caused them to fight. "Thank you both for tonight," I tell them. "I am so very grateful to you for your hospitality."

Maryam waves off my thanks. "It's not hospitality. This is your home as much as it is ours. Right, Ardishir?"

"Of course."

This is where I know for sure they *both* are wrong. This is not my home. I will have to leave it, one way or another. Either my visa will expire and I will go back to Iran, or I will get married and move to my husband's home.

I bite my bottom lip to keep my tears from flowing as I go upstairs to my bedroom. Once in the privacy of my room, I stare at myself in the mirror. My face has turned greasy from all the makeup Maryam slathered on me.

I snarl at my reflection. Perhaps Haroun is the best I can do in such a short time. Perhaps he is all that I deserve.

I let out a big sigh and rearrange the *hejab* that hangs over the corner of my mirror so it covers the whole thing, so I am hidden from seeing myself. I light my Perpetual Light candle, turn on my Googoosh music, and smear cream all over my face. I rub it off viciously, cursing my fate, hating that all my choices are bad ones.

I turn off my light and climb into bed. I burrow myself in the fluffy red comforter on my bed and turn so I can watch the flame of the candle dance in the darkness.

My bedroom has always been my refuge. Since Maryam married Ardishir and left Iran, I have had my very own bedroom. It is the only place I did not have to wear some sort of veil, some sort of mask. On the streets, I literally veiled myself—kept a grim, eyes-down countenance. At my job, I put a barrier between myself and my girls every time I pretended to them that the future was something to which they could look forward. And with my dear parents, I was the polite, obedient, understanding daughter, the one who pretended not to see Maman's glassy, tear-puffed eyes. With her so sluggishly sad, I countered with a dutiful cheer. Always a veil. It has only been alone at night that I get any sense of who I am, of who I might become. It is alone at night that I have found my greatest peace.

I realize that I will lose this, too. I will lose my nighttime peace. If I marry Haroun, I will come to imagine all sorts of rodents running through the house at night. I will begin to hear the crackle of imaginary cockroaches and the buzz of imaginary wasps as I try to fall asleep. I am sure Haroun will twist restlessly in our bed, fending off imaginary insects.

Good night. Sleep tight. Don't let the bedbugs bite.

I suddenly remember this rhyme from our days in America, from the nights our father tucked Maryam and me into the double bed we shared at our apartment in Berkeley. We used to pinch each other after he'd left the room. *Gotcha.*

The memory makes me smile. I will have to remind Maryam of this in the morning. We, too, used to conjure up imaginary bugs.

But we did it only for fun, not because we were crazy.

Maryam.

I know she is trying to help. And I know there are to be sacrifices involved in rushing into marriage. I did not expect to find my one true love in such a short period of time. I knew I would have to settle. And I know that my life is not destined to be easy. Being a woman from Iran, I would never dare to hope for such a thing. I just never realized how tiring it is, to have to constantly drum up the energy to live only a half life.

Everyone in my life that I love has had to make sacrifices. My mother and father settle every day, living in the wake of a revolution that has betrayed them.

Maman Joon. With her soft skin that smells of rosewater. Who goes to the beauty salon every week to have her hair done, her eyebrows waxed, her skin deep-cleansed, and her toes manicured. *Why, Maman,* I used to ask when I was still a child, *why do you bother when you only have to cover yourself up afterward?*

And she would look at me in kindness and explain herself to a daughter too young to possibly understand.

Because they can make me cocoon myself from the world, but they cannot stop me from feeling beautiful.

At this she would take my chin in her hand and bend close to me. *I will live in the cocoon, Tami. And you will emerge as my beautiful butterfly.*

I begin to cry as I think of my mother. Poor *Maman Joon.* She should not have to live the way she does. They should return her passport. They should let her go.

Sleep does not come to me this night. I cry all the tears that

I have stored up for so long, tears of homesickness and parent-sickness and friend-sickness. Tears for the sacrifices inherent in being a woman of Iran.

When it is very late and I am sure Maryam is asleep, I walk stealthily to the kitchen and dial my parents' home in Iran. It must be close to noon there, and I expect my mother to be home. Sure enough, after only three rings I hear the lullaby that is her voice.

"*Allo? Allo?*"

"*Salaam,* Maman, *Hale shoma chetor-e?*" *How are you?*

"What's wrong, Tami? Is everyone okay? Are you and Maryam all right?"

Tears gather in my eyes. How many years I heard her ask these same worried questions each time she received a phone call from Maryam. Her tone always roused my father and me from whatever we were doing, to hear Maryam's news from America.

"We're fine, Maman. I just wanted to hear your voice. It is very late here, and Maryam is asleep."

"Tell me how you are, *Tami Joon.*"

My tears stream down my face. I wipe them and sniffle and wipe the whole mess onto my pajama top. I no longer try to hide my sorrow from my mother. Instead, I explain to her my dinner with Haroun and the predicament in which I now find myself.

"So you and Ardishir both think he is unwell in the head. And yet Maryam does not."

I confirm this is true.

"Ardishir thinks you should not marry him?"

"That's right."

"And Maryam thinks you should."

"That's right."

"And what do you think, Tami?"

I inhale deeply. "My head tells me this is the correct and logical decision to make. Marrying Haroun would allow me to stay here, and I do love it here. He would be a good provider and does not seem too religious."

"And your heart? What does your heart say?"

"Does that matter?" There is bitterness in my voice.

"Of course it does."

"I don't know, Maman. It isn't my heart so much as my stomach, my gut. I have been unable to talk myself out of this heavy feeling I have had since dinner."

"He really asked to inspect your mouth?"

"He did."

In the moment of silence that follows, I am able to picture my mother perfectly and imagine what she is doing at this moment. She is dressed in house pants and slippers and has her hair pulled back with a barrette. She is standing at the window facing the courtyard. The curtains are open, since the window is not visible from the street. And she is watching leaves twirl through the cobblestones. And she is thinking what to say to her youngest daughter, knowing how much I depend on her wisdom. This silence brings me calm, for I know her judgment will be sound. She more than anyone knows how much is at stake for me.

"You are perhaps not ready to get married, even if it was to someone perfect in every way," Maman finally says.

This thought occurs to me frequently as I fall asleep at night, listening to my sad Googooshi music. I have so enjoyed my freedom here, and so chafed under Maryam's manageable admonitions. A husband's admonitions might not be so mild, and cannot be so easily dismissed.

"Would you marry Haroun in Iran? If not, then you should not marry him at all. *Go as far as you can see, and when you get there you'll see farther*. You must trust this will happen. You must trust that Allah has other plans for you than to become Haroun's wife. If He wanted you to marry Haroun, He would have made Haroun more stable."

"I'm sure you're right, Maman. It is just hard to walk away when I don't know what the future holds."

"I know, my love. Believe me, I know."

"If I do decide to marry him, will you support my decision?"

There is hesitation.

"You will do what must be done, Tami. I know this about you. Your father and I will support you and trust you, no matter what your decision."

"Even if that means I may have to come back home?"

There is more hesitation.

"Your friend Minu is engaged, did you know? She is marrying Seyed, the grocer's son."

This may sound like a change of subject, but it is not. Unemployment is very high in Iran. Seyed is okay, and he is employed, but poor Minu will have to live in the house of her mother-in-law. And her mother-in-law is known for her dourness and meanness to others. When you marry in Iran, you marry the whole family. All the brothers, parents, cousins, and uncles. And it seems there is always one who finds ways to be cruel.

"Poor Minu," I say. "I am sad for her, but she must have felt it was her best choice."

"I'm sure she did."

This is my mother's way of telling me that my choices would be even more limited in Iran.

"Let me talk to her," I hear my father's voice insist in the background.

"*Tami Joon,* how is America?"

"Baba!"

"How is my little black fish?"

A moan of homesickness escapes from my throat. "*Baba Joon,* I miss you. I wish you and Maman could be here with me. Our family should not be separated like this."

"Shhhh," he quiets me. "You must not say such a thing. You are our little black fish, and you will keep going and keep going and don't let the pelicans swallow you up. We are fine here. You must not think sad thoughts of missing us."

"I know, Baba," I whisper. I hide from him my sniffles. He wants to see only the brave side of me.

After we say *Khoda hafez* and hang up, I cry there in the blackness of the kitchen until deep exhaustion overtakes me. I stumble back to my bed, stopping only to turn on my Googooshi music once more.

At first, I cuddle under my covers in the middle of the bed in a fetal position, like a baby in her mother's womb. This is how I usually fall asleep. But then I realize this will have to change once I am married so I better get used to it. I scoot over to one side of the bed and lie on my back and straighten my legs. I pull the covers up to my chest and cross my hands over my stomach. I imagine myself sharing a bed with Haroun. In this imagined future, I foresee many nights like this, nights in which I feel so alone I must sneak out of bed and cry to my mother over the telephone wires. I see myself lying awake in my half of the bed and staring at the contours of the ceiling while my husband slumbers beside me.

13

"Tami, time to wake up."

I hear Maryam's voice from the doorway. With my eyes still closed, I can feel light breaking through the cracks in the window shades. I decide to feign sleep and hopefully she will leave me in peace.

It is not to be. I hear her soft footsteps approach, and the bed sags slightly as she sits on its edge.

"Tami, you must wake up or you'll be late to class." She gently shakes my shoulder.

I moan. It is all I can do. My eyelids refuse to open. I suspect the salt from last night's tears has made my lids stick together.

Maryam shakes my shoulder a little more insistently. I manage to open one eye and catch sight of my alarm clock. She is right. If I do not get up immediately, I shall be late to class. But I simply do not have the energy. My depression smothers me like a winter quilt. I shift my one open eye to Maryam's face.

"I do not feel very well today," I tell her. "I think I will stay home, if that is all right."

"Of course it's all right. Can I bring you anything?" Maryam places her palm on my forehead to feel for fever. Her touch feels so cool and pleasant that I whimper. This is what my mother did when we were sick as children. This is what I need today, someone to take care of me. Comfort me. Make me feel better.

"Do you remember when we were children in America and *Baba Joon* tucked us in our bed at night and told us to sleep tight and don't let the bedbugs bite?"

Maryam smiles. "Of course I remember. I'm surprised you do. You were so little."

"I only remembered last night as I was lying in bed. I wondered if Haroun is attacked by bedbugs each night."

Maryam slaps her hand to her forehead. "Oh, no! I bet he is, poor man."

We giggle.

"I called Maman last night," I tell Maryam when the joke has lost its luster.

"You did? Why didn't you tell me so I could talk, too?"

"It was very late. You were asleep and I didn't want to wake you."

"Did you talk to her about Haroun?"

"She says I should not rush into anything."

"She's a fine one to talk." Her voice has an ugly edge to it.

"What are you so mad at her for? Have you been mad all these years? Is this why you never visit?"

She ignores my questions and asks one of her own. "Did you remind her you *have* to rush?"

"She knows, Maryam."

Maryam sighs. "I know he's not perfect, Tami. But you

must listen to *me*. I am right here with you, and I will not let you make a decision that will ruin your life. We really do not know for sure there wasn't a bug on the ceiling or that a bug did not bite his leg."

Not this again.

"Come on, Maryam. It was all in his head."

"How do you know?"

"For one, he was looking directly at me and talking to me, when he snapped his head full around to the corner of the ceiling. There was no way he could have *seen* a bug in that corner from how his head was positioned. There's no way. It was an involuntary gesture and completely paranoid."

"You should not be so judgmental, Tami."

"I'm *not* judgmental, Maryam. I'm only trying to be honest with myself." I push my covers off and sit up. My head suffers from dull throbbing.

"What are you doing?" She separates my sheet from my blanket and covers me with the sheet once more. "You should stay in bed if you're sick."

If I stay in bed, I am sure Maryam will call in sick as well and stay right next to me and talk to me all day of the benefits of marrying Haroun. That will do nothing for my mood.

"I'm only tired," I say. "I don't want to miss class."

"At least let me drive you today."

I thank her and stumble my way through my shower, dressing, and breakfast. Maryam has perhaps realized that it is she who has driven me out of the house, for she does not say another word about Haroun. We kiss as she drops me off, and I assure her I am well enough to walk home, and that perhaps the walk will do me good.

I feel my spirits lift as I approach my classroom. There is such a crazy energy in the room, most especially from Agata and Josef and their silly behaviors. It is increasingly clear to me that he is in love with her. If she realizes it, too, then she is doing an admirable job of pretending she does not.

Today, I notice immediately that along with her brown linen dress, which she has worn every day to class, she is wearing an orange-pink-white flower pin decoration in her hair. And she is wearing bright orange lipstick to match. She looks like a clown.

"Agata!" I exclaim. "Is today a special day?"

Edgard winks at me. Agata sniggers, to let me know she is in on the joke as well.

"Josef gave me a present yesterday of this hairpin and this lipstick."

"Oh," I say admiringly, smiling at Josef. "That was a very thoughtful thing to do, Josef."

He smiles proudly. "She never buys anything for herself. Even her clothes, they are handed down from people in her church. She should have nice things that have belonged to no one before her."

"She *should,*" I agree.

"You should see her apartment," he continues. "Nothing's new. The curtains were out-of-date by the end of the 1970s. And her bathroom towels have fringes hanging from them."

Eva has walked in and heard Josef's comment. "What were you doing in her apartment, *hmmmm?*"

Edgard laughs. I smile. Of course Eva's interpretation of the situation has something to do with sex. But Nadia speaks up, as she always does when someone is in need of defense.

"Agata has lived a hard life," she reminds Josef. "When you lose both your parents and your brother in such a horrid manner as she did, perhaps things like new curtains are not so very important."

She is right, of course. I feel ashamed for smiling at Eva's joke.

"My husband and I picked out those curtains together," Agata states firmly. "God rest his soul," she adds, as she always does.

"Life goes on," Josef replies matter-of-factly. "My wife died. I still buy myself new curtains once in a while."

"Well, *bully for you*," Agata says, and turns to face the front of the classroom, using yesterday's lesson in slang against him. Josef shrugs and faces the front, too.

Eva, Nadia, Edgard, and I look at one another behind their backs and make what-to-do faces. We take our seats in silence and wait for Danny to get the overhead projector set up. I am very much relieved when Josef leans over and whispers something into Agata's ear. I do not hear what he says, but Agata slaps his shoulder and smiles at him. He smiles back. Eva raises her eyebrows to me. I smile. And then I slip my camera out of my backpack and take a picture of Agata's hair clip.

As Danny calls the class to order, Eva leans over. "Want to do something after class?" she whispers.

I nod.

Coffee. We could go for coffee.

This thought lifts my mood even more, and soon I am doing all I can to make the class lively and fun for my classmates.

When I am paired for one-on-one conversation with Nadia, I invite her to join us.

"My husband is picking me up." Her tone is rueful and she does not need to say anything more. She talks like some of my married Persian friends who are in unhappy marriage situations.

"Perhaps another time," I tell her, knowing this is not likely. And then, to make the situation less awkward for her, I change the subject. "He must be very excited about the baby."

"He wishes we were having a boy." Her eyes contain such pain that I reach for her hand and squeeze it gently.

"Men always do, don't they?" I shake my head like it is a lighthearted wish. Yet I know for many men, it is a very important matter, and they are very disappointed in their wives if they produce girls. "But girls are the best. Have you chosen a name for your daughter yet?"

Nadia shakes her head, *No.*

"What about naming her after your mother?"

Nadia grimaces. "Her name is Cyzarine. I want something less harsh-sounding than that."

"Your grandmother's name?"

"Anzhelika."

I laugh. "Well, that doesn't help much, does it?" I am pleased to see her smile, to know that my friendliness has made her feel better.

We talk about her cravings for Mexican food, which she's never even eaten before this pregnancy. We talk of what it feels like to have a living being inside you, and some of her fears of being fully and singularly responsible for a new life.

"You don't think your husband will help out much?"

"Oh, I'm sure he will," she says lightly, then immediately asks after my parents. I tell her I spoke with them just last night, and how good it was to hear their voices. Nadia prompts me to tell her about my mother, and I do. I tell her everything I love about her, including and especially knowing what she has had to sacrifice in order for her daughters to be happy.

"Your mother sounds wonderful," Nadia tells me.

"She is," I agree.

"I miss my mother, too," she says quietly. "She didn't think I was making a good decision in getting married and coming here."

"That's all my parents want for me, to come to America and get married."

"They hold you close and then push you away." She murmurs this, almost to herself.

"I'm sorry?"

She rests her eyes on me. "Sometimes the best thing a mother can do for her daughter is send her away, like yours did. She sent you out into the world so life can be better, you know? And then other times, the best thing a mother can do is keep her close, to shield her from the ugliness of the world. That is what *my* mother tried to do, but I wouldn't listen. I should have listened."

Nadia's English is difficult to follow. It takes several long moments to process her words. And when I do, I am unsure how best to comfort her, how to help her not feel she is to blame. For, really, could she have known? How could anyone really know what it will be like to live with someone day after day, year after year? Perhaps there were signs that her mother saw but Nadia chose to ignore. But must Nadia be punished for such a mistake for the rest of her life? I do not want this to be the case, for I am, myself, in not such a different situation as her.

"Maybe things will get better for you," I encourage her. "Maybe after the baby, your husband will be very happy."

Her look tells me she has no such hope.

"He's never been happy," she confides. "And as long as I'm with him, I won't be, either."

I let out my breath and we sit for the remainder of our allotted conversational time with a heavy veil of silence between us. I do not know how to comfort her.

14

After class, I take Eva into my confidence and tell her about Ike. About how he has brought me flowers and walked me home. About how he has asked that I stop by today.

"I promised my sister I would not befriend any American men," I tell her. "But this—well, this is two girlfriends only going out for a cup of coffee, yes?"

"Why do you let your sister tell you what to do?" Eva demands as we start our walk to Starbucks. I push up the sleeves on my sweater. The sky is clear and upbeat, sunny as ever. I have yet to see a cloudy day in Tucson.

"She is only looking out for me."

"Bullshit," Eva says. "She's trying to control you."

"We don't think that way in my culture," I explain. "She is my sister and she is thinking only of me. If I have a reputation that is tarnished, it will be very difficult for me to find a husband."

"Screw finding a husband!"

I laugh. Eva wears a short skirt and thigh-high boots and clops along with a sexual confidence I know I can never match. Nor would I want to. Nor do I want to swear like her, but I love it when she does. It sounds so bold. Eva has no need for taking this English class. She speaks English as well as she ever will. *Like a sailor.* She knows all the swear words and slang and uses them often. I think she only takes the class for something to do, until her green card arrives or until her husband gets back.

"If I don't find a husband, I have to go back to Iran. You must know that."

She looks sideways at me. "You're like Nadia." She does not say this like it is a good thing. "She was a mail-order bride, you know."

"A what?"

"A mail-order bride. You know, some lonely American dickhead loser can't get it on with American women and so he orders a wife on the Internet. I don't know why Russia is where they always seem to order them from, but it is."

"Her husband does not sound very nice."

"Last semester, she came in with three broken fingers one day. Another time, she had choke marks on her neck. He's an *asshole.*" She shakes her head in disgust. "I have no patience for women who put up with that shit. She needs to dump the dumbfuck before he kills her."

"She needs to survive," I defend Nadia. "She has come here from far away and has no one."

"She has us," Eva retorts.

"Maybe she doesn't think some of her classmates are so open to helping her."

Eva bumps into my shoulder and turns to me. "You mean me, don't you?"

"Well . . ." I did not mean to speak so frankly. But just because Eva has been lucky in life, it does not excuse her from being sympathetic to women less fortunate. "We should do something for her. Have a party for her before the baby comes, perhaps. She's having a girl, did you know?"

"Yippee," says Eva without enthusiasm.

I laugh. "What, you don't like girls?"

"I don't like kids, period. They tie you down. I only want men tying me down. Literally, if you know what I mean."

She winks at me lasciviously. I shrug my shoulders in apology. I just don't get most of her sexual innuendos.

"Bondage," she articulates. "Have you heard of bondage?"

She stops on the street—right in the middle of the sidewalk!—and mimics having her hands tied above her head. She squirms, thrusts her pelvis out, and moans, *"Oh, baby, do whatever you want. I'm your prisoner. Oh, baby."*

"You're the goofiest girl I've ever met," I tell her, laughing despite my horror.

She throws her arm around my shoulder. "Come on," she says. "Let me tell you some dirty jokes as we walk to see your boyfriend."

"He's *not* my boyfriend."

When a big white pickup truck approaches from behind a few moments later and slows, matching our pace, all my muscles tense. I am back in Tehran walking home from school with Minu and Leila. *The* bassidji. *The morals police.*

Eva senses my panic. "What's wrong?"

"Don't look back," I tell her. "Just keep walking." With my free hand, I reach to tuck my bangs into my *hejab,* to pull it forward on my head. No *hejab.* Panic courses through my blood.

"They're only college boys, Tami." Eva waves at them. "Hi, boys!"

I clutch her arm. *"Don't."*

They pull up to the curb near us. "Hey, ladies. We're going to Bob Dob's. Want to join us?"

"Want to?" Eva asks me.

"No!" *What is she thinking?*

"You're sure? It might be fun, having a few brewskis with the boys. They're both pretty cute."

"Eva." I glare at her.

She turns to them and smiles apologetically. "Sorry, guys. We're off to see Tami's boyfriend."

I pinch her arm. The boys in the pickup say "Too bad" and drive away. Eva pulls firmly away from me. "What was *that* all about?"

Relief floods over me. I feel loose, like my body has no joints and I might flop to the ground. Like I might start giggling or crying and never stop.

"I'm sorry. It's just that if this were Iran, we might have been arrested just now." There is no *might* about it, with Eva in her short skirt and thigh-high boots, and neither of us with headscarves, we *would* have been taken to jail.

"For what, walking down the street?" Eva's look is scornful, tough, like she could take on anyone. In Iran, she'd have her defiance beaten right out of her.

"Never mind." I finally let go of her arm and stand on my own. She will never understand how things are back home. And this is perhaps a good thing. "Would you really go somewhere with men you don't know?"

"Sure." She smiles at me. "This is how we *meet* people."

"Well, I already told you, I'm not supposed to spend time with American men."

"Ike doesn't count?"

I return her smile. "Ike doesn't count."

"But he's American, right?"

"He's American."

"And he's a man, right?"

"Right." I grin. She has caught me.

"What-ever."

I laugh and bump my shoulder into hers as we walk down the street.

"Don't be mad, Eva. I don't mean to ruin your fun. You can go along with those men if you really want to."

"No," she says in a way that tells me they're already out of her thoughts. "I want to see what this Ike is all about. I want to see what's so great about him that you're willing to break your sister's rules."

"I'm not!" I insist. "I'm only going for coffee with my girlfriend!"

"You are so *full of shit,*" she says to me with a grin. That phrase is all her own. I know what the word *shit* means, and it was not in yesterday's lesson.

Oh, my God," Eva whispers to me as we arrive at Starbucks to find Ike sitting at a table on the patio. "Is that him?"

"Mmmm-hmmm," I say back quietly. He is perhaps five meters away. If she raises her voice, he will hear what she says.

"Two words come to mind," she tells me. *"Eminently fuckable."*

I elbow her, hard. But it is too late, he has heard her. I can tell by the surprise I see sparkling in his eyes.

"He is fucking *hot,*" she continues in a low voice. "Check out those biceps."

"Eva," I scold. "Shhhhh. You are being very rude."

Ike stands, and Eva gives me a little nudge forward. I introduce them.

"Tami needs a chaperone," Eva says as they shake hands.

He smiles broadly at Eva. "Something tells me you're one hell of an unusual chaperone."

He turns from her to me and my breath quickens as we lock eyes. "I'm glad you could make it." His smile grows wider. I can tell mine does, too. It is Julia Roberts huge, only by now, it is all mine and it is for real.

And it does not need to be surgically corrected.

He urges us to join him at the table. We make small talk for a few minutes as Ike inquires how class was and Eva tells him the Agata-and-Josef story. We laugh over how goofy Agata looked, and try to figure out if she was wearing such gaudy lipstick and the hairpiece to make fun of Josef, or if she was really pleased with the fact of the gift despite how dreadful it was. Ike tells us some funny stories from his day at work, and soon enough, we are all laughing together and chatting away as if we were longtime friends.

But it feels false to me, this lightness. I feel as if I am outside of myself, looking at these three laughing people and wishing I could be one of them. This is all I ever wanted in Iran, the freedom to laugh in public. To choose my own friends, no matter if they're men. To sit in the open air at a café and talk without fear of the *bassidjis*. I would gladly wear that stupid *hejab* forever if I could just look at men in the eye and make a connection of friendship and share a table at a coffee shop without fear of my world coming to an end.

"Earth to Tami," says Eva, and snaps her fingers in front of my eyes. "You're a million miles away, and all you've left us is a dopey smile on your face."

I come back to them. "I was just thinking what a great day it would be in Iran if we were suddenly allowed to go to coffee shops and mix men and women together. To openly be friends with each other, I mean. I think a whole revolution could be prevented."

"Really?" says Ike. "You think lives will be lost before *coffee shops* are integrated?"

"Not coffee shops, but coffee tables. And absolutely. Of this I am sure. Many Iranians think things will change gradually in a bloodless revolution. But I don't."

"But going for *coffee*. That's such a simple thing," he exclaims.

I laugh. "But it's not, of course. Men aren't even supposed to *look* at women. To look at them is considered fornication of the eye."

"Fornication of the eye!" Eva loves it. She slaps her hand on the table and repeats the phrase. "Fornication of the eye! Ooh, baby, *fornicate my eye!*"

I am glad she finds it funny. I, however, cannot laugh. I am reminded of sixteen-year-old Atefeh Rajabi of Neka who was very recently found guilty of the similarly absurd crime of "acts incompatible with chastity." Poor Atefeh was hung from a crane and left dangling in public view for forty-five minutes, while the man involved received one hundred lashes and was released. The story making the rounds in Tehran is that she so incensed the judge by pulling off her headscarf and *speaking in a sharp tongue* that he, personally, slipped the noose around her neck and gave the order for the crane to rise. He, personally, ordered her lifeless body to hang there for forty-five minutes as a message to other girls: *This can happen to you.*

I fix a smile on my face and stop myself from sharing the story of Atefeh. There is no need to infect my friends with the vision of such atrocities, no need to dampen the pleasure of this afternoon. *Yet, what if the world could really see? Would it matter, would it make things different for us, if they saw Atefeh dangling from the crane?*

Ike notices my silence, my discomfort with Eva's jokes.

"You think there's going to be another revolution?" he asks.

"I don't know," I say with a sigh. "It is not so long since our war with Iraq. So many sons and fathers died, hundreds of thousands. It is too fresh, I think. We already have to make too many visits to the cemetery. You should see how large it is now. It has a playground and restaurant and takes up kilometers of land. None of my generation wants our parents to have to suffer through another revolution. The mullahs are old. They cannot live forever. Perhaps we can wait them out and things will get better. Or perhaps someone of prominence will convince them to stop forcing faith on people; it is a contradiction in terms and an insult to the religion. God does not want a government, he only wants people to treat one another with decency and dignity. This is what we think. Many of us, I should say."

"I know!" says Eva. "Maybe there could be some sort of compromise. Women and men can go to coffee shops together, but women have to wear chadors, those ones with only slots for the eyes. Can you just picture it, trying to have any type of conversation in one of those awful things? Or drink coffee! How do you drink coffee when you're wearing a chador?"

She laughs loudly. I start laughing, too. Chadors are made for isolating, not for socializing. Ike just shakes his head at us and tries not to join in.

"Or," Eva continues, "men could start wearing chadors, too, as a sign of protest! Mix everything all up."

"We don't wear chadors!" I insist through my laughter. "Only *hejab*. It is only the very religious women who wear chadors."

"Okay," Eva says. "Then men should start wearing *hejab*, too. Make a mockery of the whole thing. Ridicule as a form of protest. Yes, that's it! And now that I've single-handedly solved the problems of your country, I'm going to buy us some coffee."

Ike and I laugh as she flounces away. But it feels too weird, to sit alone with him. I look down to my lap.

"Hey," Ike says quietly after a long moment.

I look up.

"I'm glad you're here," he says, with softness in his eyes.

I smile, but I suddenly feel so very sad. I wish Minu were here with me. I wish she could have an afternoon like this. I look back down to my hands and try to move past my sorrow.

"I brought you a present," he says.

"You should not be buying me presents," I say to him, looking up to his smiling face.

"It's nothing." He hands me a plastic bag from Fleet Feet. I reach in and pull out a box.

"Shoes!" I say. I hold them up, delighted. These are the sort of shoes people wear to hike in Sabino Canyon. "This will be like walking on pillows!"

"I guessed at the size," Ike says. "I used to sell shoes in college. It was one of my many jobs."

"Thank you," I say warmly. "This is such a thoughtful gift."

"I figure you can hide them in your backpack if you don't want your sister to see them."

"Clever!" I tease.

"Try them on," he encourages.

They fit perfectly. By the time I have the laces tied, Eva is back outside with drinks.

"Hey," she says. "Nice shoes!"

"Ike gave them to me."

She gives Ike an appraising look as she sits down.

"So, Ike, are you dating anyone?" she asks unabashedly.

I will never bring Eva here again, I resolve as I stare studiously at my new shoes.

There is barely a pause before Ike responds. "There's a particular girl I like, but I wouldn't say we're dating."

My heart skips a beat. I bite my bottom lip and continue looking at my feet. *These shoes are so white.*

"She's somewhat . . . Hmmm, how to say it?" He pauses. *Reflectors, too. Very well thought out.*

"What is the word?" he thinks out loud.

My insides churn. *Can't wait to head home in these new shoes. Like walking on clouds.*

"It's not that she's shy, exactly," he continues. "It's more that she's . . ." Again he pauses.

"Obsessed with her new shoes?" Eva suggests.

"Exactly."

I smile immediately. I look up at him, so relieved he meant me.

"They're beautiful shoes," I say warmly.

He laughs. Eva rolls her eyes. "This could take forever, you two."

"We've got time." Ike keeps his eyes locked firmly with mine.

"Not really," Eva tells him.

I lift my right foot and kick her shin with my new shoe.

"So, do you like working here?" I ask brightly.

"Yeah, do you?" Eva echoes me. "I need to get a job one of these days."

"It's not bad," Ike says. "Great benefits. Great coworkers. Great experience for when I open my own place. That's my plan, a chain of coffee shops."

"How soon are you going to open them?" I ask.

"My dad and I are looking at places right now." I look at him with admiration. So he is not only a coffee shop worker.

He will be a business owner one day, too! My sister might even like him a little better if she knew this about him, I think. But no. He is a distraction, and she will never think him anything else.

"So I can work for you, then," Eva suggests.

"Only if you tell me all of Tami's secrets."

"You're on," Eva agrees. "Speaking of which—"

"*Eva!*"

"Speaking of what?" Ike asks innocently, raising one eyebrow at me and looking back to Eva.

I jump up. "Come on, Eva. We've got to go."

"I think I'll hang out here for a while and chat with Ike some more. I'll catch up with you tomorrow in class."

I put my hand on my hip. "There's no way I'm leaving you all alone with him."

"Afraid I'll learn all your secret plans and clever tricks?" Ike grins mischievously.

"Afraid I'll seduce him?" Eva grins mischievously, too.

Ike watches me, curious to see my reaction.

"You can seduce him all you want, if that means what I think it means." Ike's face falls. "Only not tonight. You're coming to dinner at my house, *remember?*"

"Why does *she* get to meet your sister?" Ike pouts.

"Aha!" Eva jumps up from her chair, excited. "Dinner with the Wicked Witch of the Middle East. *This* should be fun!"

I grimace as I realize it's equally dangerous to have Eva spend time with Maryam as it is to have her spend time with Ike. She is a land mine waiting to detonate.

"When do *I* get to meet your sister?" Ike asks.

"Never," I tell him, and smile sweetly. "But thank you very much for the shoes."

I remember my camera, and bend to pick it up. I feel

awkward, very on display, but I want proof of this day. I snap a picture of our three coffee cups, their round rims on the round table, the lack of hard edges. The rim of Eva's cardboard cup is splashed with sheer red lipstick; she has made her mark. I take a picture of Eva from her waist down—the thigh-high black boots and the leather miniskirt. Then I take one of my new white running shoes, chaste and cheery.

"Let me take one of you and Ike," Eva orders, and reaches for the camera.

"Nah," I say casually, and turn to photograph the three blond college girls at the next table. Each wears a formfitting, sleeveless shirt and talks on her cell phone. They are together yet separate. Their nails are fake-long and manicured; their teeth are too white. They are very much the same, interchangeable. Barbie doll girls. Not one would dare to wear a hair clip like Agata's.

"Here, let me take one of you and Ike," Eva demands again.

I snap the plastic cap back onto the camera lens. "That was my last shot. No more film."

"Then what did you waste it for, taking pictures of people you don't even know?" My friend Eva is not very polite.

"Tami's trying to spark a revolution when she goes back to Iran. Aren't you?" I look at Ike quizzically. He's not joking.

"What do you mean?"

"I don't know," he admits. "But you seem to be taking them with some sort of purpose. To use in some way."

Eva stretches her arms and strikes a sultry, kissing-the-camera pose. "Take another of me and staple it up on all the light posts in Tehran. *I am freedom.*"

You are pornography, I think but do not say. I giggle instead. "I'm looking for more . . . what is the word?"

"Subtlety?" Ike suggests.

"Yes," I agree. "More subtlety."

"You are looking for freedom in all its often overlooked details. You want to document some of the little choices that free people make."

"Yes!" I am amazed, openmouthed amazed. He grins at me like he has figured me out, and continues, "You are photographing tiny acts of everyday rebellion."

I gasp. "How? How could you know this? What makes you think it? I have only taken four pictures just now."

He shrugs. "But look at your choices. I can totally imagine you back in Iran showing them to all your girlfriends."

I step back, startled, and stare at him in awe. He hardly knows me. And I am not going back to Iran, he is wrong about that. Yet he is right, too. I do take my pictures with the hungry, yearning eyes of Leila and Minu in mind.

How did you do that, look into my soul like that? This is what my eyes ask his. Ike's eyes are as blue as the Tucson sky, with not a cloud in them. *I don't know,* they twinkle back. *But it's pretty cool, isn't it?*

Eva interrupts the moment. "Hey, Ike. How big is your biggest belt buckle?"

"I beg your pardon?" He looks from her to me. I shrug. I cannot be responsible for her silliness.

"We're taking Tami dancing at The Rustler. Want to join us?" I clear my throat at her to indicate this is not a good idea, but she just smirks at me.

Ike has seen my discomfort. "Ah . . ."

"I'm sure he has other plans," I say quickly.

"We don't even know when we're going yet!"

"Still," I insist, looking imploringly at Ike. "I'm sure he has other plans."

He studies me before responding. I hold my breath as I wait for him to answer.

"Actually, you're right," he says. "I probably can't make it."

I nod in gratefulness. But Eva just rolls her eyes at the two of us.

All the way to my house, I drill into Eva's head that while in my house, she must not mention Ike. Must not. Must not mention the men in the pickup. Must not mention Ike. Must not mention the shoes. Must not mention Ike.

"I get it, Tami."

"I don't think you do, Eva. We come from different worlds. Mine is not so flexible as yours. It's not like maybe things will be okay if only we bring them up a certain way. If my sister knows that I am spending time with Ike, she will not let me walk to class. She might not even let me go to class anymore."

"I get it." Eva sighs, clearly tired of my admonitions. "What about your shoes?"

Good point. We are three blocks from my sister's house. I bend to take them off and replace them with my boots. Ike suggested that I hide them in my backpack, but to have them in the house is too dangerous. I look around. We are in front of a pink adobe house. The house of the woman with the silly red hat I took a picture of the other day, from a distance with my long-range lens. Her yard is overgrown with native plants and long grasses. I push some grass aside and shove the shoes in, then cover them up with the grass. There.

Eva shakes her head. "This is crazy."

"Not a word about the shoes," I warn.

"Shoes?" she asks innocently. "What shoes?"

"You're incorrigible, Eva." I laugh, and link arms with her. "And I mean that in a good way. I think."

15

We walk into the house to the wonderful scent of *Dolmeh-yeh Seeb-Zamini* being prepared, one of my favorite dinners. Maryam must still feel bad about this morning. Or else she wants something from me.

"That smells so good," Eva says to me in a quiet voice.

"It's delicious," I whisper back. "Let me go tell my sister you're here."

I take off my boots and point Eva toward the couch. After she sits down, I lean over.

"Remember, not a word about you-know-who."

Eva mimics turning a key to lock her lips and throwing the key over her shoulder. I laugh gratefully and head to the kitchen. Maryam stands at the stove, stirring tomato paste into the onion and lamb. She smiles to see me. I walk to her and we kiss hello.

"I brought my friend Eva home for dinner," I say. "I hope this is all right."

"Tonight?"

"Is this okay?"

"Sure," she says. "I am glad you have made a friend. Of course it's fine."

"She's in the living room. Will you come meet her?"

Maryam washes her hands quickly and follows me to the living room. Eva stands as I introduce them and they shake hands. *She should have taken her boots off. I should have told her to take her boots off.* Eva comments on how delicious the food smells.

So far, so good. Keep it up, Eva.

"My husband will be home in a few minutes," Maryam says. "Please, sit down and enjoy yourselves. I will get some tea and fruit for us."

She disappears back into the kitchen to prepare the tea, and I feel awkward suddenly, unsure what we should talk about. It is only Eva who is at ease.

"This place is beautiful," she murmurs, looking around at the Persian rugs on the walls, the gold-plated vases with silk flowers. At the ornate porcelain samovar displayed on the coffee table, and the hookah in the corner.

"Do you smoke pot in that thing?"

"Pot?" I ask. "What is this word?"

"Marijuana. Hashish."

"Oh, no. We use a highly aromatic tobacco. You inhale the smoke through the urn of water right there, which cools the smoke before inhalation."

"Very cool," she says. "Where's the cat?"

"What cat?" I never told her we have a cat.

"A Persian cat. That's all this place needs to make me feel like I'm in Iran."

"Iranians don't keep cats," I inform her. "They're dirty."

"Except for Persian cats, right?"

"*What* are you talking about?"

"*Persian cats,*" she enunciates loudly and carefully. "You need a Persian cat."

I furrow my eyebrows at her. I wonder if maybe it is this house that makes people crazy. I know Eva was not crazy before she came inside, yet now she is acting as oddly as Haroun and his bugs. *That's it. This house makes people crazy about invisible animals.*

"Eva," I say firmly. "I need you to stop talking about cats."

She stares at me, dumbfounded. "Why?"

"Do not, under any circumstances, mention cats to my sister."

"What was that you were saying, Eva?" Maryam asks, coming back in the room with a tray of tea, cups, and a bowl of fruit.

"Nothing," I say with a warning tone in my voice. "Eva was only saying how much she likes this house and thank you for inviting her here, and I was saying don't mention it."

Maryam smiles, pleased by Eva's compliment. She pours three cups of tea and, upon hearing Ardishir's car pull into the driveway, pours a fourth cup. I pop two sugar cubes into my mouth and savor the tea as it warms my mouth and disintegrates the sugar cubes and slides comfortingly down my throat.

Eva plops a sugar cube into her tea and takes a sip. Maryam opens the front door for Ardishir. He comes in, kisses her gently on both cheeks, and removes his shoes. When he catches sight of Eva, he smiles.

"Hello," he calls out. "You must be a friend of Tami's from school."

Eva stands and Ardishir walks over to her for a handshake.

"That's right. I'm Eva. I see that I should have taken off my boots."

"Don't worry about it. It's not necessary. It's very nice to meet you, Eva." He turns to me and kisses me on both cheeks, and then he takes a chair near the coffee table.

"Tea!" Ardishir says happily. He pops one sugar cube in his mouth and takes a long gulp of tea. "Ah, nothing like a nice cup of tea after a long day."

"I was just telling your wife and Tami how lovely your home is, with all these beautiful rugs and Persian things."

"Thank you," Ardishir says.

"I was telling Tami that I feel like I am in Iran. Or what I imagine Iran must be like."

"Have you seen the Persian cat yet?" he asks her with a smile.

Eva snaps her head toward me and waits for my explanation. She looks at me like *I* am the crazy one.

"We don't have a cat," I assure her, and turn to Ardishir to scold him in Farsi. "Why would you say something like this?"

He laughs and replies in English. "That's the first thing Americans always ask when they come to our home. *Where's the Persian cat?*"

Eva looks victorious. "That's exactly what I asked, and Tami acted like I was crazy!"

Now Maryam giggles.

"What *is* a Persian cat?" I demand. "I grew up there and I've never heard of such a thing."

"They're those beautiful long-haired cats. Sometimes they have blue eyes that look like they glow," Eva tells me.

"I've never seen such a cat," I insist. "Nor have I heard of such a cat."

Ardishir chuckles once more. "I had to look them up in the encyclopedia at the library when I first came here. Back then, I never wanted to say I was from Iran, what with the hostage-taking at the American embassy. So I always said I was from Persia, and few people knew what I was talking about. Without fail, they'd say, *'Oh, you mean where Persian cats come from, and Persian rugs?'* I'd always say, *'Yes, where the rugs come from, exactly.'* "

"I think the cats actually come from England," Maryam says.

"Is this all people know of our culture?" I ask in wonder. "Cats and rugs?"

"Pretty much," Eva says. "Except now we also think of veils and hostages. And angry, bearded men in the streets yelling 'Death to America.' "

"This is horrible," I say in exaggerated misery and clutch my hands to my hair.

Maryam shrugs. "They see what the news shows them."

"But we're wonderful people," I insist. "We are good people making the best of a bad situation."

"Has anyone been mean to you since you've arrived?" Eva asks me.

"No," I tell her. "I have been met with nothing but kindness."

"Even when they know you're from Iran?"

"It seems like especially then."

"Well." Eva shrugs. "That's how it is. Germans were hated, too, after Hitler. And now most people like Germany just fine. This hard time for your country will eventually pass."

"It's the ebb and the flow," says Ardishir philosophically. "The ebb and the flow."

We are halfway through dinner and I am breathing easier. Maryam seems to like Eva just fine. More than fine, actually. Eva is on her best behavior; I have never seen her so polite and well mannered. She asks how the food is prepared. She accepts a second and a third helping. She says no, there is not too much salt in the dish. She inquires after my parents. She does everything right.

The trouble comes when Ardishir innocently asks what Eva and I did that day after school.

"We went for coffee," Eva says quickly. "I took Tami to Starbucks, since that's such a symbol of America."

"But Tami has already been there," Maryam says. "Did you go to the same one as where you had the run-in with the police?"

"What run-in with the police?" Eva asks me.

"It is nothing," I tell her, embarrassed. "Only a misunderstanding."

"Well," asks Maryam a second time, "is that the one you went to?"

Did you see that man again? That is what she is really asking.

I nod, guilty as charged.

Maryam's eyes turn suspicious. I look at Eva. Her face betrays nothing. She waits to follow my lead.

"It was a lovely time," I say quickly, nodding at Eva. "We began to plan a baby shower for our friend Nadia. She is soon to deliver her baby."

"Her husband is not very nice to her," Eva says. "So we want to do something very special."

Maryam softens. "That's very kind of you. What did you have in mind?"

As we didn't actually plan anything, I am at a loss. But not Eva. She takes full advantage of the moment.

"We decided to have a slumber party at my house," she says.

Maryam looks as confused as I feel. "A what?"

"A sleepover," Eva explains. "Where Tami and Nadia and even Agata from our class spend the night at my house. We will do one another's hair and makeup and stay up late and have a girls' night in."

"That sounds so fun!" I detect some wistfulness in Maryam's voice.

"You can come, too," I invite her. Eva nods.

"No, thank you," Maryam declines. "This should be a special time for Tami, for her to have her very own girlfriends."

I feel guilty for the relief that spreads over me. It *will* be more fun without Maryam. I will be less restricted in my words.

"Soon enough, she will be married and won't be able to do such things," Maryam continues.

My heart sinks.

"Why not?" Eva asks, friendly enough. "I'm married, and I can. You would be able to come if you wanted, right?" She looks from Maryam to Ardishir and waits.

"Of course," Ardishir says.

"But I would not have wanted to be away from my husband so soon after getting married. That is all I meant. When Tami is a new bride, she surely will want to be at home in the evenings with her husband."

"Hmmmmmm," Eva says, as if this idea has never occurred to her.

"When is Nadia to have her baby?" Maryam asks.

"Early May," I tell her.

"That's a beautiful time of year to have a baby. There will be the scent of honeysuckle in the air." Again, I note a wistfulness in Maryam's voice that I have not heard before.

"Do you two plan to have children?" Eva inquires.

I cringe inside. I have never even asked this question of my sister.

Maryam looks at Ardishir before she responds. "Perhaps someday." Ardishir smiles encouragingly at her. "But it's enough for now to look after Tami."

"Tami is hardly a child," Eva says. "And it sounds as if she'll be married off soon enough, anyway."

Maryam clears her throat. "You are right, of course. Would you excuse me for a moment?" She pushes back from the table and I see that she bites her bottom lip as she hurries to the bathroom.

I feel Eva's eyes on me, but I turn mine to Ardishir. "We're trying," he says matter-of-factly, readying a spoonful of *Dolmeh-yeh Seeb-Zamini*. "But we perhaps should have had children when we were younger. We thought we had plenty of time. But it is not so easy to get pregnant as one ages."

"I'm sorry for you," I say. "You both would make wonderful parents."

Ardishir excuses himself and goes off after Maryam.

Eva raises her eyebrows at me. "Maybe he can't get it up," she whispers with a crooked grin, and winks at me.

I do not wink back. Instead, I narrow my eyes.

"What?" Now she is defensive. Now she is innocent.

"You should not ask such sensitive questions."

"How am I supposed to know what's sensitive and what's not?! You've got your own little wacko rules. We can't talk about Ike. We can't talk about a pair of shoes. We can't talk about Persian cats. But war? Hostages? Government overthrows? Go for it. I'm sorry if I don't understand your rules of protocol, Tami."

Now I feel bad. She is right. It is tricky to eat dinner with us. "I'm sorry. You could not know her distress over having a baby."

"Did *you* know about it?"

"No." I smile. "Or I would have told you not to mention it."

She grins at me. "All is forgiven."

"So I suppose you'll pop out a bunch of kids after you get married," she says after a few moments of companionable silence.

"It depends."

"Will you have any say in the matter?" She asks this with a derisive tone.

"I would think so." I would *hope* so is what I mean.

When Maryam and Ardishir return, Maryam seems different. Hardened somehow. I have never been good at gauging Maryam's mood, but it seems to me that caution would be in order. Her smile is fixed and her posture is unnatural. Too straight.

She is deliberate in taking a few more bites of her food. When she does finally speak, it is to me.

"Haroun called earlier today."

I take a long drink of my water and avoid looking in Eva's direction.

"Did he mention to you that he is to be out of town for several weeks?" Maryam's lips are pursed with disapproval.

I shake my head. "No, he didn't. Did he say how long exactly?"

"He wasn't sure. His company is bringing a new computer system online and he is very involved in the project. They are expecting some problems as it launches."

"Who is Haroun?" Eva asks.

"No one," I quickly reply before my sister can assign him as my fiancé.

"A nutcase," Ardishir says at the same time. Maryam glares at him.

"He did give me the number of his doctor so we can make an appointment for you. He's Persian, the doctor."

Why must she bring this up now?

I try to keep my face from turning into a pout. I do not like this doctor business at all.

"Are you sick?" Eva asks me.

"Not at all."

"Then why the doctor?"

"It's complicated."

I look directly at Maryam. "We can talk about this later, can't we?" It is more of a demand than a plea.

"Who's Haroun?" Eva repeats.

"Tami's fiancé," Maryam tells her.

"He is *not* my fiancé."

"But he will be," Maryam insists.

Ardishir has been quiet since we returned to the table. But now he looks up from his plate and looks at Maryam. "I will not give my permission for Haroun to marry Tami. Not ever."

"What's wrong with him?" Eva asks.

"Nothing," says Maryam.

"Everything," says Ardishir. "Tami is not going to marry him."

Eva turns to me. "Well, Tami? What do you have to say about all this?"

I put down my fork and wipe my mouth with my napkin, which I fold carefully before responding.

"Apparently, what I have to say about this is not so very important." I keep my tone light and wait for someone to dispute this.

But no one does.

16

The next morning, I grumble a good morning to my sister and brother-in-law. They do not even seem to notice my dark mood as I flop down at the table and bump it so their teacups tremble.

Ardishir reads with his face hidden behind his *New York Times*. Maryam, who has never been much of a morning person, slumps at the table in her bathrobe, her hand propping up her head. She thumbs idly through a recipe book of South American dishes.

"Why do you bother?" I ask her. "It's not like you ever cook anything other than Persian food."

She doesn't raise her head to me, but only lifts her sleepy eyes to look at me across the table. She says nothing. I am being ignored, yet again.

"Well?" I insist. "Would it kill us to eat burritos once in a while? I mean, we do live in a city where half the population is Mexican."

"Are you unhappy with the dinners I have prepared for you?" Her look has turned sharp, yet she maintains a neutral tone.

"I just don't know why you think the Persian way is always the best way. The only way."

"You are welcome to cook dinner anytime you wish, Tami."

She holds out the recipe book until I take it. Then she gets up and kisses Ardishir on the forehead. He smiles, but does not look up from his newspaper. Maryam puts her dishes in the sink and announces she is going to take a shower.

Alone now with Ardishir, I make as much noise with my silverware as possible. I clink my teacup while stirring cream into my tea. I drop my knife onto my plate twice. I clear my throat a few times. Finally, he lowers the newspaper.

"Tami, is there something you wish to discuss?"

Yes. I want you to stop running my life.

But I cannot say this to him. He is my brother-in-law. He paid for my ticket to America and welcomed me into his home. And in most matters, I trust his judgment completely.

"No," I respond sullenly, not meeting his gaze.

"You're sure? Speak up if there's something on your mind."

It's now or never. I came to America for the freedoms it offers. One of those is the freedom to disagree with those in authority. And here, that means Ardishir.

I swallow hard and look up at him. "I think I should be able to marry whomever I decide to."

"I see," he says, nodding at me. "And do you really want to marry Haroun?"

"That's not the point."

Ardishir folds the newspaper and sets it on the table. He

places his hands in his lap and gives me his full attention.
"What is the point?"

"The point is . . ." I stop, suddenly flustered.

Oh, yes. I am a grown and university-educated woman.
I have as many brains as Ardishir or any man. And where
there are decisions to be made about my future, it is I who
should make them.

"The point is," I continue in a voice that is less shaky with
each word, "it's only tradition that demands Haroun ask you
for permission to marry me. It's only a formality. You need to
honor my wishes in this matter. After all, I am the one most
affected by it."

"True," he says. "Very true. Yet both of us know he's got
some issues. I think marrying him would be a mistake, and I
doubt I'll change my mind about that."

"You don't have to change your mind," I tell him. "You
only have to respect my decision."

He looks long and intently at me. I feel my bottom lip
quiver, but I do not look away.

"I have seen how you let Maryam push you around."

I open my mouth to protest, then fall silent. He is right. I
do let Maryam push me around. But she is my older sister,
and she is only looking out for me. She wishes for me only the
best. And Ardishir already knows this.

He continues. "Regarding this marriage, as much as
Maryam pushes you in one direction, I will push you in the
other."

Tears fill my eyes.

"Just to provide a balance," he assures me. "Just to make
sure you are seeing all sides. But I will respect your decision.
The choice is yours, Tami."

"Thank you," I choke out. *The choice is really mine.*

"And if you decide you do not want to marry him, you must make sure I know this. I'll make sure that no marriage takes place, and I'll shoulder the burden from Maryam's anger."

I smile at him as I blink back tears. "That is very brave of you."

He chuckles.

"I am so ashamed of my behavior, Ardishir. Please, forgive me for thinking the worst of you instead of the best."

"There is nothing to forgive. You took my words at face value," he says lightly. "Sometimes it is not good to be so direct. Sometimes, it is best to hide one's true thoughts."

He reaches again for his newspaper. He unfolds it and raises it to block his face. It occurs to me as I watch this kind man hide behind his newspaper that it is not only Iranian women who wear veils and curtain themselves from the world.

I leave my house and walk toward school with my heart much lighter. It is a beautiful and cloudless morning. I am addicted to Tucson's fresh air. I allow my lungs to breathe deeply here in a way I never did back home.

I smile as I walk, for each step brings me closer to my new life in America. I am eager to get to class, enjoy my classmates, and perhaps see Ike on my way home. I will have dinner with Haroun when he returns and I will observe him to see whether he is someone I can marry. I am hopeful he is. After all, he showed so many good qualities when he came to our home. He was gracious, well spoken. Polite, loves to travel. Successful in his profession, able to provide. Not unattractive. This morning, in the bright spring sunshine, his

odd behaviors seem only to be quirks, not negative judg-
ments about his character.

I walk with my head held high, looking at each house and
yard as I pass it. I must say, the native desert landscaping has
grown on me. The saguaro cactus, the cholla, the creosote
bushes and mesquite trees. But the colored rocks that people
dump in their yards for decoration are simply awful. Natural
dirt, the desert floor, is so much more pleasing than these
horrid manufactured rocks.

I slow and look around as I approach the yard where I have
hidden my walking shoes. When I reach the spot where I hid
them, I squat down and reach into the grass.

But they are not there. Puzzled, I poke through more of
the long grass, but yank it back when I see an iguana scurry-
ing away. I do not understand where my shoes could have
gone and wonder if perhaps an urban coyote might have
taken them to eat.

"Looking for these?"

The voice is friendly, but I close my eyes in embarrassment and keep my head down. I've been caught. I no longer
think such a transgression will land me in jail. I only wonder
what sort of explanation I can give. Slowly, I crawl back from
the bush and look up to the voice.

"Hello," I say with a chagrined smile. Before me stands an
older woman beginning to crumple into herself from age.
But her green eyes sparkle, still young. She is clearly amused.

I rise to my feet and brush myself off before I approach her
to retrieve my shoes. "I'm sorry for leaving them on your
property. Please, excuse me for the transgression. I will not
do so again."

"What nationality are you?" She peers at my face, trying
to figure it out.

"I'm Persian."

"Well, you're beautiful, that's what you are. I'm Rose McClellan." She extends her hand and I step forward to shake it.

"Hello, Mrs. McClellan."

"No *Mrs.* I'm not married. Never have been."

My skin tingles with excitement. *Never been married!*

"I'm sorry," I say quickly. "Forgive me for assuming."

"Just call me Rose."

"Thank you. I'm Tami. Tami Soroush. I am in town visiting my sister."

Her eyes twinkle again. "Why are you hiding your shoes in my yard?"

I sigh. "It's complicated."

"I see." She gives me an appraising look, as if to tell me it probably is not so very complicated. And she's right. But I feel so mortified at moments like this, moments when Americans catch me acting crazy. I worry that Americans will base their opinions of all Iranians on their opinions of me. I want to tell them: *No, no. Don't let me reflect badly on them. I represent only my silly self.*

I think that perhaps I have offended her by my reluctance to confide my secret. "I won't leave them here anymore," I assure her.

She leans toward me, peers at me. "Did you steal them?"

"Of course not!"

She winks to tell me she is joking. "Are you hiding them from your sister?"

I must visibly cringe, for she laughs out loud. "You're welcome to leave them here. In fact, I'll put a basket on my front porch and you can throw them in there."

"Oh, no. That won't be necessary."

"Oh, but it will! Or else my sprinkler system will drench them each morning before you collect them."

"Well, thank you. You're very kind."

"Here, come on the porch and sit in my rocking chair and put them on."

I do not know how to refuse her offer, so I follow her to the porch and sit in her bright red rocking chair. While she disappears inside the house, I quickly unzip my boots and lace up my walking shoes. I watch the door, waiting for her return, noting the hand-painted sign above it, *La Casa de Rosa*.

She emerges a moment later with a white wicker basket, which she places next to her door.

"Here! You can keep your boots here and then switch back on your way home. I just love the intrigue! I feel like I'm involved in espionage of the highest order."

I laugh. "I know this is so silly."

"I have only one condition." Rose has lowered her voice to make it sound serious. "I'll guard your shoes only if you promise to stop in for a cup of tea sometime and share with me this so very complicated secret of yours."

"I, ah...It's not a very good secret," I confess. "And I don't want to bother you."

"It would be no bother," she says lightly. "I'd enjoy the company."

"Thank you. You're very kind."

"Come soon, Tami."

I nod and we say our good-byes.

I find myself smiling the rest of the way to class. I like Rose. Unmarried Rose. I wonder if she lives in that big house all alone. I wonder what she does all day by herself. Does she play her music loud? Paint her toenails while watching television? Read until late into the night? Does she try new recipes for fun, knowing she has to spice them only for her palate and pleasure? Does she sleep in the middle of the bed? Does she think I am a crazy girl, to be hiding my shoes in her yard?

I grin at that thought. For maybe I am crazy, but she has invited me into her home, nonetheless. It's nice to meet someone who wants to know my secrets and who, I suspect, will still like me, anyway.

17

The weeks pass. One day after class, I invite Eva to join me for a coffee, but she tells me she has other plans, so I walk alone to Starbucks. My nervousness increases the closer I get. So far, every day I have gone, he has been waiting for me. But all the other days, I have been with Eva. *Will he be there? Or won't he? Which is better? Which do I hope for?* As soon as I see Ike waiting for me on the patio, I know the answer. I am very happy to see him. Very, very happy. So happy I cannot stop smiling like a fool.

Haroun is still out of town; his business trip has stretched on and on. But I do not mind. We talk most evenings on the telephone and the situation is very friendly between us. When he tells me that he will try to stop traveling so much after we are married, I urge him not to change a thing about his career for me.

If I am to marry Haroun, I would like for him to be a traveling husband. And in the meantime, I am well aware that I will, perhaps, never again be as free as I am right now. So yes, I am glad to see Ike waiting for me.

"Hey there, Persian Girl," Ike greets me. "Where's your sidekick?"

"Eva? I think perhaps she is growing tired of me."

"No one could ever grow tired of you." Ike smiles at my blush and continues, "She's trying to set us up, you know."

I pull back like I am startled at the idea, although in truth, I know this very well to be true. I hear the words *Ike* and *eminently fuckable* from Eva's mouth about ten times each day. In response, I always *tsk-tsk* her and roll my eyes, and I fear this just encourages her. She remains committed to corrupting me.

"Will you join me for a proper cup of tea?" Ike asks and offers me his arm.

"Not that horrible mango tea?" I say this with a bit of a tease in my voice.

"Today, we're going to have real Middle Eastern tea like you're used to."

"Really?" I link my arm through his and feel very daring.

"Yep. Come right this way." He leads me around the corner of the coffee shop. We walk past Starbucks, past the hair salon, and past a French bistro in the Geronimo Square plaza.

"Are we going *there*?" I point ahead to a restaurant that has gaudy purple silk curtains framing the door. Sinbad's, it is called.

"Indeed we are."

He holds the door open for me. Now, this is not a Persian restaurant, but I think perhaps a Jordanian one. Yet I feel at home, with the music and the smells of familiar spices.

We seat ourselves and in an instant, a Middle Eastern man brings us menus. He greets us first in English and then greets me a second time, in Arabic.

"I'm sorry, I do not speak Arabic."

"Farsi?" he asks. I nod. He brightens. "I'll send out Cyrus. He's Persian. He'll be right with you."

"What's good here?" Ike asks.

"I thought we were only having tea."

"I'm starving, actually. Let's have an early dinner. Or a late lunch. Whichever."

But I cannot take a meal with him. That would make this a date.

"Kebabs are always a good choice," I advise. "But I am not hungry. I'll have only tea, or perhaps a *laban*."

He scans the menu and reads the description of the yogurt drink. "Is it sweet?"

"No, very tart."

"Like Eva." He grins at my confused look. But before he can explain, Cyrus approaches our table.

Salaam, we greet each other. He asks me, in Farsi, what I would like to eat. I order my *laban*. He asks if Ike speaks Farsi. At this I laugh and tell him no. He asks, *"Does your boyfriend work at Starbucks? I think I've seen him there."* This is the closest a Persian man will get to being nosy, to ask his questions in a roundabout way. He does not care where Ike works. He only asks to see if I will correct him about Ike being my boyfriend. Which I do, of course.

After Ike orders and Cyrus leaves, Ike leans back in his chair and crosses his arms. "Was he hitting on you?"

"No, of course not. He didn't raise a hand to me. You saw everything."

Ike chuckles at my mistake. "Hitting *on* you, not *hitting* you. Was he flirting with you? Asking you out?" He makes goo-goo eyes and a kissy face.

"Don't be silly," I tell him, smiling. "Nobody's *hitting on me.*"

"Would you even know if they were?"

He clears his throat and his face reddens. He is very cute when he is embarrassed.

"I might not know," I admit.

Ike sits forward and unrolls the silverware from his white cloth napkin. He sets each utensil in its proper place on the wood table and flattens his napkin in his lap. I watch how he avoids my eyes as he does this. But then, abruptly, he leans toward me.

"Would you want to know? If someone was flirting with you, I mean?"

I draw back from him while my heart thunders in panic. I suspect that I know what he is asking. I open and close my mouth like a fish, unable to form a response.

"You know what I think, Persian Girl?" he continues.

Persian Girl. I am not sure I like this special name he has for me, for I have not felt like a girl since I was forced to wear a veil many, many years ago. But I do like that he *has* a nickname for me.

"I couldn't possibly know what you think, American Boy."

And I'm not sure I want to know.

"I think you're falling in love with me."

I scoff. "Persian girls don't fall in love."

"Bullshit. Everyone falls in love."

"Tell me, American Boy, what does it mean to fall in love? How exactly does one go about it?"

He laughs heartily, but then he sees I am not joking. He waits until Cyrus has delivered his plate of food and retreated. Ike picks up his knife and scrapes the lamb kebab off the stick and onto his rice. Then he looks at me.

"All right, then. Well, I'd say you know you're falling in

love with a person when you think about them constantly. You can't stand being apart from them. You feel the world is yours for the taking, as long as you have them in your life. Have you ever felt that?"

I firmly shake my head. "Dating in Iran is like . . . I don't know. There are so many restrictions that the focus, and the fun, it seems, is all centered around beating the system. You know? Like walking down the street together and not being stopped. That's the thrill, the not getting caught. I think we fall in love with the feeling that we're getting away with something, more than with an actual person."

"So, like, you're looking for a partner in crime more than a boyfriend?"

I laugh, but he's not too far off.

"Well, I've had boyfriends here and there, but you can't date proper, like you see in American movies. You talk on the phone a lot. A *lot*. And you can meet up at parties, but . . . I don't know, the parties are so crazy and it gets really tiresome. At least for me it did. Trying to date was more of a hassle than anything."

"So no one ever rocked your world, huh?"

I chuckle as I work through that slang. "You know how you said when you fall in love it feels like the world is yours for the taking? Well, I can't know what that feels like because the world *isn't* mine for the taking. With or without a boyfriend. With or without a husband. Period. It's mine for the bearing. And so, at least from my perspective, the best a girl can wish for is to find someone who makes things a little more bearable. Does that make sense?"

"Whew." He lets out his breath. "That sucks. You need to stay in America, then. Let somebody *rock your world*."

I am momentarily unable to answer, so great is my shock.

Does he know what I have to do to stay? He is not, in any way, suggesting some way to help me...is he? I clear my throat.

"Iranians are more focused on getting married, on having a partner in life, than...um...having their *world rocked.*"

"That sounds like a huge generalization, Tami." He shovels a huge amount of food into his mouth and then adds, matter-of-factly, "You should try it sometime."

"What, generalizing?"

"Having your world rocked."

My face feels quite hot. Embarrassed, I take a long drink of my *laban.* I must get the focus off me. "How about you? Have you ever been in love?"

"Sure, yeah." He nods and then shifts his gaze away for a moment, to the couple at the next table over.

"What happened? Why did it end?"

Did it end? That is my real question.

"We dated in college, our senior year. It started out not very serious, because we both knew it couldn't last. She and a girlfriend were planning an extended backpacking trip to Europe after graduation."

My eyes grow big. How brave she was.

"It was the trip of a lifetime." He shrugs. "And, you know, I was finishing up my business degree and planned to work in a coffee shop for a while before opening my own. I'd been planning it forever; it was all outlined in my Franklin Planner."

"What is this, Franklin Planner?"

"Oh, right. A Franklin Planner is, like, this system of planning out your whole life, according to your values. You figure out your values and your dreams and then you set goals based on them. And then you make lists of all the little steps you've got to take along the way to get there. And then you take *those* steps and put them in your daily planner. So, basically, every task you do in your daily life is directed toward realizing your dreams."

The enthusiasm in his voice builds as he talks, and I can see how exciting the idea is to him, that every single thing he does every day is, in some way, getting him closer to living his dreams. The thought dares to cross my mind: *What is this, then? How do I fit into your dreams?* I don't ask these questions, of course.

"This girl," I ask instead, "she did not make it into your Franklin Planner dreams?"

"She wanted to get married."

"Oh."

I can't fathom how a girl would approach such a topic. How someone like me, for instance, would approach it with someone like Ike.

That's simple, you wouldn't.

Ike shrugs. "I said I'd wait for her, that she should go and I'd stay and get working on all this. But she said she knew that if she left, she wouldn't come back. That she wouldn't be the same person a year down the road and she had to be free to see where life took her."

He swallows hard. "I understand that. She was going to lose herself. Find herself. Whatever. So it was either marry her and she'd stay, or don't and she'd leave forever."

"You preferred to lose her rather than marry her?" My voice feels far away.

He pauses, considering his answer. "It was simply the worst timing possible. I'm living in my parents' guesthouse. My job barely pays above minimum wage, and I've got a bunch of lean years ahead of me before I'll turn a profit with my coffee shop." His voice deflates. "It just wasn't meant to be."

"I'm sorry," I tell him.

"I get a postcard every now and then. She was right, she didn't come back." He smiles sadly. Bravely, I think.

"It sounds like you really loved her," I say quietly.

He considers it, then nods. "But, you know, you're right. She wasn't in my Franklin Planner dreams."

I am happy to hear it.

I have a question for you," Ike says as we finish our meal.

"Mmm-hmm?" I let my caution sound through, telling him to be careful with his questions.

He sits back, crosses his arms. "Tiny acts of everyday rebellion. If you were in Iran right now, with your camera, what would you photograph?"

I wouldn't. That's my first thought. I'd be afraid of drawing attention to myself. But his inquiry is an interesting one to consider.

"I'd take a picture of a woman in *hejab,* sitting at a computer in an Internet café, telling the world about her life and dreams through her blog."

Ike bites his lower lip and nods, *Go on.*

"Well, of course, I'd photograph a group of girls wearing bright headscarves pushed very far back on their heads. That's a *total* sign of protest. The most obvious form of protest."

"What else?"

"Men and women crammed into a taxi together. Satellite television dishes. Girls on cell phones talking to guys across the street."

Ike raises an eyebrow and smiles. I continue.

"Nail polish. Beauty salons."

"I have an idea," he says.

"What's that?"

"When you go back, take pictures of all these things, and send them to me. I'll get them framed really nicely and I'll exhibit them in my coffee shop once it's opened. I'll call it *Everyday Acts of Rebellion*."

"That's an interesting idea, Ike. I'll keep it in mind."

Ike walks me most of the way home. When we arrive in front of Rose's house, it seems a good place to stop. I explain to him my elaborate shoe-hiding ritual, and he climbs onto the porch with me to wait while I switch back into my boots. My boots have now reached the point where they would probably be comfortable to walk so far in, but I have grown to like stopping for a moment at Rose's house to sit in her rocking chair and change shoes. She often pops her head out the front door to say hello.

And today, she does not disappoint.

"Hello, you two," she says. Ike nods to her. "Tami, I will see you for tea soon, yes?"

"Yes," I promise.

Rose pulls her head back and closes the door. I suspect she will watch us from behind the curtain and try to hear our words through the glass window.

"Here, let me." Ike gets down on one knee to untie my shoes. I feel like Shirin, a fairy-tale Persian princess, to have a man at my feet like she had the adoring Farhad at hers.

His bangs fall across his forehead and I am tempted to reach out and brush them back.

He catches me looking at him and smiles as if he knows what I am thinking.

"Will you go on a date with me sometime, Tami?" he bursts out.

Panic stabs my heart.

"I, ooh, ah . . ." I stumble badly over my response. In my sudden nervousness, I have forgotten my English.

"Just a yes or no will do," he says with a smile. "A yes would be the preferred response."

I cannot say yes, yet I do not want to say no. So I decide to stall, instead. I reach for my boots from the wicker basket and zip them onto my feet. I stand from the rocking chair and then I ask, "What do people in America do on dates?" I do not look at him as I ask. Instead, I focus on putting my walking shoes in Rose's basket.

Sex, drugs, and rock-and-roll. This is what Eva has told me Americans do on dates. But by now, I know better than to listen to everything she tells me.

"We could do anything you want," he says gently. "We could go to dinner, or to a movie. Or we could really live it up and go to dinner *and* a movie."

His voice is so eager that I must look at him. And my heart breaks when I do. Poor Ike, his eyes are full of hope. Part of me thinks I should trade a potential marriage to Haroun for one date with this lovely American man, who has shown me nothing but kindness. But I could not justify to my parents my willingness to trade an evening of enjoyment for a lifetime of repression, and he has made it very clear to me that he is not ready to be married.

"I just can't," I tell him over the lump in my throat.

He licks his lips, nods once, and shifts his gaze toward the street. I have hurt his feelings, and I feel awful.

"Ike?"

He gives no response. I step toward him and put my hand on his arm. He visibly calms from my touch and turns back to me.

"I don't get it. Am I reading something wrong here? Do you just not like me?"

I shake my head. My heart feels so swollen I fear it may burst.

"I like you," I whisper.

"Then what? Is it your sister?"

My breathing is labored. I raise my shoulders in a shrug. He leans closer to me, and his eyes turn soft. "You do know that you're killing me here, Tami, don't you? I mean, you know how I feel about you, right?"

When he sees my panicked expression, he reaches out and strokes my cheek. I want to melt into his touch.

"You just met me," I whisper.

"I think you've been in my heart my whole life, Tami." His voice is husky. "You feel like home to me."

I cannot look at him anymore, at his ocean eyes. It would be too easy to drown in them. I look away quickly, and see Rose yank her head back behind a curtain. This jolts me out of the moment.

"I need to go."

"Don't go," he says. But now his tone is light, playful. And so I smile and repeat myself.

"I need to go."

"No you don't."

"I do."

And with that, I turn and descend the steps on Rose's porch. Ike follows. When we reach the sidewalk, he stops. I must cross in front of him to head in the right direction, and when I walk past him, he reaches for my wrist. I want to cry and he must see this because he shakes it gently and then lets me go.

"Bye, sweet Persian Girl."

"Bye," I whisper, and try to smile. I walk away as fast as I can and stop only when I am safely inside my house, and then I lean against the door after closing it behind me and bend over to gasp for air. *Breathe, breathe,* I tell myself. *Do not drown in this man.*

"Tami?"

I straighten up and see Maryam walking into the living room. She does not notice my affliction.

"Haroun called. He'll be back in town soon and wants to take you to dinner next Wednesday. I think he might ask you!"

She beams with excitement.

"Great," I manage to reply.

After Maryam disappears into the kitchen, I rush to my room, collapse on my bed, and sob for fifteen minutes straight. *Maman Joon* once told me that sometimes there is nothing like a good cry to make a woman feel better. This is not one of those times. My American Boy has stirred feelings inside of me that I have never had before, and they have shaken me to my very core.

18

For my dinner date with Haroun, I wear stark red nail polish and the same low-cut dress I wore my first night in Tucson. I will dare him to disapprove of me. When the doorbell rings exactly on time, I answer the door myself and brace for his reaction to my appearance. Startled, he just stares at me for a moment.

"You look amazing, Tamila," he finally says.

"Oh! Well, thank you!" I am pleased by his reaction. His eyes are not covetous, but rather proud. This is good, I think. I need to remind myself that Haroun is not the bad guy. He is a good guy. He might be the one who saves me.

"Come in, please," I welcome him. He hands me one of the two bouquets of tulips he brought. "These are for you. I brought some for your sister as well."

"That is very kind." I reach for my bouquet. "Let's go to the kitchen so you can give them to her."

We chat pleasantly in the kitchen with Maryam for

several moments. Then we take our leave and drive in his spotless black Mercedes to the west side of Tucson. We are going to a steak house in the desert that used to be a ranch, and when we arrive, the host is expecting us.

"Mr. Mehdi, how are you this evening?"

I am impressed. This must mean that Haroun eats out often. This is also good, for I do not want to be tied to a kitchen my whole life.

"I am fine, thank you, Mr. Hiller. May I introduce you to Tamila Soroush?"

Mr. Hiller and I shake hands.

"Please, come right this way. Your table is ready." He leads us to the patio and to a table close to the open-pit outdoor barbecue. "I have a shawl for you, Ms. Soroush." He slips a warm black shawl over my shoulders, for which I am thankful because of the mid-March chill.

Haroun smiles at me once we are seated. "The flame from the fire sparkles in your eyes. It makes them even more beautiful."

"Thank you." How nice. His eyes, too, sparkle pleasantly.

When the waiter comes, Haroun suggests we order margaritas along with our steak dinners. I barely hesitate before smiling and nodding my acceptance.

"So you are not opposed to alcohol?" I ask once the waiter has taken our order.

"Not at all," he says. "I never overindulge, that would be wrong, but a glass of wine or beer every now and then is one of the true pleasures of life, I think."

"That's what my father says," I tell him.

He smiles. "Mine, too. Does your father secretly brew beer in the basement as well?"

I laugh and cover my lips with my index finger. "Shhhh. You never know who might be listening."

He winks at me. "I think we're safe here."

When our drinks come, we clink glasses. "To our fathers," Haroun says.

"To our fathers."

As I take a sip of my first margarita, I am reminded once again that the best things about America are the little things, the little freedoms that Americans don't think twice about. The freedom to sit outside with a man and watch the fading sunset. To wear a little makeup and smile at a man without being accused of corruption. To sip a margarita in the chilly desert air.

I also realize that I am having fun with Haroun. He is handsome and attentive. He dresses well and there has been nothing so far to dissuade me from accepting his marriage proposal, when it officially comes.

Time to get to work. I take a gulp of my margarita and feel the alcohol burn its way to my stomach, giving me courage. I need to be bolder now than I have ever been before in my life.

"So, tell me what you want from a marriage," I say. "Tell me what you want from a wife."

Haroun sets his drink down and puts his hands in his lap. I look into his eyes and see gentleness.

"I want someone to go through life with," he says. "Someone to travel with and have dinner with and care for. I want my wife to be my best friend."

My heart softens when I hear his response. But I persevere in my tough questioning. "Are you traditional in how you view your wife?"

He shakes his head. "I think the traditional way has left many women in Iran very unhappy."

"So your wife could work outside the home?"

"Sure."

"Would you let your wife go on a trip with her classmates to, say, Lake Havasu City to see the London Bridge?"

"Of course!" He smiles broadly at me. "I want my wife to be happy. To have many friends and not feel isolated like so many women in Iran do."

My heart is suddenly full of song.

"So you are not one who believes a woman's place is in the home?"

Haroun shrugs. "I have a housekeeper who comes twice a week to clean, prepare meals, and do my laundry. I do not see that this would change. It took me a long time to find the right housekeeper, and I am very pleased with her attention to detail. I would not want something such as housework coming between us."

Our steaks arrive still sizzling. They have been prepared right before our eyes on the grill. Haroun's is charred, it is so well done. I ordered mine medium rare, over his mild protests.

"These look delicious," Haroun tells the waiter.

I cut into my steak, and with the first bite I am in ecstasy. It practically melts in my mouth.

"Mmmmmmm," I say. "I have never tasted such wonderful meat."

"I am glad," Haroun says. "I only hope you don't catch mad cow disease."

Mad cow disease? I put down my fork. "What is this mad cow disease?"

"Oh, it's nothing."

"Then why did you mention it?"

He shrugs and goes on cutting his steak into bite-size chunks that he carefully places on the right side of his plate. Piece after piece, very methodically. I find him annoying all of a sudden. "I am surprised you have not read about this," he tells me. "It's all over the news. It's a European and American disease you catch by eating meat that is prepared too rare. The brain wastes away and you go crazy and eventually die."

My stomach threatens to throw up what I have just eaten. "Why did you not tell me about this before I ordered? Why did you not tell me to order mine well done like you did?"

"How would that make me look?" he says. "I do not want to control you. You should be able to decide things for yourself."

"But if I'd only known about this disease, I surely would not have ordered mine rare!" I sputter through my sudden anger. "I do not want to catch a brain disease that has no cure! You should have told me of this."

"I'm sorry," he says. "In the future, I will make sure to inform you of such things. Should we send your plate back and ask them to cook it properly? Or would you like something else?"

My appetite is ruined from the very idea of crazy cows. I push my plate away. "I'm not hungry. Why would a restaurant even serve food that can make people sick?"

"America is all about freedom of choice."

"There is such a thing as taking freedom too far, I think."

"I agree." Haroun raises his arm and the waiter quickly approaches. "Please take her plate away. It is covered with brain-disease germs."

"Yessir, of course." He immediately clears my plate. Behind him, I watch the cook accept a ten-dollar bill from another waiter and tuck it into his front shirt pocket. They laugh openly at the waiter bringing back my plate.

Hmmm. It seems there has been some sort of wager regarding this dinner date.

"Haroun, the host who seated you seemed to know you quite well. Do you come here often?" I say this like it is small talk. And I down another large gulp of my drink.

"Oh, yes. It is my favorite restaurant for steak in town. I like that I can watch the cook prepare my food. Plus, I have inspected the kitchen and it is very clean. Top-notch."

Grrrrrr. Of course a restaurant wouldn't serve food it believed would be harmful to its customers. This is just more of Haroun's craziness.

"Haroun," I say, "I have something very important to tell you."

I have his full attention.

"There is nothing wrong with my smile."

He looks at me, puzzled. "Of course there is not."

"I mean, I will not agree to have corrective surgery on my mouth, because there's nothing wrong with it."

He looks incredulous. "Of course there's not! Why ever would you be concerned with such a thing? Your smile is full of hope and joy," he says. "I have never seen one more beautiful."

I sit back, stunned. "But the night we met, you told me it needed repair."

"No I didn't." He laughs very loud. "I only said there is no repair that could be made on such a beautiful mouth as yours."

"Oh. I must have misunderstood."

I didn't! I didn't!

I take another two gulps of my margarita.

"And another thing," I say, leaning forward. "I have some concerns about . . ."

I stop and swallow hard. It is hard for me to say things so directly. It is not how I am used to behaving. But this is my life, my future, I'm deciding on. Haroun will just have to forgive me for my words.

Or not.

"You have concerns about what?" he asks, as if he has no cares in the world.

I look at him with kindness to show I do not mean him any offense. "You seem perhaps overly concerned about cleanliness."

He nods in agreement. "Cleanliness is very important to me."

"I mean, I wonder if it's an unhealthy way of being." I brief him on my observations—the quite earnest handwashing, the mad cow disease concern, the paranoia about a potential bug in the corner of our dining room, the illusionary spider bite.

Haroun places his fork down on the corner of his plate and reaches for my hand. My heart rate spikes at his touch.

"It is true I am concerned about my health," he says. "I value my life and all life. I want to live it to the fullest and enjoy a future with a lovely person for a wife and, God willing, children someday. Is that so wrong?"

He gently strokes my hand with his thumb. He makes it all sound so reasonable.

"No, of course not."

Haroun's eyes darken and sadness falls across his face. His hand becomes limp in mine.

"I will tell you something that I usually never talk about. My only sister died from an infection when she was eight. She suffered greatly and it was a needless death due to carelessness at the hospital."

I squeeze his hand and feel tears come to my eyes. "I'm so sorry, I didn't know. Your poor parents."

I receive a small smile. Haroun's eyes have turned watery.

"It was a very bad time for my family," he says. "I loved her very much. This is why I am careful. I know how quickly life can be lost."

I pat his hand. "Thank you for telling me."

"You remind me of her," he says, looking into my eyes

with great kindness. "Your hopefulness. Your zest for life. These are qualities to cherish. To protect."

I blush. I am pleased he has recognized these traits in me. It is good, for a husband to want these qualities to remain in his wife.

"Tami," he says quietly, intertwining his fingers with mine. "You would make me a very happy man by agreeing to be my wife. Will you do me the honor of marrying me?"

Ike.

I take a deep breath. My heart pounds. My mouth is so dry I have to lick my lips before responding. But when I speak, it is with a strong voice. "Yes, Haroun, I will marry you. It would give me great pleasure to be your wife."

His smile is huge. I smile back and am relieved to find that I do not feel sadness. I certainly do not feel the joy one would hope for, but joy is not required, only willingness.

And I am willing to marry Haroun. I shall marry him and stay in America.

Haroun pats my hand one last time and then raises his margarita glass for a toast. I raise mine as well.

"To us," he says. "To my new bride."

"To us," I agree, and smile at the man who is soon to be my official husband.

And then I gulp the rest of my margarita while he devours his well-done steak.

19

I had hoped that when I arrived home from dinner with Haroun, I would be able to slink off to my bedroom and collapse into my bed. To think this situation through in silence, in darkness.

But Maryam is still awake, and so my hope is dashed. She and Ardishir are together on the couch in the living room watching the Persian news on the satellite from Los Angeles. Ardishir barely turns his attention from the program. But Maryam, who has been lying with her head in Ardishir's lap, jumps up and rushes to kiss me hello. Her eyes beg with curiosity as she waits for me to offer information.

"How was dinner with the macadamia nut?" Ardishir calls over before I have a chance to say anything. Then he gives me a wink and a smile.

"Don't you listen to him." Maryam takes my hand and pulls me toward the love seat by the fireplace. We sit down together and she keeps my hand in hers. "Well, little sister, how did things go? Was dinner everything you hoped it would be?"

"Please," I ask, "what is this illness called mad cow disease and how does one contract it?"

From the couch, Ardishir hoots a loud laugh. Maryam shushes him.

"Haroun doesn't think he has it, does he?" She asks this as if she is afraid to hear my response, for it would confirm his craziness if my answer is yes.

"No, but he thinks I may get it from eating my steak medium rare."

There is another loud laugh from Ardishir. "Mad cow!"

"Hello, no one is listening to you, Ardishir." Maryam's anger is palpable, but Ardishir doesn't even see her glare, he is so bent over with laughter. She turns back to me. "Ignore him."

"Well, what is this disease?" I persist.

"It is something strange and rare, that is all I know. And cows go crazy from it. But I don't think people in the United States have gotten it. I have only heard of some cases in England many years ago. You surely would not get it from eating a steak tonight."

I should have known. I missed out on a perfectly delicious steak because of his craziness. The sacrifices have begun already. I withhold a sigh.

"Haroun asked me to marry him and I agreed. He will come to speak with Ardishir soon."

Maryam cups my face in her hands and kisses me on both cheeks and my forehead before responding. "Oh, little sister! This is such good news! Ardishir, did you hear the good news? Tami will be able to stay in America, right here in Tucson!"

Ardishir has stopped his laughter. He looks over at me

with a severe look upon his face. "He is crazy, yes? You have not changed your mind on that, and yet still you agreed to marry him?"

I know Ardishir told me he would play the role of the doubter and forbidder up until the last moment, but his tone is so serious that my voice falters.

"I, um, no, I do not think he is crazy. Only a little overly cautious about his health. His sister died from an infection when he was young. This is why he behaves this way."

"Oh, poor Haroun, to have lost a sister." Maryam's eyes well with tears, and she looks to Ardishir, I think, to see if she is convincing him to pity Haroun.

This is, I think, a good strategy. "He says I remind him of his sister."

"Now, that's disgusting. Why would he want to marry his sister?"

"Ardishir, enough from you!" Maryam boils over with rage. Her voice softens when she asks me, "Shall we call our parents and share the good news?"

"There is no need to bother them, because I forbid the union. I will not give my permission." Ardishir is so stern that again I am taken aback.

"It's not up to you," Maryam spews at him. "Asking you is only a formality, and we can skip it if you're going to act this way. Why aren't you happy for my sister?"

"It will be important for Haroun to receive permission from Ardishir," I say. "It is practically all he talked about from the moment I agreed to marry him."

That, and my need to be examined by his doctor.

"Ardishir will give his permission. It is what my parents want, and his role is to represent their wishes here."

"It's my job to act in the best interest of *Tami*. Marrying someone who should be locked away in a mental institution

is not in her best interest, and I won't be convinced other-
wise." He shakes his finger at Maryam as he says this.

I am dumbfounded. He talks so seriously.

I stand up from the love seat. "I'm going to bed. You two
can work this out between yourselves. I only know that
Haroun intends to visit soon to speak with Ardishir."

"Good night, Tami." Maryam pulls me close for a hug.
"Don't worry about my husband. He will be reasonable
when the time comes."

With Maryam hugging me, she cannot see Ardishir's
face. I am hopeful to receive another wink and smile behind
her back. But it is not to be. He narrows his eyes and says
good night sternly, like a disapproving father. Perhaps if he
grows tired of his job as an orthopedic surgeon, he can become an actor, because he plays the part of new-sheriff-in-
town so very well.

Later that night, hours after Maryam and Ardishir have
gone to bed, I tiptoe to the kitchen and dial Iran. I am desperate to hear Minu's voice, to have her reassure me that I am
making the correct choice in marrying Haroun.

"Oy!" she squeals when I greet her. "Is it really you, my
American friend? You must tell me how you are! Your girls
ask after their favorite teacher all the time, they want to know
all about your adventures in America, but I must tell them to
use their imaginations, for she is far too busy to call me with
the details."

Minu is a teacher also. Her classroom was next to mine.
She is short and slight and wears her hair in a pixie cut. She
talks with grand gestures of her hands and great theatrical
expressions. I can see her now, exactly, as if I were standing
in the room with her. She is performing for me.

"Please forgive me," I beg. It is not a joke, to abandon my best friend. My voice drops to a choked whisper. "I miss you so much, Minu . . . it's so hard to think of you there and not with me. You're on my mind all the time, I think of you constantly, but in my thoughts you are here with me, and we are finding our way in America together."

I have these photographs in my head, these daydreams, of Minu and me seeing R-rated movies that are uncensored. We play Frisbee at Himmel Park. Laugh at the world. *Check out the fine dudes.* We are laughing, laughing, always laughing. We are riding our bicycles through the university campus. Buying our own red scooters and zipping around town, letting our hair blow free in the wind.

"I'm getting married, Tami, did you hear?" Her voice sounds bright.

"My parents told me. I suppose I should congratulate you."

We sigh at the same time.

"Oh, Tami, I don't know what I'm going to do." She sounds desperate in a way I have not heard from her before. My heart breaks for her.

"What's wrong, *Minu Joon*?"

"Oh, Tami," she weeps. "I don't know what I'm going to do."

She repeats herself and it alarms me. Her mother committed suicide when Minu was a baby, and each time we hear of a girl who has ended her life, Minu presses for details. She finds the idea of suicide admirable, for it is a way for a woman to seize control of her life, if only for the briefest of moments.

"*What do you mean, Minu?*"

"His parents are so awful. His father is very rough, very demanding."

"Of you?"

"Of his wife. Of Seyed. He treats them so badly, I wonder sometimes if he is on drugs. And his mother, oy! No woman would be good enough for her son, least of all silly old me."

Here is a joke Minu and I have laughed at over the years: A young Persian man excitedly tells his mother he's fallen in love and is going to get married. He says, *"Just for fun, Maman, I'm going to bring over three women and you try to guess which one I'm going to marry."* The mother agrees. The next day, he brings three beautiful women into the house and sits them down on the couch and they chat for a while. He then says, *"Okay, Maman, guess which one I'm going to marry."* She immediately replies, *"The one on the right."* The son claps. *"That's amazing,"* he says. *"You're right. How did you know?"* The Persian mother replies, *"Because I don't like her."*

This joke is really not very funny. I don't know why we ever thought it was.

"Oh, Minu," I commiserate. "Does Seyed know of your concerns? Perhaps he might agree to live apart from them."

"They've got an apartment for us above theirs," she informs me glumly. "And now I fear that Seyed will be like his father in marriage. It is what he learned. It is all he knows."

Oh, my poor Minu. My sweet, dear Minu. She is as deserving of happiness as anyone. And yet it will be denied her. She knows it; I know it.

"You just tell them the bride has gone to pick flowers," I tell her. "And then run out of there, down the street in your wedding dress, as fast as you can!"

She laughs. During Iranian weddings, the man performing the ceremony asks the bride if she agrees to marry the groom. When the bride does not reply, the guests cry out, *"The bride has gone to pick flowers."* The woman is asked again, *"Do you agree to marry this man?"* Again, she stays silent. Again, the guests cry out, *"The bride has gone to pick flowers."* It is only after the third time she is asked that the bride says yes.

"That would be a sight, wouldn't it?" Minu asks, her voice breaking.

"I'm sorry, Minu," I whisper.

"Me, too," she whispers back.

We both know it will not happen. Our bride will not get to pick flowers. And I no longer have the heart to share my concerns about marrying Haroun. Next to what she faces, I should consider myself lucky.

20

When I arrive at class the next day, everyone else is already there. Conversation stops. All eyes turn toward me. Even Danny, who usually keeps himself out of the conversations until class begins, looks at me with a worried look.

"Well?" Eva demands.

"Well what?" I do not like being put on the spot in front of everyone like this.

"How was dinner?" Eva asks. "Any interesting news for us?"

She has told them all. This bothers me, for I would have preferred for my situation to be private. I would have preferred to arrive at class one day already married, and simply share my news then. But now they all know of my dilemma, my quest. I look at each of my classmates in turn. Edgard raises his eyebrows at me. Nadia looks scared. Agata looks mildly curious, and Josef looks ready to pounce.

I sigh. I may as well get this over with now. "I expect that I shall get engaged very soon, perhaps as early as this weekend. And this is good, I am happy, because I will get to stay in America. My fiancé is a very nice man."

"Hooray!" yells Agata, raising both fists in the air in a victory cheer. "Hooray for Tami!"

Josef comes up to me and pats my hand. "Good girl, good girl. I am sure you have made your parents very happy."

"I hope so." I smile at him.

"When's the date?" Edgard asks.

"I don't know exactly, but sometime in the next few weeks."

Nadia smiles bravely at me, but I can tell my news makes her want to cry.

"We need to have Nadia's baby shower soon, then, so we can have your wedding shower the weekend after that," Eva pronounces.

"You don't need to have a party for me," I protest.

"*Girlfriend,* if you're getting married, you need some serious lingerie and, a-hem, bedroom toys."

Bedroom toys!

Even after all these weeks, Eva still shocks me speechless on a regular basis. I give her the wide-eyed look of disapproval that she has come to know so well.

"Eva! These are not matters to discuss in front of everyone!"

Edgard and Josef snigger like teenage boys. "Please, discuss away. Pretend we are not even here," Edgard says with a wave of his hands. "Right, Josef?"

"Absolutely. We are not even flies on the wall."

"We could combine parties," Nadia suggests.

"Oh, no," I disagree. "Having a baby is such a special thing. You must have your own party."

She makes a face. "I do not think I will be able to go to your party if it is not held at the same time as mine."

"That man is such a—" Eva starts in on her like she always does.

Agata quickly interrupts. "He vill let you a-go to your own a-party, though, von't he?"

Nadia nods. "He knows we need things for the baby. Especially with his hours cut, every little bit will help. So if we could combine my party and Tami's, it would be for the best."

Her eyes have dark circles under them, and her hair looks stringy, as if she has not shampooed it in several days. I am so worried for her. I reach out and squeeze her hand. "It'll be fun to have it together."

Danny has let us converse well into the start of the class, but he finally calls us to order. We work for over an hour on practicing proper use of participles and how to avoid dangling them. I pay careful attention and participate fully, as always, and soon enough, class is dismissed.

"Come on," says Eva, pulling me up from my chair. "Let's go tell your boyfriend that you're going to marry the fruitcake."

My eyes sink shut. I am tired of her lack of sensitivity.

"Haroun is not a fruitcake," I say. "He is going to be my husband."

"Not if Ike has anything to say about it."

I grab Eva's arm and dig in with my nails. "He must never know."

She shrugs. "You know he's going to find out."

She tries to pull back, but I keep my grip on her. "He's not. You need to promise me—*promise me*—you will never breathe a word of it."

"Is that what you *really* want, Tami?"

She yanks her arm away.

"Yes."

"Then fine. I won't say a word about it."

"I don't want to go to Starbucks anymore," I tell her. "I don't think it's right, now that I'm almost engaged."

"Good. I'm sick of coffee."

We decide to go to Park Place Mall and shop for baby gifts for Nadia. While waiting for the bus, we sit on a bench and close our eyes and lift our faces upward to bask in the beautiful March sun. I have peeled off my sweater and sit there in my Levi's and turquoise camisole and I feel like my soul is healing somehow with each ray of sun that pierces my skin. Feeling the sun on one's body should be a basic human right afforded to all. Chadors. *Death out for a walk* is how Guy de Maupassant way back in the nineteenth century described women in chadors. *Never again*, I resolve. Never again will I veil myself from the sun.

"You know what?" I tell Eva. "Marrying Haroun is good."

"If you say so."

"I say so."

"Did he do anything goofy last night?"

I chuckle. I tell Eva how he took out an antiseptic wipe after touching my hand across the table and methodically wiped all evidence of me from his body.

We share a laugh.

I tell her how he slammed on his brakes on the way home, claiming a dog had run out in front of the car, which was completely his craziness talking.

We share another laugh.

I tell her how he asked me to open all the doors—to the restaurant, to my house, to the passenger side of the car where I sat, so he would not have to absorb their germs.

I sigh. "But other than that, we had a really nice time."

She kicks my shin with the side of her leg.

"I bet you'll die a virgin," she says.

I laugh and I feel the sunshine even on my teeth. "Somehow, I doubt that."

"Sex isn't exactly a sterile endeavor, you know."

"Well, it wouldn't be the worst thing to have a marriage without sex."

Eva reaches over and slaps her hand over my mouth. "Blasphemy!"

I bite her hand, and she pulls it back. "Seriously, Eva, if it means I get to stay in America, that's just fine with me."

"You've never had sex, right?" She asks this scornfully.

"Of course not!"

"Ever had an orgasm?"

"I don't even know what that is."

"Oh, girlfriend! We are going right to Borders when we get to the mall. I'm going to buy you a book about sex. A very graphic book about sex."

I feel my cheeks redden. I am so very grateful we are alone at the bus stop.

"And then you can hide it in the grass next to your shoes!" she jokes.

I laugh. "I won't have to hide it! I am getting married now. Maryam won't mind if I have a book about sex. She might even buy me one herself."

She rolls her eyes. "Jesus, you people are nuts. Porno books are okay, but walking shoes are not."

Then she gets an idea. Her mouth opens very big and she clutches my arm. "I know! I think before you're willing to give it up forever, you should at least *have* sex, so you know what you'll be missing! So you can make an informed decision!"

She nods at me like this is a brilliant idea.

"*Right.* And how am I supposed to do that?"

She raises her eyebrows at me a few times and grins. "I'm sure Ike would be willing to help out in that regard."

"Are you *crazy?*" At the very mention of Ike's name and the word *sex,* my body feels all squishy and warm.

"You're the crazy one," she insists. "Ike's totally hot."

"Haroun won't marry me if I'm not a virgin."

"He'll never know."

"He wants me to see his doctor for a full physical to make sure I'm completely healthy before we get married. So trust me, he'd know."

Eva looks disgusted. "What *is* this?" she demands. "Why are you letting yourself be treated this way? Aren't you humiliated that he'd even *suggest* such a thing?"

Aaargh. Eva only sees the world from her happy, sex-filled, gender-equal, German perspective. Telling her things about my life is really pointless. I don't know why I bother.

"This sun feels wonderful, doesn't it?" I say, turning my face back up to it and closing my eyes once again. "In Tehran, there is so much smog it feels as if the sun never gets through like it does here."

"Living under the clouds of smog," Eva drawls sarcastically. "That's so symbolic."

I elbow her and open my eyes because I hear a bus roaring down Broadway Boulevard toward us. I stand and grab her hand to pull her up. She swishes her hair from side to side, then grabs hold of her breasts and repositions them so they are as perky as can be, and tugs the waist of her skirt so it rides as low on her hips as possible. Her flat, tanned stomach is on display for all to see.

My friend Eva, I think with sudden affection. *She wouldn't last an hour on the streets of Tehran.*

• • •

This is my first bus ride in America, so I let Eva lead the way. We board at the front of the bus. She pays the driver by slipping change into the dispenser, then grabs the first available row she can find, which is just a few rows from the front. I sit next to her and look around, at the advertisements, the male passengers in front and behind us, and marvel at the modernity of the bus. Back home, the buses are pre-revolution.

I turn to Eva with indignant glee. "I can't even tell you how much I enjoy doing these sorts of things. Back home, women have to board the bus in the back and stay in the back so the men do not even see us. This is so crazy—I am not being corrupted just from riding a bus!"

Here's an example of how topsy-turvy things are in Iran— we have these restrictions on buses, yet men and women cram into taxis together. As a joke, we call dating "going for a taxi ride."

Eva leans her head against the window and looks at me. "What would happen in Iran if you moved to the front of the bus and sat down?"

I snort with incredulity. "I never would."

"Why not?"

"I'd be dragged off the bus and arrested."

"What if every woman moved to the front of the bus?"

"They wouldn't!"

"But if they did?"

I raise my hands and speculate. "We'd all be taken to jail. Beaten, maybe."

"And if you kept on doing it?"

"What, do you think we're insane?"

"I'm just saying, there's power in numbers."

"There's power in guns," I tell my naïve friend.

I can tell Eva is frustrated with me. "Do you know who Rosa Parks was?"

I shake my head.

"Danny told us all about her last semester. It used to kind of be the same way here, only not with men and women but with blacks and whites. Blacks had to ride in the back of the bus and had to give up their seats to white people if all the seats were taken. And after doing this for years and years, one day Rosa Parks refused to give up her seat."

Terror strikes my heart. "What happened?"

"She got arrested. Then she got bailed out and the whole city of Montgomery, Alabama, exploded. Blacks started striking and refused to ride the bus until they could sit where they wanted and didn't have to give up their seats to anyone. And the whole town more or less ground to a standstill. Economically, the town couldn't survive without the black workers."

"Did they ever get the law changed?"

"You bet." Eva nods proudly, as if she took part herself. As if we could all just do the same thing in Iran and things would get better for us.

"Well, America is all about the money. That's why it worked. In Iran, the government runs most businesses. It wouldn't matter if we stopped riding the buses. They wouldn't care. They wouldn't care if we stayed in our homes forever and never came outside. In fact, they would probably prefer it. They'd give all the jobs to the men."

"You're such a defeatist. You think like a total victim."

I am a total victim. I feel a sudden rage toward her.

"I don't want to talk about this anymore," I tell her in a voice that is not very friendly.

"It really bothers me how you let people walk all over you!

You're marrying this *weirdo* who's going to hold you back. Once you're married, he's not going to let you out of the house, just you wait. Too many germs. He's going to keep you a prisoner, in some germ-free little bubble. And if you ever do have kids, it'll be through artificial insemination so he doesn't have to touch you and dirty himself. But he won't have kids, you mark my words, because they're so germy with their snotty noses and they'd have to go to school and breathe in germs from all those other kids."

"Eva, enough!" I say this loudly, firmly.

"No, it's not enough." She is equally loud, equally firm. "This conversation is long overdue. You deserve better. You need to learn how to stand up for yourself, Tami."

"And you need to learn to *shut up*. How dare you say I deserve better? My girlfriends in Tehran deserve better. So does my mother. So does every Persian living in Iran and longing for the chance to live in a free society. I'm not any more *deserving* than they are."

The bus pulls up to the mall entrance. I rush off the bus. She follows. I keep walking, and when she calls out to me, I turn around.

"Come on," she coaxes. "I'll drop it. Let's find some things for Nadia."

"*No.*" I yell this at her louder than I've ever spoken to anyone before. "You're just going to judge poor Nadia and mock her the same way you do me. And I'm sick of it, Eva. I'm sick of having you, simple little *you* with your simple little life, tell us how all our lives would be so much better if we would just stop being victims."

"If the shoe fits . . ." She has this stupid, pleasant look on her face like she hasn't heard a word of what I've said. And I want to slap it right off, I really do.

"I don't even know what that means!" I scream. "For the

first time in my life, I get to make a choice about my future. It's *my* choice! *Mine, nobody's but mine!*"

It occurs to me that I have totally lost control of myself, but I am too far gone to care.

Eva raises her hands in defeat. "What-*ever*, Tami. I didn't mean to set you off. *I'm sorry.* Let's just get on with our shopping. I'll buy you that book about sex, and—"

She hasn't heard a word I've said.

"Fine, Eva. You go buy me a book about sex. I'll wait right here."

She looks at me quizzically. "Are you sure? Why don't you come in with me?"

I wave her off. "No, no. I'm too shy. You know that. You go buy it and I'll wait here and calm myself down."

"Okay," she agrees. "And then we'll shop for Nadia. Right?"

"Right."

But I am so sick of people shoving their opinions down my throat that the moment she disappears into the bookstore, I turn and start running. I run all the way to the other side of the mall. To Macy's. To Maryam, who is working today.

She is my big sister. And she understands in a way no one else ever can.

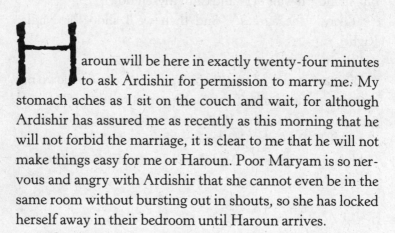

21

Haroun will be here in exactly twenty-four minutes to ask Ardishir for permission to marry me. My stomach aches as I sit on the couch and wait, for although Ardishir has assured me as recently as this morning that he will not forbid the marriage, it is clear to me that he will not make things easy for me or Haroun. Poor Maryam is so nervous and angry with Ardishir that she cannot even be in the same room without bursting out in shouts, so she has locked herself away in their bedroom until Haroun arrives.

As for Ardishir, he sits cheerily next to me, casual and unconcerned. Oblivious to my nerves. He wears jeans and a cable-knit sweater as a concession to Maryam, who sank to the floor and beat her arms upon it when she realized he intended to receive Haroun wearing his oldest gray sweatpants and his University of Arizona T-shirt with the holes in it.

"You could just stay here," he suggests. "You know, keep

on doing what you're doing. Taking your classes and living with us."

I do not bother to answer him. We have talked about this several times already. I do not want to put my life on hold in such a manner. I do not want to be a criminal and always in fear of deportation. Living in fear is what I am trying to get away from.

"You could postpone any acceptance of his engagement until after *Noruz*. This way, you are still able to meet other men who might make more suitable husbands."

I shake my head. "It is better to move forward with what we know."

"You could apply for an extension of your visa," he suggests.

"*Ardishir.*"

"Oops, he's here!" Ardishir rises and calls out to Maryam, "Honey, the pistachio nut is here!"

I laugh despite my frustration and move as if to hit him. He dodges my arm and goes to the door. I follow, and Maryam joins us in the foyer. She squeezes my arm in support. "Ready?" she whispers. I nod with a closed-lipped smile.

Salaam, we all greet one another and exchange pleasantries about the weather and ask after one another's families. We enjoy a cup of tea in the living room, and after it is finished, Maryam rises and asks for my help in the kitchen. Haroun smiles at me and nods his agreement that I should go with my sister. Once in the kitchen, Maryam and I huddle as close to the door as possible in a way that allows us to hear every word, which we know from testing out this position last night.

I hear the clink of the teakettle as Ardishir pours more tea for Haroun and himself. It is only after a bit more tea that Haroun begins his appeal.

"I am aware of Tamila's situation with her visa," he begins. "I know she needs to marry soon in order to stay in the United States. And I have grown very fond of her in the time we have known each other. I believe she is fond of me as well."

Maryam squeezes my elbow. I smile and try to relax the tension I feel in my body, try to stop holding my breath.

"If I receive your permission, I would like Tamila to become my wife."

When Ardishir replies, his tone is very welcoming. "I am glad we have had the chance to meet you. Tami seems to think you are a suitable match."

"Yes, I believe so."

"How is that spider bite, if I may ask?"

Aaaaargh. Maryam flinches and covers her eyes with her hand. *Come on, come on, don't do this, Ardishir. It's not funny.*

Haroun sounds surprised to be asked such a question at this time. "It is fine, fine. I took antibiotics my doctor prescribed and the swelling has gone away completely."

"Good, good. That's very good."

There is a heavy silence as Haroun waits for Ardishir's answer and Ardishir acts as if the question has never been asked. Finally, Haroun speaks again.

"I am going to visit my uncle in Albuquerque over *Noruz* and I was hoping you would allow Tami to accompany me so he could meet her before our marriage. I assure you, our behavior would be entirely proper."

"You're going away for *Noruz*?" Ardishir sounds pleasantly surprised.

"Yes, for eleven days. One day to drive out there, nine days to visit, and another day to drive home."

"Yes. Hmmm. Why not just fly?"

Maryam and I shake our heads at each other. She looks as unhappy as I feel.

"By driving, Tami and I would get to spend a large amount of time together getting to know each other better and making plans for our wedding and our married life."

"Not to mention, that recycled air on those planes is disgusting."

"Oh, isn't that the truth! The last time I flew, I was sick for a month afterward."

I narrow my eyes at Maryam. I do not like Ardishir making fun of Haroun like this. "I'm going in there if he doesn't stop this," I whisper.

"Just wait," she whispers back.

"I'm afraid that I cannot allow Tami to go with you unaccompanied," Ardishir tells him with a regretful tone. "If I might suggest, why don't you go and bring your uncle back with you? We can do the official engagement upon your return. We'll have a dinner party for your uncle and set a wedding date then."

"No," I whisper angrily to Maryam. I know why Ardishir is doing this. It is the safest way he can think of to postpone the engagement so I can perhaps meet another man over *Noruz*. But I do not want to meet another man. I have settled on Haroun.

"That's fine, I understand, that's a good idea," Haroun agrees gracefully, politely. "I am sure my uncle would like to be part of everything."

I will have none of this. It is a horrible idea. Who knows, maybe his uncle will not like me. Or maybe he will introduce him to some clean-freak beauty in Albuquerque and Haroun will fall in love with her. Before Maryam can stop me, I stride into the living room and take a seat beside Haroun.

"I have an idea," I say in my most optimistic voice. "I have never been to Albuquerque and would very much enjoy going—"

"Tami, I cannot allow it. What would your parents think, you going without a chaperone? I couldn't—"

"I was *saying*," I glare at my brother-in-law, "I would very much like to celebrate *Noruz* with Haroun and his uncle."

"Tami, I just—"

I hold up my hand to stop Ardishir. "If Haroun and I get married tomorrow or the next day at the courthouse, then it will be no problem for me to go with him."

Haroun's eyebrows perk up as he considers the idea. "I would be amenable to that."

"Tami deserves to have a nice wedding," Ardishir insists. "It's bad enough that her parents won't be able to be here. The least we can do is make sure she has a proper wedding ceremony."

Maryam joins us from the kitchen. "That's a great idea, Tami, to get married right away! We can file the immigration paperwork while Tami and Haroun visit his uncle. And then we can take our time to plan a big celebration. There will be no rush for it, as long as the paperwork is completed."

But Ardishir will have none of it. He turns to Haroun. "I am very concerned that we show your uncle the proper respect. He is an old man, and it would be best to honor him. You should bring him here so we can meet him and show him our respect for your family."

"I don't think he'd mind," Haroun says.

"And yet, we are not in such a rush that we have to exclude your family from their own nephew's wedding. We will wait. There is time."

I clear my throat and glare at Ardishir to remind him, *It's my choice. You need to support my decision.*

Haroun laughs and reaches for my hand when he sees the look I give to Ardishir. He pulls me close to him on the couch and rubs my back. "It's okay. I'm disappointed, too, that we cannot be married right away and take this trip together. But Ardishir is right; this is the best way. We'll get engaged as soon as I return with my uncle, and after we're married, we'll take many, many trips together."

I let out all my breath and sag back against the couch. I feel thoroughly defeated by the situation and betrayed by my brother-in-law.

Did you forget your promise to me? Those words were the only ones I spoke to Ardishir after Haroun left. The rest of the time, I sat on the couch with my arms crossed and shook my head at him. I just listened as Maryam berated him for hours.

The next morning, Maryam must work, but Ardishir stays home and makes phone call after phone call on my behalf. It seems he calls every Persian he has ever met and inquires after the marital status of their brothers, their uncles, their sons, and themselves.

And nothing works out. To make matters even worse, one of the two *Noruz* dinners we have already scheduled with potential fiancés cancels due to a serious illness in the family. So we are down to one confirmed meeting, and Maryam has already warned me that this family may be more religious than she expects I would like.

A horrible sense of dread has knotted itself into a ball inside my stomach ever since Ardishir postponed the engagement. I think this morning is the first time I have actually, really and truly, believed my quest might end in failure.

"Do you want me to drop you off at school today?"

Ardishir asks when it is already past the time I should have left.

"I'm not going," I reply.

I am flopped on the living room couch, covering my eyes with the palm of my hand to shield them from the bright March sunlight that streams through the windows. I have lain like this for hours.

"Come on," he urges. "You need to get up and do something. You're making me feel bad just lying there like that."

"Good," I spit out. "You should feel bad. You should have made all these phone calls *before* you ruined things with Haroun. Then you would have known what a gift he was offering and been nicer to him. It is not so easy, finding someone to marry."

His tone remains pleasant. "Nothing's ruined, Tami. Everything will work out the way it is supposed to. Don't worry." He reaches for my hands, pulls them away from my eyes, and hauls me up off the couch.

I yank my hands back and narrow my eyes at him. "I could have married Haroun today at the courthouse and been done with it."

"So you'll marry him in two weeks." Ardishir shrugs.

"I could have already filed my immigration papers."

"In two weeks," he says. "It will all come together in two weeks. You just need to make sure that nothing happens between now and then that causes him to change his mind."

22

Nadia comes to class sporting a brave smile and a broken left arm. She stands at the entrance to the classroom, almost as if she is afraid to come in.

I am the first to notice her. Agata and Josef are too busy with their flirtatious argument. Edgard is reading a medical journal, Danny is making copies of our worksheets for class, and Eva has not yet arrived.

I meet Nadia's gaze and immediately go to her. I direct her back outside the classroom.

"Nadia, what happened?"

Her eyes are dull and resigned, with no fight left in them.

"Lenny got arrested for drunk driving and I didn't answer the phone when they called me from the jail to come down and get him. So he had to stay overnight in jail, and when he got home, I told him I was going to leave him."

I gasp. "What happened?"

"He pushed me down the stairs outside the trailer."

"You could have lost the baby!" It is all Nadia lives for, this baby girl she's about to have.

She gives me a grim look. "I think that might have been the plan."

"Nadia!" I clutch her right hand, her unbroken hand.

Her eyes well with tears. "I am so stupid for even saying such a thing to him. Of course he would react in this way. Oh, Tami. I don't know what I'm going to do. I can't go on like this!"

Nadia's tone is just as desperate as Minu's was on the telephone the other night.

"What do you mean, Nadia?"

"Tami." She looks at me with pleading eyes. "He told me that if I leave him, he will call immigration and tell them I tricked him into getting married. He said I will have to leave the country and my baby will stay here!"

"Oh, Nadia, how awful!"

"Is this true, do you know?"

"I'm sorry, I don't."

"Could you find out for me, please?" she begs. "Could you ask your sister or someone who would know? *Please,* I have no one else to ask. If it wasn't for this baby shower coming up and the gifts he thinks we will get, I don't think he would even let me come to class anymore."

I look at Nadia standing there with her stomach bulging in Lenny's *It's Miller Time* T-shirt and with her arm in a cast. There is an old Persian saying, *I used to feel sorry for myself because I had no shoes, until I met a man who was dead.*

"Of course I will," I promise. "You just keep being so brave, and together we will figure this out."

Poor, poor Nadia. She needs all the help she can get. I put

my arm around her for strength. "Are you ready to go in-side?"

She nods glumly but resists stepping forward. It must take all the energy she has to face the outside world after being treated so badly at home.

"Nadia?" I begin to ask.

She looks sideways at me, waiting for my words, and I see so clearly the humiliation she feels that I do not continue with my question. *Couldn't you tell he would be like this before you married him? Weren't there any signs at all?*

"Hold your head high," I tell her. "You've done nothing wrong."

But she disagrees. "Yes, I did. I married him."

We start later that day than usual because everyone huddles around Nadia, worrying over her and encouraging her and hugging her. Everyone, that is, except Eva. She comes to class late and sits in her chair with her arms crossed and watches while we fuss. She looks mad. Mad at Nadia and mad at me.

"You ditched me the other day," she accuses when I finally take my seat next to her. I look at her and think, *It's not all about you, Eva.*

"I'm sorry, Eva," I apologize. "It was rude and unkind. I'm sorry I yelled at you."

She waves away my apology. "Don't worry about it. I'll bring the books tomorrow."

Danny begins the class by sitting on his desk with his gui-tar around his neck. His eyes look sad. I imagine this is be-cause of Nadia's situation.

"Eva asked that we spend some time talking about the

civil rights movement," he begins. I smirk at Eva, knowing she's asked him to do this for me. He strums a few melancholy chords on his guitar and then adds, "I think today, with one of our friends newly injured, is a good day for a serious lesson from your teacher." I swallow hard as he plays the same chord again. This time he hums along. The tune feels mournful, heavy, as if it contains a history of heartache.

Danny looks at each of us in turn. We're German. Czechoslovakian. Iranian. Russian. Polish. Peruvian. And we've all got something we're trying to leave behind. We've all got our sad stories. Nadia is the one Danny wants to hold eye contact with, tries to hold eye contact with, but she won't look at him, so he rests his eyes on me. I am too courteous to look away.

"I tend to get all worked up when people talk about their *rights*," he says. "Any kind of rights. Civil rights. Human rights. Women's rights. I don't know, quite honestly, if anybody anywhere *has* any inherent rights. Says who, you know? Who decides what these rights are? Who bestows them?"

I am tense all over, especially in my shoulders. This is not the Danny I thought I knew. *Just like a man,* I think. *Just like a white man from America, to so casually toss out the only ounce of belief I've been able to sustain all this time, all these years, the idea that somewhere, somehow, I would get my rights, maybe even take them if the opportunity comes along. But I have them, Danny, I do! I do have rights!*

Again, he plays the same chord, a little faster this time. The tone of his hum has changed, too. It's less mournful, more determined. It fuels my curiosity, makes me willing to hear him out. Where's he going with all this?

"Talk to me instead about responsibilities," he continues. "And I'm paraphrasing Gandhi here. But I think we're all put on this earth to make it a better place, plain and simple.

And I think that everyone—*everyone*—has a special contribution to make. A *God-given potential*. And I believe it's a crime against God not to find out where your talents may lie and develop them. And I think it's a crime against God to hold other people back from contributing in the way He intended, whether it's a husband or a government that's doing the holding back."

He turns from me to Edgard. "What if you, with your doctor's brain, are the one who's supposed to find a cure for cancer, but instead you're washing dishes in a restaurant?"

He turns back to me. "What if you are supposed to bring about this oxymoronic notion of peace in the Middle East—*what if you're the one who can actually do it*—yet you've received no training in persuasion, in negotiation? Can you really be expected to stand up for the whole world when you've never been allowed to stand up for yourself?"

I stood up to Eva yesterday, I whimper in my head. The ugly word *victim* thuds back at me from the recesses of my brain.

"I'm going to sing a song for you all in just a minute, and what I want for you to think about while I'm singing it is this: What are you waiting for? I happen to think that if you only have the courage to hope for a better someday, you've barely got any courage at all." Now he stares at Nadia. I want to elbow her, in her unbroken arm, so she sits up and pays attention, because I know what Danny means now, at least in relation to her. "If the best you're willing to do is hope that things will one day be better for your children, forget about *you*, then you're selling yourself short in the eyes of God. You're ignoring that hint of greatness God put inside of you, and isn't that the saddest thing of all?"

He strums the chord again, harsher. But briefly, no humming this time. He's got his final point to make, this ponytailed man who's now got the eyes of a zealot. "I used to wonder, what do they have to lose, these people who hold others back? These husbands, these parents, these governments? And I've come to realize *that's the wrong question.* The correct question is: How do we help them realize what *they have to gain* by letting us, encouraging us, insisting to us, that we develop our God-given talents and put them to good use in the world?"

"We Shall Overcome."

That's the song he sings to us, teaches us, then insists we sing along with him.

We shall overcome, one day.

Haroun calls that night, full of complaints about his eight-hour drive to Albuquerque. The truck stop was filthy, so he didn't want to use the bathroom and went outside behind a tree instead, but got bitten by a mosquito in a place he won't mention, and so itched the entire way to Albuquerque. He itched so badly he almost drove off the interstate several times. And his eye began twitching from tiredness after three hours on the road, so he had to stop and buy some medical supplies so he could fashion an eye patch for himself.

"It must have been hard driving with that eye patch," I offer, glaring at Ardishir, who sits at the kitchen table flipping through old address books, looking for any eligible Persians he might have overlooked. He makes big eyes at me, eager to hear of Haroun's latest strange saga.

"It was. I wish you were with me," Haroun says with affection.

"I wish I were there, too," I say through a gritted smile.

Ardishir nods at me, like, *Keep up with the compliments, Tami,* and all I think is, *My, how the worm has turned.* He finally realizes how desperate the situation is.

I squeeze my eyes shut. "I miss you," I tell Haroun. "I'm counting the days until you return."

But what I am really counting is the number of days until my visa expires.

It is now down to eighteen.

23

Maryam brings me a pink cowboy hat, a pair of Tony Lama boots, and tight blue jeans with a boot-cut leg. She also brings me a fitted white blouse and a bolo tie and a belt with a turquoise buckle. Tonight I am finally going to the country-western bar, and she wants me to have fun. She also wants me to look cute, because the owner is Persian and, you never know, maybe he wants to get married before my *crazy* fiancé gets back. I know this because I overheard her talking to Ardishir.

"Well?" I come to the living room and spin around. I have done my hair in braids and tied pink ribbons around each end.

Maryam claps. "You look *adorable*."

"You do," Ardishir agrees with a laugh. He reaches for his wallet and pulls out fifty dollars. "Buy a round of drinks for your friends."

"Thank you."

"And don't drink more than two drinks," Maryam tells me for the third time.

"I won't."

"And don't lose the camera. Americans steal, you know."

I burst out laughing. Her generalizations sometimes are quite amusing.

Ardishir holds out his hand for my camera, and I pose for several photos.

"Take a photo of my boots," I tell him. "Only my boots."

He does. I take off my cowboy hat.

"And now a close-up of me and my braids."

"Yes, ma'am," he jokes. Then I put the hat on Maryam and throw my arm around her shoulder. "Take one of me and my sister." As he is doing so, Edgard pulls up in a battered old station wagon and honks the horn.

"They're here!"

Maryam frowns. "Can't they come in? It would be good for us to meet your friends."

"Let her go." Ardishir hands the camera back to me and opens the door. "Have fun."

"Thanks." We have made our peace. I know he only wants the best for me.

The Rustler is big, loud, and packed. But Agata and Josef came early for happy hour and got a table for us right near the dance floor, so we have a place to sit. Eva leads me to the bar and she orders a pitcher of beer and I see right away who the Persian owner is. He looks like he is sixty years old and he wears a wedding ring and so I do not even bother to introduce myself.

Haroun it is.

This bar mesmerizes me. Music, alcohol, and couples dancing. Three big no-no's where I come from, where having fun is against the law. People go around in a big circle on the dance floor. Promenading, Edgard informs me, pointing out the lanes on the dance floor that are only for couples. Other times, line dancers take over and all the people do the same dance moves at the same time. Men on the sidelines stand with their thumbs in their belt loops, and the women have the biggest hair I've ever seen.

Eva drinks a beer very quickly and then hitches on to the group of line dancers.

"Want me to teach you how?" Carrie offers. She is Edgard's wife and we have just met and I like her very much because she treats Edgard with such respect, and she brought him back with her from Peru and gave him a chance at a new and better life.

"Come on." Agata pulls me up and leads me to an open spot at the edge of the dance floor. She and Carrie teach me the grapevine and the hot turn monterey and the sailor left and sailor right and the kickball change. It is very fun, but by the time I learn the steps, the song is over. So we go and drink a little bit of our beer and practice some more, and by the time "Boot Scoot'n Boogie" comes on, I feel confident enough to let them drag me out with all the others.

All I can say is, thank goodness for the beer! I make many mistakes, but I don't care. My cowboy hat has fallen off my head and hangs down my back, and my braids bounce with each step I take. But it is so fun! We continue into "Friends in Low Places" and then "Electric Slide" and by the end of "Electric Slide," I am dipping low like Eva and pushing my chest out when I land on my heel.

And I am laughing, laughing, laughing with all my friends. This is the most fun I have had since arriving in America.

"Someone's got his eyes on you," Eva yells to me. With her arm around my shoulder, she continues to dip low and drags me down with her, so low I can see my own cleavage. I feel like a *badjen,* and I like the feeling. But when I look up to the edge of the dance floor, I stop dancing. I freeze, and Eva yanks me back up with her. But I can barely go through the motions of this electric slide.

For, standing at the edge of the dance floor, looking more handsome than I've ever seen him before—in his light-brown, well-worn leather cowboy boots, faded blue jeans with a hole in the knee, and a crisp white T-shirt—is Ike. I don't need to take a picture with my camera. I know I will remember this image of him forever. Of Ike, standing there, watching me. Beautiful, wounded Ike.

"How did he know we would be here?" I yell at her over the sound of the music.

"I have no idea," she says with that devilish grin of hers.

I duck out of the line and my friends continue the dance without me. I have to sidestep and pause and dash my way around the other dancers as I make my way to Ike. I stop a few feet in front of him. I will try for humor.

"Howdy, pardner." I put my cowboy hat back on my head and latch my thumbs through my belt loops and pose like I have seen the men do. I give him my best smile. He remains serious.

"Howdy, Persian Girl."

Tears fill my eyes.

"Are you very angry with me?"

"For how you blew me off?"

I look at him quizzically.

He asks again, without slang. "Am I mad that you stopped coming to see me?"

I nod.

"No." After a pause, he adds, "I just miss you, is all."

"I've missed you, too," I tell him quietly.

He watches my friends dance for a moment. "You look good out there on the dance floor."

I laugh. "No I don't."

"You look happy."

"Do I?" I can hardly contain my surprise.

"Definitely."

"*Really?*"

He looks at me quizzically. Our eyes lock, and his turn serious. "We're wasting time, Tami. We should be spending every minute together."

I look to the ground. He reaches for my hands and squeezes them. In response I step forward onto the toes of his cowboy boots.

"Hey!" He feigns offense, but I just give him an evil-Eva grin.

"I like you far too much to spend time with you, Ike."

"That makes no sense at all," he chortles.

I pull on him. "Come have a beer with me. Tonight is for fun. I don't want to be sad."

"Sometimes I don't think Persian girls even know *how* to be happy," Ike grumbles as I lead him to our table. I feel very daring, to be holding his hand like this in public. And I also feel desired. What a nice feeling this is, to be wanted. I am sure Ike is not going to pull out an antiseptic wipe and scour my germs out of his skin.

When we get to the table, I introduce him to Edgard and Josef and point out Carrie and Agata on the dance floor. Then I pour him a beer and hand it to him.

"Just how many Persian girls do you know," I ask him, in a teasing voice, "to be able to judge that they do not know how to be happy?"

He gulps a few sips. "One," he admits, chagrined.

"Meaning me?"

"Meaning you, Persian Girl."

I pull down the brim of my hat so it sits low on my fore-head. "I'm not a Persian girl," I inform him. "I'm a cowgirl."

The skin around Ike's eyes crinkles when he bursts out laughing. As I watch him, a sudden recognition comes over me: Tonight, I can be anyone I want. Tonight, I am with Ike and my friends, and they enjoy me and maybe being happy only means living in the moment, appreciating the exact moment you're in and not thinking about the worries of the future. And I think, *I can do this.* Tomorrow, once again, I can be the girl who settles. Tomorrow, I can be the girl with a fiancé who likes but doesn't love her. Tomorrow, I can be the girl who might perhaps never have laugh lines of her own.

But tonight, I can be a cowgirl.

Eva, Agata, and Carrie make their way back to our table after a while to have a drink. When the music turns slow, the dance floor shifts from line dancing to something akin to a slow promenade around the perimeter of the huge dance floor. Couples hold each other and effortlessly move in rhythm, turning and stepping and gliding as if they were one. I stare openmouthed. They are so beautiful, these couples.

Ike stretches out his hand to me. "Dance with me," he requests.

I shake my head. "I don't know how."

"I'll teach you."

"I can't."

"I'll dance with you," Eva offers. But Ike ignores her.

"Come on," he urges me, gesturing with his head in the direction of the dance floor. "I dare you, Cowgirl."

Well, that just does it. Faking a confidence I definitely do not feel, I walk ahead of Ike to the dance floor. I hold my hands up like I have seen the couples do and wait for Ike's direction. He takes my hands and keeps a proper two-foot distance between us. Still, my heart pounds.

"Okay, this is a waltz," he tells me.

"A waltz," I repeat, and nod to let him know I am ready.

"We step forward on the left," he instructs, and steps to the side. I follow him. "Then step right beside the left." This, I also do. But it soon becomes too complicated, all this stepping left in place and then stepping forward on the right and stepping left beside the right and backward on the left and then cross left over the right. I become flustered and fall several steps behind and Ike smiles gently at me and acts as if he doesn't care, but every mistake I make only confirms that this world of slow dancing with a man is beyond me.

I stop trying halfway through the first waltz. I simply halt. Ike stops, too. I try to pull my hands back, but he keeps holding on.

"You're doing great, Tami," he assures me.

"I'm sorry," I tell him, my beautiful Ike with the laugh lines. "I just don't know how to do this."

"You'll get the hang of it."

But I know I will never get it right, and all of a sudden, it is about so much more than the dance. Tears spill over before I can even try to fight them back.

"Hey," Ike says softly, and pulls me toward him. "Come here."

I step into his hug and he wraps his arms around me and holds me close. "You fit right in," he murmurs.

I smile into his shoulder. It is how I feel, too, like he is a part of me. *You're not a Persian girl tonight.* I remember this and tighten my embrace. I take in Ike's clean-soap smell, the smoothness of his freshly shaven cheek. And then, without thinking, I do something I would not have thought myself capable of doing.

I kiss his neck.

It is warm and so very soft and I feel him smile when I kiss it and he smells so good that I kiss his neck again in the exact same spot. And then I realize what I have done and step back.

"Sorry." I smile sheepishly.

"No need to be sorry." He leans forward and I shake my head to warn him that I lost myself for a moment but now I remember who I am and I cannot kiss him anymore. As we look at each other, happy and miserable at the same time, the overhead lights flicker on and off and on and off.

"What is this?" I ask, looking around me. The place looks not so special in the harshness of the light.

"Closing time." He swallows hard. "Can I give you a ride home? Please?"

I take a deep breath and hold it for as long as I can before exhaling. Ike watches me, and I can tell he already knows my answer from how I am breathing. I don't even have to say it.

I am back to being a Persian girl, and there is no way I can agree to what he has proposed.

24

Maryam picks me up after class on Monday and drives me to see Haroun's physician, Dr. Saeid Haji. I have never been to a male doctor before. I sit looking out the window, rubbing and twisting my hands.

"You're in America. Don't be scared, *Tami Joon*," Maryam reassures me. "There's nothing wrong with a male physician examining a female patient."

"I know this, logically," I tell her. "But it's hard nonetheless, when you're told your whole life by the government that it is wrong."

Maryam reaches over and pats my knee. "I know. I still get nervous myself."

Based on how Dr. Haji has decorated his office, I think he must see mostly Middle Eastern patients. There are photographs of geographical sights in the Middle East. There are health pamphlets written in Arabic and Farsi. And there is a stack of prayer rugs in a basket. This makes me swallow hard. *Great, he's religious.* I should have worn *hejab.*

Maryam gives me one last smile of reassurance, but remains in the waiting room when a Middle Eastern nurse wearing a headscarf comes for me. She takes me to a small examining room and points me to a chair.

"Dr. Haji will be with you in just a moment."

My voice sounds frightened when I speak. "Should I lie on the examining table? Should I change out of my clothes?"

"You're here at the request of Haroun Mehdi, is this correct?"

I nod.

"You are to marry him?" She shows no expression, so I don't know how to take this question.

I nod again.

"The doctor will be in shortly."

I am so nervous that when Dr. Haji knocks gently on the door to the examining room, I cannot even tell him it is okay to enter. I am bent over, clutching my stomach, tensing all my muscles.

He enters on his own after a moment and looks concerned to see my posture. He is about my father's age, bald with very pale skin.

"My dear, are you in pain?" He takes a seat on a rolling stool and slides close to me.

"Just nervous," I whisper.

"Is this your first visit to a male doctor?"

I nod.

"You're new to America?"

I nod again.

"Well, I think you'll find this to be quite painless." He

pats my knee and smiles. I watch the skin around his eyes crinkle. Laugh lines. I take them as a good sign.

I breathe deeply and make myself sit tall. He nods encouragingly.

"So, you're marrying Haroun Mehdi?"

"Yes."

Dr. Haji pulls out a penlight from his breast pocket and peers into my ears. He shines the light in each of my eyes, and has me open my mouth so he can examine my throat. His hands are smooth and soft and kind as he presses against the glands in my neck. His gentle manner relaxes me, as do his questions about my parents and the neighborhood I am from in north Tehran. He is from north Tehran as well.

Dr. Haji scribbles a few notes in my file. With his eyes averted, he asks, "How well do you know Haroun?"

"I met him a couple of months ago."

He looks up. "You are here on a tourist visa?" It is more a confirmation than a question.

I nod. He studies my eyes, and after a long moment nods back. I can tell he knows exactly what my purpose is in marrying Haroun.

He clicks his pen closed and puts it in his breast pocket. He crosses his arms and clears his throat.

"Haroun has been my patient for many years, so I know him well," he says. "From a medical standpoint, anyway."

"He speaks very highly of you," I tell him.

At this, Dr. Haji's mouth breaks into an involuntary smile. "I'm sure he does."

I think back to my restaurant meal with Haroun, how the staff placed bets on his behavior. I can only imagine the crazy things Dr. Haji has heard from Haroun's mouth over the years.

"I am restricted in what I can say to you, due to doctor-patient confidentiality laws," he says.

"I understand."

"But I have to wonder if you know what you're getting into with him."

My voice is shaky as I reply, "I know he is quite concerned about his health and germs in the environment."

Another involuntary laugh from Dr. Haji. "Yes, this is true. You put it very kindly."

He stops for a moment as if measuring his words, and when he speaks again, his voice is quiet, like he is breaking bad news to a family with a member in the hospital. "I want to tell you something about America, Tamila."

"Please," I encourage him. I can use all the advice I can get.

He keeps his eyes locked on mine as he speaks. "Divorce laws are very different here than in Iran. It is nothing, to get a divorce here. It is so easy and common, you can do it by mail. You don't need to prove your husband is unfit, and you don't have to go before a judge."

My heart pounds as I listen to him. I look at him questioningly. *What do you know about Haroun that I don't know?*

Dr. Haji reads the question in my eyes and shakes his head. He cannot tell me. He leans closer.

"You can file papers without the other person even knowing. You don't need your husband's permission, is what I am telling you. Do you understand?"

I let his words sink in, and then I nod at him. I am sure my eyes are now very big and scared.

He again pats my knee like a father. "I will give Haroun a clean bill of health on you. And I will tell him that I want to see you every month for the next year for a quick checkup." He grins at me. "He will like that."

Now I am the one who laughs without intending to.

"And when you come in, we will have honest communications about your marriage." Dr. Haji's eyes turn stern. "I will ask you every time how you are doing. And I want you to tell me the truth. Do you agree to this?"

I nod and feel the tears forming.

"I will ask, *Are you okay? Are you safe? Are you ready to file some papers?* I will have papers right here in my office. Do you understand what I am saying?"

You are saying Haroun is mentally unstable. You are saying I must be careful. You are saying that maybe what I am doing is not so smart.

"Is he dangerous, Dr. Haji? Do you think he might hurt me?"

He shakes his head. "I don't think so. But he's never shared living space with anyone since developing his . . . his health concerns. I am not sure how it will affect him. It may be a huge stressor. I want to watch the situation closely."

"Thank you."

"And make sure he takes his medication."

"All right."

"Do you have family here in town?" he asks.

I tell him about my sister and Ardishir. He recognizes Ardishir's name, has met him at various gatherings over the years. Dr. Haji is so pleasant, so nice, I am tempted to ask him if he has any sons just sitting around waiting to get married. But I am sure this is not the case. I am sure if he has sons, they are off living exciting lives of freedom, dating and marrying anyone they wish.

"Do you have any daughters?" I ask instead.

He beams. "I do. My youngest is a girl. She lives in Colorado." He pulls out his wallet and shows me a picture of a ravishingly beautiful woman whom I'm sure has had a nose job, based on how perfect her profile is. She is posed with an American man and two beautiful children.

"She's beautiful," I tell him. "So are your grandchildren."

He thanks me.

"Your daughter looks very happy."

He gives me another smile, and again I am struck by his laugh lines. *I want laugh lines.* He pats me one last time on the knee before standing and walking me to the door.

"You'll be happy, too, one day," he says. "Life is very long, and you just have to get past the bumpy parts as quickly as you can."

"Thank you so much," I tell him. And it is all I can do not to throw my arms around him and hug him like I would if he were my own father.

"I'll see you soon, Tami," he says by way of good-bye.

"I'll stay in touch," I promise.

Maryam and Ardishir are celebrating their wedding anniversary tonight with a dinner at Anthony's in the Catalinas, so when we arrive home from seeing Dr. Haji, she heads to her side of the house to soak in a bath and make herself even more beautiful than usual for her husband.

My plan for the evening is to be as scruffy as possible. As soon as they leave, I will change into sweatpants and a T-shirt and flop on the couch to watch movies in the dark.

On the way home from the doctor, Maryam and I stopped at Casa Video, where I rented the movie documentary *Divorce Iranian Style* by Ziba Mir-Hosseini. It shows actual divorce cases in Iranian court and it is clear how badly women are considered in Iranian divorces. Maryam has already seen it, and she insisted I rent it, especially in light of Dr. Haji's comments. I also rented *Bend It Like Beckham,* since Ike has mentioned this movie to me more than once.

I am in the kitchen making for myself a cheese sandwich on wheat bread with mustard and lettuce when the doorbell rings. I hurry to answer it and find a skinny man dwarfed by a gloriously fat bouquet of flowers. *From Ardishir for Maryam,* I think as I accept the flowers and thank the deliveryman, but then I notice it is my name and not Maryam's on the card.

My heart pounds from the fear of getting caught by Maryam with this card in my hand, for I know Haroun well enough to know these are not from him. I would expect to receive flowers from him on special occasions, but not as everyday demonstrations of affection. He is too measured, too organized, to be spontaneous in such a manner.

I set the bouquet on the coffee table in the living room and hurry upstairs to my bedroom, thankful Maryam has not called out to see who was at the door. I close and lock my door and sit on my bed and stare at the handwriting on the envelope. *For Tamila Joon.*

My breathing slows and my fear dissipates as I determine perhaps I was wrong about my soon-to-be fiancé. These flowers must be from Haroun. Ike does not know my full name, and he certainly doesn't know the term of affection favored by my family. *Joon,* or loved one. Or does he? The moments we've shared are already blending into memory.

I slide open the envelope and pull out the card. My hands start shaking almost immediately. The flowers are indeed from Ike.

Please, Tami, don't stay away. It's too soon to say good-bye. I need to see your smile. If I don't see you tomorrow after class, I will come to your house and pound on your door until you let me in. Love, Ike.

Love, Ike.

Love, Ike.

Love, Ike.

These are the words I read over and over. Somewhere along the way, I lose the comma between them.

Love Ike.

I hear the front door open. Ardishir is home.

"Where's my beautiful bride?" I hear him call out.

"What lovely flowers!" I hear Maryam say.

The flowers. I sigh. Why can nothing be easy for me?

I force myself up from the bed, when all I really want to do is bury myself under the covers and hide. I tuck the card from Ike along the edge of the mirror. My *hejab* cloaks it from sight. I stick my tongue out at myself in the mirror before heading back to the living room.

I walk in and find Ardishir and Maryam kissing passionately in the foyer. Ardishir clasps his hands around the small of her back, under the depths of her long black curls. She is on her tiptoes kissing him back, with one hand resting on his buttocks and the other clutching a grocery-store bouquet of flowers. They press each other close, so close there is no space between them. I should leave, but I cannot move. The thought strikes me: *I will never have this sort of romance. I will marry Haroun and we will peck each other on the cheek as brother and sister.*

I grab the remote control and turn on the television at full volume. They jerk back from each other and look to find the source of the interruption.

That would be me.

"You don't mind, do you?" I ask with raised eyebrows.

Ardishir looks amused, as if he knows I am looking for a fight and he isn't going to humor me.

He squeezes Maryam's arm. "I'll go get ready."

Maryam smiles at him and pointedly ignores me.

"Nice flowers," I say.

"Not as nice as yours." Her bouquet is less than half the size of mine.

"But you've got the nicer marriage."

Her eyes soften and she comes over to me. She reaches out to stroke my cheek. "I'm sorry, *Tami Joon*. I wish it were a better arrangement. We needed more time, didn't we?"

I let my cheek rest in her soft hands. "You've never looked more beautiful, Maryam."

She gives me a smile of thanks, but her eyes look sad, even on such a special night. In her sadness I see the sorrow of every Persian woman I know.

Why must we all be so sad in our hearts?

"You're the best sister a girl could ever hope to have." I kiss Maryam on both cheeks and reach for her anniversary flowers. "Here, let me put these in a vase for you."

When Haroun calls later that night, I am watching the end of *Bend It Like Beckham,* at the part where Joe shows up at Jesminder's door demanding to see her. His is the last voice I want to hear just then, so I let the machine get it.

25

I should not have watched *Bend It Like Beckham* last night, for I am not allowed a happy ending. I approach Starbucks with one thought in mind: I must say good-bye forever to my good friend Ike.

I am fifty yards away when he catches sight of me, and I see such relief in his eyes. He keeps his eyes locked on mine as I approach, and he stands beside his table and waits for me. My resolve falters before I even reach him.

It is like in a movie. Life may go on all around us, but there is no one in the world but the two of us.

You're here to tell him good-bye.

I feel heaviness in the pit of my stomach. I hope it doesn't show in my face. I want Ike to remember this moment and see only my smile.

"My God, you're like a vision," he says when I reach him. He pulls me close for a hug and reaches to cradle my head in his hands.

When Ike steps back and takes both my hands, he looks at me earnestly. "We've got to make the most of the time we have left, Tami. We can't waste a single minute."

I let out all my breath slowly and feel my smile leave my face. How can I hurt him like this? He has been nothing but kind.

"Let's sit," I urge him while squeezing his hands. He does not release mine as he takes his chair. We seem to have crossed some threshold at The Rustler in sharing our feelings for each other.

"I want you to meet my family." He looks at me earnestly. "I want you to come to dinner and get to know them. I want them to know you, too."

"I can't," I say softly with regret.

"You can," he insists. "I've researched this, and there are tons of Internet cafés now in Tehran. So we'll be chatting on-line all the time until you can come back again, and I want you to meet my family so that when I tell you stories about them, you'll have their faces in your mind."

"Ike, there's no way."

"I'm inviting your sister and her husband, too," he says with conviction. "They've got to get to know me, too."

"Ike—"

"I'm not taking no for an answer."

"This isn't a movie." I smile sadly. "I'm not Jesminder and you're not Joe. This is real life, and I've come here today to tell you good-bye."

Ike furrows his eyebrows. "That's ridiculous. I don't accept it."

"You can't reject my good-bye!" I say indignantly.

"Yes I can. You don't leave for, what, ten days or so?"

I'm getting married, Ike! Married!

But I do not say this, of course. I can barely stand to even think it.

I shake my head. "It's too hard, being with you."

"I told you, I'm going to make sure your sister loves me."

My lips are suddenly very dry. I lick them and bite the bottom one, and when I get my courage up, I reach out and stroke his cheek. "It's not that."

"Then what is it?" His impatience is playful. Endearing. He is my dear. He is my heart. I lower my eyes and take his hand. I try to memorize the path of his veins. "I won't be coming back. I will probably get married when I get back to Iran. It's time."

"Don't." His breathing becomes very heavy.

I look up. "Don't what?"

"Don't get married." He shakes his head and his voice takes on an increasingly desperate tone. "Don't just do it because that's what's expected of you. Be the one who's different."

"That's exactly what you don't want to be in Iran."

"Fuck Iran, Tami."

"What does that even mean, *Fuck Iran?*" I feel my blood boil. I am sure my face is red with anger.

"Don't go back."

"You think I want to go back?" I say bitterly. "You think I'd rather be there, wearing a veil and being afraid whenever I go out in the street, when I could be here, sipping coffee in the sunshine and taking pictures and laughing the day away with you? You think I'd rather have every last thing I do determined by corrupt old men? *Do you think, Ike? Do you think I wouldn't do anything I could in order to stay?*"

"I'm sorry," he apologizes.

But I do not accept his apology. Instead, I slap my palm to

my forehead. "God, you Americans, you make me crazy! You think everything's so *easy*. And maybe it is for *you*, but for the rest of the world, you know, well, lots of us struggle just to get through the day alive, and then we wake up to go through it all over again another day. Our lives are like a nightmare that never ends."

"*Groundhog Day.*"

"What?"

"*Groundhog Day.* With Bill Murray. It's a movie."

"What-*ever*, Ike." I stand, exasperated. "It must be nice, to be able to base your view of the world on nothing more than the movies you've seen, but they're *not real*. All the American movies end happily, haven't you noticed? And that's not how it really is, in case you didn't know."

Ike looks at me like I've lost my mind. Like I am hurting him just for spite, and maybe he's right. I've said too much, and of course, it's not what I really want to say. I have not spoken the words closest to my heart. Nor will I.

I sigh. "Listen, I've got to go. Things are really crazy from here on out. My sister's got a bunch of things planned and we might go out of town for a while. . . ."

He stands, too. "We're not ending things like this, Tami."

"Ike, what do you expect from me? I've got to spend time with my family, with my sister. I have no idea when or if I'll be seeing her again."

"Fine," he concedes. "But this isn't the end. Today, I mean. Today is not the end for us. Our last day is not going to be spent fighting."

I grab my backpack and head toward the sidewalk. "We weren't fighting."

He follows, calling out, "You're so argumentative today, Tami. What's gotten into you?"

I close my eyes to stop the tears, but they pour out too

strong, so I stand there like a fool and cover my face with my hands and try to steady myself.

"Hey," he whispers in a husky voice, and pulls me to him from behind. "I'm sorry."

I turn into his hug and bury my head into his shoulder. My tears immediately stain his shirt and wet his neck. His arms tighten around me.

"*You've* gotten into me," I whisper. "My heart is just breaking, and I don't know what to do about it. I never meant for this to happen. I promise, Ike. I never meant to hurt you." My words are reduced to a jumbled sob by this point.

He steps back and lifts my chin. He lowers his lips to mine. And then he kisses me, and it is the softest, most soothing kiss the world has ever known. I never knew a kiss could be so gentle. It is like I am a child in my mother's arms, and for this moment, there is no such thing as fear. I had forgotten I could ever feel so safe.

"Ohhhh," I murmur, and close my eyes so I can imprint this feeling in my brain. I reach for his face and press my fingers against his cheekbones. I trace an outline of his ears and press my fingers onto his lips. So soft. His warm breath envelops my fingers, and then he catches one of my fingers in his teeth. He bites it playfully and caresses it with his tongue. *He is so alive.*

I love this man.

I open my eyes to smile at him and find that his eyes have been closed this whole time as well. He, too, is trying to memorize this moment.

"Ike," I say softly, and when he opens his eyes, the love in them is more than I can walk away from. He kisses me again, and such a surge of tingling warmth rushes through me that my knees threaten to give out. Ike feels this and presses me back, against the ledge of the Starbucks patio. He kisses me deeper and uses his tongue this time, and in my mind is a big white swirl with a little round black hole anchored in the middle. Amidst all the swirling white, my only goal is to get closer and closer to the hole in the center. I lean into Ike and whimper at how he feels against me. I try to drink him in, his taste, his tongue, his touch. I don't even know where I am anymore.

"What do you think you're doing?"

All of a sudden, I hear the screech of Maryam's voice and the smack of her presence behind Ike. I flinch and push him away. I am drunk from kissing Ike and paralyzed by the anger in Maryam's eyes.

"Did you forget you have a hair appointment? I've been waiting for you at home for over an hour."

"I'm sorry," I beg her. "I'm so sorry."

"You," she hisses at Ike and shakes her finger at him, "don't you *dare* ruin things for my sister. You stay *away* from her."

"You must be Maryam." Ike fakes composure, but I can tell how shaken he is. My sister glares at him with narrowed eyes.

"I've got to go," I tell him, making big, telling eyes at him to beg him not to argue with my sister. My heart races so much that I am sure if I looked down, I would see it beating through my chest. But I don't look down. I look only at him, telling him good-bye and I love you with my eyes.

"I think we should—" he begins.

"We need to go," Maryam says firmly, reaching past Ike to take my arm.

"Tami," Ike says in a stern voice.

"Please don't," I say back, my voice breaking. "I have to go. I'm so sorry." I squeeze his arm once as I rush past him to

Maryam's car. I hurriedly buckle my seat belt as Maryam gets in after me and starts the car.

"Don't look at him," she tells me after glancing in the rearview mirror.

But of course I do. And she is right; I should not have looked. Poor Ike stands there with his arms crossed in front of him, bending over a little as if he'd been kicked in the stomach. I feel my heart collapse in upon itself as my eyes meet his. His blue eyes reach out to me, plead to me to come back to him.

My poor Ike, with eyes as blue as the Caspian Sea. He has finally realized that this truly was our good-bye.

I sink my head back against the headrest. I know that the vision of him standing there will haunt me forever.

"Are you okay?" Maryam asks after we have pulled away.

"No," I tell her in a dull, dead voice. "But then again, that's not really the point of all this, is it? So don't bother with such silly questions."

Later that night, Maryam taps on my bedroom door. Knowing she will enter anyway, I do not answer. She finds me on my back on the bed, my eyes reddened from crying. The picture of me and *Maman Joon* from that day at the ocean lies facedown on my chest. I have studied it for hours and still do not have the answers for which I search. Maryam sits beside me on the bed and picks up the picture to study it.

For a long time there is silence.

"Do you remember if it was foggy that day?" I ask her eventually.

She looks at me quizzically. "Probably. It was always foggy in the mornings." After a pause, she asks, "Why?"

I let out my breath. "I just wonder, that's all. She looks *so happy.* And I just have to wonder, didn't she know? Couldn't she tell? That was her moment, her moment in the sun. She would never have such a perfect day again, a day of pure happiness. She looked like a song that day, don't you think?"

Maryam nods and swallows hard.

"I just can't imagine what it must have felt like, to be her," I continue. "To have all this freedom, all this happiness, and then to have it taken away so suddenly. It was like there was a tsunami forming, and it would drown her so soon, and she had no idea."

Maryam watches me like she is listening to a stranger speaking in a foreign tongue. I take the photograph back from her and study it some more. I study *Maman Joon*'s eyes. She looks like the world is hers for the taking, she really does.

Maryam reaches to wipe my hair from my face. "I keep forgetting how young you were," she says quietly. "You don't really remember any of it, do you?"

She leans to kiss my forehead. "I like your version of what happened." She smiles gently at me. "Hold fast to it. Keep it close to your heart."

"What, isn't it the truth?"

"Sure it is, *Tami Joon.* It's *your* truth, and that's what matters."

26

Look, promise you won't kill me," Eva says to me the next day after class. She pulls me aside and pushes me down onto the bench outside our classroom. "But I did something I need to tell you about."

I sigh. After yesterday's horrible situation with Ike, Eva's antics are so insignificant. I simply cannot summon the energy to care all that much about what she has said or done this time.

"I won't kill you." I try not to sound as lethargic as I feel.

Eva clutches my hand and squeezes it in excitement. "Okay, I know you don't want me meddling, but the stories you told me about Haroun just freaked me out, plain and simple. He's clearly a fruitcake, even his doctor basically said so."

I just sigh and look at her, waiting for her to continue so we can conclude our conversation and I can go home and crawl into bed.

"Have you heard of Internet dating?" she asks.

"Internet what?"

"You know, where you meet someone online through an ad on the Internet, and then if everything goes well, you meet them in person and go on a date."

"Don't tell me," I say to her, giving a small laugh of exasperation. "Please, please, don't tell me any more."

"But listen!" she says. "They have all sort of groups and subgroups as to how you meet people. You know, if you love chess, there's like a chess-lover's dating forum. All kinds of shit like this. So, I just found a couple websites for Persian singles who are looking to meet other Persian singles."

I smile despite my mood. "Persians running personal ads on the Internet? I don't believe it! We're way too hung up on the traditional way of doing things."

"Apparently, not all of you. So," she says, looking at me with undisguised glee, "do you want to know what I did, or not?"

I cannot help but grin at her enthusiasm.

"Tell me, what did you do?"

She looks so smug. "Well, after you told me all that stuff about Haroun, I just decided that if I had anything to do with it, I wasn't about to let you marry some weirdo, Persian or not. There had to be someone better. *Had to be.* So, I placed a little ad of my own, on your behalf."

"You didn't use my name, did you?"

"No, no, no," she assures me, and holds up a folded piece of paper. "You do these things anonymously. So, do you want to know what your ad said?"

I cover my mouth and giggle and giggle. My crazy friend, Eva. I nod and keep giggling.

She ceremoniously unfolds the piece of paper and flattens

it against her leg. She clears her throat and begins. *"Single Persian woman searching for a good man to marry."*

She pauses and looks up at me to get my reaction.

"Oh, my God!"

I am awarded another Eva grin.

"Single Persian woman searching for a good man to marry. Save me from current prospect, an obsessive-compulsive neat freak! Visa expires April, but desperately want to stay in America! Marriage of convenience strictly okay. I'm young, sexy, will look great by your side. Save me, marry me!"

"Oh. My. God!" I sink my face into my hands and laugh until the tears burst forth uncontrollably. The thought of Haroun reading this ad strikes me as hilarious. Oh, my God. Oh, my God. Oh, my God!

Eva waits for me to regain my composure.

"We got a perfect response," she tells me. "Out of all the responses, we got the one we needed."

I am already laughing.

"No, Tami, I'm serious. I talked to this guy on the phone, and I think he's the answer to your prayers."

"Eva, there is no time for this! Haroun gets back to-morrow!"

"There is. Listen, his name is Masoud Something-or-other and he's a real estate developer in Chicago and he's in Phoenix *right now* visiting his parents for whatever-the-hell Persian holiday y'all are celebrating."

"Noruz. It's the Persian New Year."

She waves me silent. "Whatever. Not the point. The point is, I talked to him at length several times about himself and what he's all about. I talked to a bunch of his friends and they all seem normal. He sent me his picture and he's pretty decent-looking. A big nose, but no bigger than any other

Middle Eastern guy I've met. He cleans up pretty good. I pulled a credit report on him, I checked to see if he's ever been arrested. This guy has never even had a driving violation. I'm telling you, Tami, he's perfect."

"There's got to be something wrong with him or he wouldn't be so interested in this."

She opens her mouth to respond and then stops herself. "Just meet him, see what you think."

"It's too late," I tell her. "Haroun is bringing his uncle for dinner tomorrow. We're doing the official engagement tomorrow night."

"It's not too late," she insists. "Listen, just meet the guy. If he's not a million times better than Haroun, you've lost nothing but half an hour of your life. He's waiting for us right now at Chuy's."

"What?! I thought you said he was in Phoenix!"

"We're meeting him at Chuy's at four o'clock. He drove down just to meet you."

"Eva! Aaaahhhh!"

"Nothing to lose, everything to gain. It's right on your way home."

"What's wrong with him?"

"He's perfect for you," she insists.

We walk into Chuy's and I spot him right away, as Persians can always recognize a fellow Persian. He dresses in a white polo shirt and wears a *pooldar* gold wristwatch. On the table before him is a bottle of Corona with a lime squeezed into it, a basket of tortilla chips and salsa, his car keys, and his cell phone. He looks at the walls, which consist of company-sponsored graffiti. He appears very comfortable, very casual. A fine-looking man. Actually, quite handsome.

He stands as we approach and looks first and foremost at Eva. "You must be Eva," he says happily, and reaches to hug her. Friendly guy, must have been in America a long time. *Or he's a letch.*

When they step apart, he smiles at me. "*Salaam,*" he says in Farsi.

"*Salaam,*" I say back, and extend my hand, which he shakes congenially. Eva nudges me with her elbow and tells me she is going to buy us margaritas. I tell her to get me a Diet Coke. For a moment after she leaves, I avoid looking at him by focusing on the graffiti behind his head. *Marriage is the only war where the enemies sleep together.* Startled, I shake the inauspicious words from my mind and lower my eyes to Masoud's face. His skin looks soft, pampered.

"So you're Tami." He smiles after we take our seats across from each other in the booth. "I feel like I know you already, from all that Eva has told me."

I feel my cheeks redden. "I had no idea she put that ad on the Internet," I assure him. "I would never have permitted such a thing."

He shrugs and smiles. "Why not? There's no shame in it."

"It's just *very* different from what I'm used to."

Masoud studies me, but it is not with eyes like any of the others. It is not so much with a judgmental eye as a curious one.

"So you like America," he says.

"Very much so." I cannot help but to smile broadly.

Masoud smiles back. He looks to be in his late thirties, possibly his early forties. About the same age as Haroun.

"When I came here for college, I met and married an American woman. She sponsored me for my citizenship. It was so kind of her. I always thought that someday I'd do the same for someone else, if the chance arose."

Eva slides into the booth next to me and hands me a margarita. I shake my head and smile at Masoud. "She's incorrigible."

"Did you tell her yet?" Eva asks Masoud.

"No, I was warming her up first."

I slug my margarita. "I'm warmed up. Spill it. Tell me your secret."

He takes a deep breath. He doesn't lose his confidence, but just seems to choose his words carefully. "My parents would very much like for me to be married."

"That's not so unusual," I reply slowly, knowing there is probably more to it than this. All Persian parents want that for their almost-middle-aged sons. They all want the grandson.

"Me being married would be good all around," he says. "It would stop the constant questions, the not-so-subtle invitations of young women to dinner whenever I visit."

I laugh. "How many have you met this week?"

He laughs back. "Three."

"Any takers?"

"Nah. They're all daughters of my parents' friends."

Eva can't stand the small talk, our indirect approach to things. It's too Persian for her.

"Oh, for God's sake! He's gay!"

My mouth drops open and I can feel my eyes grow big. "You're *gay*?"

Masoud nods.

"But your parents don't know it, right?"

He nods again and grins at me.

"I see your dilemma," I tell him.

"And I see your opportunity," he replies.

We study each other for a long moment. Without taking his eyes off me, he takes a drink of his beer. Without taking my eyes off him, I sip my margarita. It looks like it's killing Eva to keep quiet, but she does so, admirably.

"We have quite the interesting situation here, don't we?" I finally say.

"We do indeed."

We both smile.

"*Aghar moush va gorbe hamkari khonand vaubelahe doekhandar*," I say in Farsi. *When the cat and mouse agree, the grocer is ruined.* If he and I agree, we can trick everybody.

"My thoughts exactly."

We laugh together.

"Oh, my God," I say, shaking my head in disbelief. "This could be perfect."

"I was hoping you'd think that. Your friend Eva wasn't so sure."

"She's quite the proper girl," Eva says sarcastically.

"There's nothing wrong with proper!" I say defensively. "It's just everything is *this close* to being a completed transaction with Haroun."

"Let me tell you what would work for me," Masoud offers. "This all will either work or it won't. Hopefully, it will, but if not, that's okay, too. I need to be married to get my parents off my back, and they need to think it's a real marriage. I'm already settled in Chicago with my business, so you'd have to move there. We'd have separate bedrooms and each have our privacy, that's very important to me. I think in public we should behave as a married couple. In private, we're just friends."

"Would you—act on your, um, your homosexual impulses?" I blush as I ask it but am proud of myself for being so direct.

"*Act on his homosexual impulses!*" Eva hoots with laughter and slaps the table.

I narrow my eyes at her, a look she always ignores. "*What, Eva?* Now what did I say that's so wrong?"

"Is he going to fuck other men, that's what you want to know. Right?"

"*Eva!*"

I make apologetic eyes at Masoud.

"Don't worry," he tells me. "*Marda be adab, adab amoukhout az beadabon.*" *Courteous men learn courtesy from the discourteous.*

"That's for sure," I agree.

"Hello!" Eva declares. "There's three of us at this table, and one of us doesn't speak Iranian! How rude!"

Masoud adopts a serious tone. "In answer to your question, there is someone I've been seeing for a long time. We have been discreet and will continue to be so. He's a very good person. I'm sure you'd like him."

"Does Tami get a stud muffin on the side, too?" Eva asks. Stud muffin?

"I—I don't know," he stumbles. "I hadn't thought about it."

"I wouldn't see anybody else," I assure him. The idea is just too strange.

"You don't want to promise that," Eva insists. "You might meet some hottie and want to jump his bones. And why shouldn't you? Your husband just told you he's going to fuck his way through the phone book."

"*Eva.*"

"*Tami.*"

"*Eva.*"

"I'm just saying, don't agree to give up your sex life when you don't even know what it is you're giving up," she advises, and turns to Masoud. "She's a virgin," she explains. He raises his eyebrows in amusement.

That's it. I've had it with her. I shove my elbow into her upper arm so hard I know it will leave a bruise.

"Enough rudeness!" I say firmly.

"Hey! I'm just looking out for your best interest."

"You can take my best interest and *shove it up your ass!*" This is Eva-speak; I swear I learned it from her. She brings out the worst in me.

"Nice one!" She is proud of me and with her laughter brings the argument to a close.

"Oh, boy!" Masoud laughs. "And will you be visiting often, Eva?"

"She's a very corrupting influence," I say. "I suggest she be banned from the house."

"But I'm the one who brought you two together!"

Masoud winks at me, and I know from that wink that he's the one. He's got a good sense of humor and doesn't lose his cool. Haroun would *literally* be washing out Eva's mouth and my mouth right now with soap if he had just heard our conversation.

"Do you have a housekeeper?" I ask.

He laughs. "Is that your biggest concern?"

"That's my first concern," I tell him. "I have several more."

He chuckles. "Okay. Yes, I have someone come in twice a month. We could bump it up to once a week if we need to, that would be just fine. Next question?"

"Do you have any mental illnesses I should know about?"

"You go, girl!" Eva applauds my questioning.

"Except for this gay thing, I'm a very normal guy. Pretty stable, mentally."

"Tami wants to be a photographer," Eva tells him.

"Excellent."

"She would want you to fund any sort of training she

might need and then set her up in business. Wouldn't you, Tami?"

I feel a broad smile cross my face. "Yes," I say firmly. "That would have to be part of the deal."

"Not a problem," Masoud informs me. "It sounds like a fun endeavor."

Oh, my God!

I can't think what else to ask him. But there should be more. I can't just agree to marry him after ten minutes, can I? Yet I already know he's a million times better than Haroun.

"I'd also want a dowry paid to my brother-in-law," I tell him. "In case things don't work out."

"That's fine."

"Eva?" I cringe. "I almost hate to do this, but what questions would you like to ask him?"

I sit back and let her take over.

"How much do you make?" she asks.

"Last year I cleared a quarter million dollars, and that was a bad year."

"Holy shit," she says. "Would Tami get her own money or would you be some Middle Eastern control freak where finances are concerned?"

I shake my head and roll my eyes.

"My bookkeeper takes care of all the bills and investments and savings. I expect we'd have a shared household account and each have our own money as well. Does that sound amenable to you?" He looks at me for my reaction.

"That sounds fine." It occurs to me I never spoke about this with Haroun.

"I would, of course, expect a legal agreement that in the case of divorce, all assets obtained prior to the marriage revert to me."

"That sounds fair," I tell him.

"Kids. Tami wants kids," Eva states.

"So do I," he replies.

"You do?" This surprises me.

"Absolutely."

"But how . . . ?"

He shrugs. "There are ways. I've *been* with women before; it's not like I *can't* be with my wife in that way. And there are scientific methods to help in that regard."

"Artificial insemination," Eva says.

"Exactly," Masoud agrees. "That is probably the best way. But I definitely want kids, and sooner rather than later. My parents are elderly. It is something they would like to enjoy before their passing."

"This all sounds just perfect," I say. "*Baad avardera baad mebarad*—but what is brought by the wind will be carried away by the wind. What am I missing? It cannot be so easy as this."

"Maybe it is as easy as this," he says simply. "I'm sure you deserve for things to be easy once in a while, don't you?"

I think of all the trouble I've caused, with Ike and Haroun, and tears come to my eyes. The truth is, I don't deserve for things to be easy. I deserve to have a hard road ahead of me for all the pain I have caused.

So I look at him and swallow hard. "What do we do now?"

He raises his eyebrows. "I suggest we go talk with your family."

"Tonight?"

"I have to go back to Chicago tomorrow evening. There's some business Friday I have to be there for."

I clear my throat. "We'd have to do this within the next week."

"That's fine. We'll have the ceremony and a little celebration Sunday and then file the license at the courthouse Monday. Does that work?"

I nod.

Eva grabs my arm. "This is so exciting!"

"I don't know," I say. "I don't know what to say."

"Say yes, Tami," Masoud urges me. "Make it easy on yourself and just say yes."

I shrug my shoulders. *Make it easy on yourself.* Haroun or Masoud, which one's easier? There's no contest. There's no point in thinking about it for even one moment longer.

"Yes," I tell him. "Yes, yes, yes."

He raises his beer bottle for a toast. I raise my margarita glass, and Eva raises hers.

"To happy endings," he says.

"To happy endings," I agree.

We all drink happily.

"Well," I sigh. "I hate to ruin such a pleasant moment, but we'd better go tell my sister."

"What do you think she'll say?" he asks.

"All I know for sure is this: We're not asking her. We're *telling* her. How she takes it is entirely up to her."

27

I borrow Masoud's cell phone and leave a message for Maryam on hers: *I am bringing a friend home, and we will prepare the dinner. You take it easy.* Eva decides not to join us for what might be a volatile evening, and she leaves to go home.

Masoud and I finish our drinks and stop at the Wild Oats Market just up the block to buy ingredients for chicken burritos. Masoud thinks cooking dinner will impress Maryam. I think he has no idea what he's getting into. We buy two cream-colored taper candles and several orchids. Masoud's concern about the presentation of the table makes me laugh because that is how we joke back home that a man might have homosexual leanings, if we notice him doing the pretty part of women's work, such as gardening, home decoration, and the like.

"You better be careful, or my sister will have her suspicions," I tell him in a joking manner.

"Have no fear," he says. "My parents have no clue, and they know me better than anyone."

I somewhat doubt this. Most parents, I think, have a pretty good idea of the sexual orientation of their children, even if they pretend they don't. Especially in Iran, where dissembling is an art form, I am fairly certain Masoud's parents could know and he'd have no idea of that. I saw a bumper sticker on a pickup truck here that said, *Denial Is Not a River in Egypt.* And I found that very appropriate to my culture, where denial and keeping secrets are done for the sport of it as much as out of necessity; it's one more way we veil ourselves from one another. But then again, Masoud does carry himself in a very masculine, knock-them-down sort of way. Aggressive, which I always view as manly. Haroun with his engineer's hands and constant infirmity seems more of a sissy than Masoud.

We are both cheerful from our alcoholic drinks and giddy about our situation, so we find several things very funny as we play married couple at the grocery store. Masoud is like Ike in this way, in how he makes even everyday things very fun. *Look, honey, the tortillas look so fresh today,* he says. *Yes, dear,* I reply, *and I notice the chicken's on sale.*

It takes only about twenty minutes to get the dinner in the oven and the table set, so Masoud and I sit on the living room couch and start in on one of the bottles of wine we bought for the occasion.

"Oh!" Maryam says in surprise when she arrives home and finds me on the couch with a man. A Persian man, no less. "I thought you were bringing Eva for dinner." She smiles graciously and looks at me curiously.

"This is Masoud," I announce, and he quickly stands to shake her hand. "He lives in Chicago."

"Oh, how nice." She shakes his hand and smiles at him in

her endearingly Maryam way. "And what brings you to Tucson?"

Her kindness to Masoud offends me after her rudeness to Ike yesterday. I suddenly want to offend her in return.

"Masoud and I are getting married," I announce.

"I thought we were going to tell them after dinner," Masoud says pleasantly, turning to me with a fixed smile on his face.

I shrug. "Perhaps I should not have had this glass of wine."

Maryam's eyes are huge as she looks from me to Masoud and back to me again. "Tami, what are you talking about, getting married? You are already engaged. Are you feeling all right?"

Her tone implies she thinks I perhaps have been coerced by Masoud and am having this discussion against my will. She thinks I need her to save me yet again.

"Haroun's crazy," I remind her. "I don't want to be married to him."

"And who's going to tell this to Haroun?"

"Ardishir," I say firmly. "If it weren't for him, I would already be married and then we wouldn't be in this mess. None of this would have happened."

"You can make it unhappen, Tami."

"I don't want to. Masoud's great. He's normal and decent and wants to be married. He understands the position I'm in and wants to help me out. He's going to help me get my photography business established."

She looks at me incredulously. "How long have you *known* him?"

I look at my Mickey Mouse watch for effect. "About ninety minutes."

Maryam snorts at me in disgust. "Ninety minutes."

"What?" I demand. "We knew after ninety minutes that Haroun was crazy. And yet you thought it was fine for me to marry him. Just because I found Masoud instead of you, you think it's a bad idea. If you'd met Masoud on the street earlier today, you would have dragged him back here yourself. You know you would have. Look at him. He's perfect."

He stretches his arms outward with his palms facing up. Like, *Here I am, not so shabby.*

"How *did* you meet him?" Maryam asks after giving him a once-over. *"At a coffee shop?"*

My mouth drops open from her meanness.

"Eva ran an ad on a Persian singles website," I say defiantly.

Maryam covers her mouth in horror, as I knew she would.

"It's a nice website," Masoud offers. "Very tasteful. Persiansingles.com."

"Do you meet many women this way?" Maryam is so snide.

"Tami's the first woman I've met this way."

The first *woman* he's met this way. I laugh at his choice of words.

"Maryam, he cooks!" I offer up.

She looks at me like I am crazy. "So what?"

"So he cooks! And he lives in *Chicago.* That's good, *don't you think?"* I can see Maryam process that one. It will keep me from running into Ike.

"As long as someone exercises a little *self-control,* there is no need to move halfway across the country," she admonishes me.

"Oh, don't worry, we'll still visit," I say sweetly, misinterpreting her on purpose. "Masoud's parents live in Phoenix and he visits them several times a year. *Isn't that right, honey?"*

I lay it on thick. People with no self-control tend to do that.

"I'm calling Ardishir," Maryam threatens in a huff.

"Fine." I shrug. "He hates Haroun. That's why we aren't engaged already, because he hoped someone better would come along. And someone did."

Maryam glares at me for a moment. Then she throws her purse and sweater on the couch and stomps off to call Ardishir.

Masoud grips my arm as soon as she leaves the room. "What was *that* for? Now she's going to think I'm a total jerk."

"She and I have been arguing lately." I am shaken by his anger and try to take my arm back but he keeps his hold firm.

"You and I had a deal and the deal was we'd tell them after dinner, after they'd gotten to know me." He shakes his head in disgust. "I went through all this trouble to fix them a nice dinner and set the stage for a serious discussion about marriage. I want them to like me. It is very selfish of you to behave this way."

"I'm sorry."

He finally lets go of my arm and turns on his smile. "Okay, then," he says pleasantly. "No harm done. Let's go make this happen."

I walk ahead of him to the kitchen and I am glad he cannot see my face, for I allow myself to snarl at his behavior. Who is he to grab my arm and tell me what to do? He is not my real husband, not yet. He needs to remember that I am doing him a favor just as much as he is doing a favor for me. I resolve that I shall remind him of this every time he forgets it.

Starting right after the wedding.

• • •

When Ardishir arrives for dinner, he is polite to Masoud and open-minded and they find out through the course of conversation that Ardishir knows one of Masoud's cousins, who is an orthopedic surgeon in San Francisco, having met him at several medical conferences over the years. And this is enough for Ardishir to be swayed that my marrying Masoud is the best thing to do.

I stop drinking at the dinner table, and Maryam starts. I observe her as she grows to like Masoud over dinner, despite her initial opposition. Her eyes twinkle at his funny stories. She eats seconds and then thirds of his Mexican cooking. She asks him many questions about his family and his real estate business. She watches how he is respectful to me, making sure I am involved in the conversation and praising my good nature.

After dinner, Masoud and Ardishir go into the living room while Maryam and I stay behind in the kitchen to prepare tea and fruit. She grasps my arm in the same spot Masoud did and squeezes it happily.

"You found yourself a good one, Tami. He's great."

"I'm sorry I was so rude before."

"You weren't rude." She lets go of my arm and reaches into the cupboard for the teacups. "I know I can be bossy."

The four of us enjoy tea and sweets, and then Masoud announces he must leave. He and Ardishir have made arrangements for Ardishir to drive to Phoenix the next day and have lunch with Masoud and his parents before Masoud flies back to Chicago for his Friday meeting. Masoud's uncle will perform the ceremony on Sunday evening.

I walk Masoud to the door and his warm hug tells me he has forgiven me for my rudeness to my sister.

And so has Maryam. She kisses me good night on both cheeks and hugs me close.

"I'm so happy for you, little sister," she whispers.

"Thank you." I squeeze her back. "He's very nice, isn't he?" *Isn't he?*

"He's much better than Haroun," she assures me. "You're right, Haroun is crazy."

"But also very nice."

"Don't worry, Ardishir will meet with him tomorrow after he gets back from Phoenix and tell him the engagement isn't going to happen."

I can't help but feel sorry for Haroun. Not sorry enough to change my mind and not sorry enough to tell him in person instead of making Ardishir do it for me. But I do feel bad, for among him, Masoud, and me, he is the one who most wants to be married.

And for all the right reasons, too.

28

Maryam drives me to Eva's slumber party that Friday, and we stop by Nadia's trailer home to give her a ride as well. She waits in the car while I go to the door to fetch Nadia, and my stomach churns the whole time because I so dislike her husband.

Nadia rushes to answer my knock.

"I'll be ready in just a second. I have to get my stuff."

"Let me help." Nadia looks worried, but she steps back to let me enter. "You have a lovely home," I offer.

She smiles. "Thank you."

It is not a lovely home. It is shabby and old, but it smells of bleach and home-cooked meals.

"I'll get my bag." She disappears into the bedroom.

I am left alone with her husband, Lenny, who does not introduce himself or acknowledge my presence. He slouches on the couch with his alcohol-swollen stomach and watches a basketball game on television. I do not interrupt his game.

I only stand at the door with a friendly smile on my face, so that if he should look over, he will have a favorable impression of me. I want this, for Nadia. To make things easy for her.

I rush to take Nadia's bag when she comes back in the room. Huge with baby and awkward with her broken arm, she looks miserable.

"When're you getting back?" her husband asks, not taking his eyes off the game.

Nadia looks at me. *Any time,* I mouth.

"About noon," she tells him.

"I don't want no rag head in my house. You tell her to keep her ass outside next time. You hear?"

Nadia blushes and looks at me apologetically. I don't even know what he means by this, *rag head,* but I know it refers to me and is unkind. I smile to show her I've taken no offense.

"It was nice to meet you," I tell him cheerily. He looks over at me with a snarl on his face. As Masoud reminded me, courteous people learn courtesy from the discourteous, so I smile sweetly at him. "I've heard *so much* about you."

I feel Nadia's mood lift as we drive away from her husband, and by the time we arrive at Eva's, she seems downright relaxed and cheerful, thanks in large part to Maryam's pleasant chatter. Maryam has asked me many questions about Nadia since learning of her situation, and so she goes out of her way to make Nadia feel safe and welcomed in her car. As we get out of the car, Maryam holds out an envelope for Nadia.

"Here," she says. "I got you a little something."

I look back at her, surprised and pleased. How very thoughtful my sister can be sometimes. She has already brought home many items of baby clothing that she got on sale using her employee discount at Macy's.

Nadia reaches to take the envelope with her one good hand. "I don't know what to say, except thank you so much."

Maryam gives her a smile to remember. "It was nice meeting you, Nadia. I am glad Tami has such a good friend as you. You take care of yourself, now, you hear?"

Nadia nods. "Yes, ma'am." ·

I bend over to kiss my sister good-bye. "Thank you," I whisper. "You are such a good person."

"So are you. See you tomorrow. Have fun!"

Surprise! Surprise!" Eva and Agata yell as they answer the door.

"What is the surprise?" I ask, confused.

"Don't be a spoilsport," Eva snaps happily, and pulls us farther inside. She takes both our overnight bags and dumps them in the bedroom. Then she comes back to the living room and claps her hands together. "Is everybody ready to party?"

"I am," I say, and look around. "Eva, this looks wonderful!" She's made a hand-painted banner that reads, *Congratulations, Girls!* There are white and pink balloons and streamers decorating the living room, and while I know this party is mostly for Nadia, I am so touched to have made such good friends in America in such a short period of time that all I can do is put my hand over my heart and soak it all in.

"Do you live here alone?" Nadia asks wistfully.

"Sort of. My husband went back overseas after we'd been here for six months. So I've been here on my own for the last six."

"Ven does he get-a back-a de next time?" Agata asks.

Eva blows off her question with a wave of her hand. "He

keeps getting extended. I won't believe he's back until I see him on the tarmac."

"You must miss him so much," Nadia says quietly as she stares at their wedding pictures on the fireplace mantel. "You look so happy together."

This is true, I realize as I study their photographs. He is handsome and fit and proud, with an American military look I am familiar with from watching *Top Gun* so many times in Iran on bootleg video. And in Eva's eyes, there is a laughter that runs deeper than I have seen in person.

"Yes," Agata determines, peering at the photos as well. "Our vriend Eva is . . . vat is dat eggspression?"

"Crazy as a loon?" I offer, and delight in Eva's smirk.

"All de bark and no de bite," Agata declares. "She talk like she ees-a de tiger, ven really, she ees-a de pussy cat."

"You know, that's true," I say.

"That is *not* true," Eva quickly contradicts me.

"Really? Have you ever cheated on your husband?" I demand.

She blushes. Eva. Blushes. That can only mean one thing: She has not been unfaithful to him.

"You!" I slap her playfully on the arm. "Giving me all this woman-of-the-world advice. I assumed you were just partying it up while your husband is gone. But you're not, are you?"

"Who's ready for a drink?" She asks this brightly.

"You know zat I am." Agata laughs in her husky voice.

"Me, too," I say.

"Water for me, please," Nadia says gamely, pointing at her stomach.

"We're drinking Cosmopolitans tonight, ladies," Eva informs us as she serves them to us on a tray. We toast to

Nadia's new baby and to my new fiancé, and Nadia and
Agata listen with close attention to the latest updates in my
saga. I tell them how Ardishir spared me from having to tell
Haroun I would not marry him. And, when I am well into
my second drink and on the receiving end of a pedicure by
Agata, I tell them the secret I will not tell my sister, that my
soon-to-be husband is gay.

"It's too bad, too, because he's kind of hot," Eva tells
them.

"There she goes again," I say, grinning at her. "All bark
and no bite."

"What do you think of that, Agata?" Eva asks. "Tami is
going to be a married virgin. Isn't that pathetic?"

Agata frowns. "A contradiction in-a ze terms."

"There are plenty of people who have sexless marriages,"
Nadia defends me. I smile my thank-you.

"Not you, obviously," Eva vollies back. Nadia blushes.

"All I wish to say is that it is better to have a good marriage
with no sex than a bad marriage with good sex." Nadia's
blush spreads all the way to her neck. "Or a bad marriage
with any sex."

"Good point," I tell her.

"No, no, no!" Agata practically yells, sticking her index
finger in the air and weaving it in a drunken manner. "You
must-a haf a good-e marriage *and* a good-e zex."

"Or no marriage and good sex," Eva says.

"No bite, no bite!" I laugh at her. She has completely lost
her ability to make me cringe at her crudeness now that I
know it is only an act.

She ignores me and focuses on Agata. "Speaking of which,
are you and Josef getting it on?"

"Getting it-a ze on." Agata grins at the phrase. "Yes, I-ah
vould say-a ve are-a getting it-a ze on qvite nizely."

"You go, girl," Eva commends her.

Clink, clink. We all turn toward the window. Nadia jumps and cringes away.

"Do you think it's your husband?" I ask her.

She shakes her head. "He doesn't know where Eva lives," she whispers. "And he lost his driver's license." But her already pale face fades a shade more and the fear creeps into her eyes.

Agata and Eva jump up and run to the window.

"It's Josef and Edgard!" they squeal like they are schoolgirls. Eva slides the window open and they lean out. "What do you troublemakers want?" Eva yells. "It's girls only! I'm not letting you up!"

"I haf come to sing a song to my-a bee-utiful Agata," Josef calls to us.

"Oh, this is so romantic," I pine, clutching my hand over my heart. I go to the window and peer down. Edgard stands back, with his hands in his pockets. He looks at us like we are crazy and drunk, and we are, a little bit of both, on this night of all women. He, perhaps, is here only to provide Josef with courage. Josef wears a suit and tie and has his hair smoothed down with pomade.

I retreat from the window to get my camera and take several photographs as he croons a Czechoslovakian love song to Agata. She listens with tears in her eyes until the song ends, then makes her way downstairs to the sidewalk in front of Eva's apartment, to where Josef waits for her. She slaps her hands on both his cheeks and gives Josef a youthful, tongue-laden kiss. I take a picture of this, too.

But then all of a sudden, I feel light-headed. I sink back from the window and set down my camera. With all the excitement, it is easy for me to make my way to the bathroom without anyone noticing that I am falling apart.

29

Thirty minutes later, the doorbell rings.

Nadia again gets that terrified look, thinking that perhaps it is her husband. But I know the doorbell is not for her the instant I see the troublemaking grin on Eva's face.

"I'll get it!" she calls out.

No, no, please, no.

I jump up after Eva and leap over the coffee table to get in front of her. I cannot see him. I cannot go through another good-bye.

"Eva, please, no, I can't. Please, no, you've got to make him go away." My words rush out and I push Eva out of the way and block the door.

"What's gotten into you?" She tries to push me out of the way, but with my adrenaline rushing the way it is, there is no way she can move me.

"No, Eva. I can't. *I cannot see him.*"

"It's not Ike," she tells me coolly.

"Right." I know her. It is exactly the sort of thing she would do.

"It's not, Tami. I promised you that I'd butt out and I did. So if you'll just move your ass and let me open the door, you'll see."

I cross my arms and plant myself. Nadia rises from the couch and comes closer, ready to offer her assistance if I need it. Agata goes to the window and looks out.

"*Vat-a ze hell?*" she asks in confusion.

"It's for Tami," Eva says in exasperation and goes to the window to whisper in her ear. As she does, Agata's face turns from confused to buoyant with excitement.

"Ah." She gives me a reassuring look. "It ees all right, Tami. It ees not your boyfriend."

He's not my boyfriend.

"You're sure?"

She nods. "This ees some-a-thing to a-make you laff."

The doorbell rings again.

"Be right there!" Eva calls. And then she snarls at me, "Move!"

Against my better judgment, I do.

"Go back and sit on the sofa," she orders. "Everybody, have a seat and close your eyes."

With my eyes closed, the beauty of the Arabic belly-dancing music that floods the room is overpowering. I am lulled into the enchanted world of the Middle East until Eva calls, "Open your eyes."

I do, and am confused to find a woman wearing a full chador standing . . . no, make that swaying . . . before us, with a big radio at her feet. Nadia looks as confused as I feel. Agata and Eva laugh at us. My eyes shift back to the woman and I watch as she weaves around in a circle and, with her back to us, waves one arm in the air in a gesture I have never seen before from a woman in a chador.

Women in chadors do not make sensual moves.

Oh, my God.

Eva has hired a stripper.

The instant I realize what is going on, the music changes to an erotic Arab dance-club number and the stripper starts unbundling herself from the chador. She wears high heels and a red garter, which we are able to glimpse as she attempts, gamely but not very gracefully, to extricate herself from the cumbersome chador.

Eva and Agata begin to yell, "Take it off! Take it all off!"

"Stop!" I jump to the radio and fiddle with it until I find the off button to the tape deck. The stripper stops and waits for direction from Eva.

"What's wrong?" Eva asks me. "It's just a joke."

"Please." I hold up my hands. I may be tipsy, but I am not so tipsy as to allow this. "I know this is all for fun, but it is a very serious offense to my religion."

"I thought you weren't religious," Eva protests. "I wouldn't have done it if I thought it would offend you."

"It's okay," I assure her. "I'm not offended. But really, it cannot continue."

Eva sighs. "I booked her when you were still marrying Haroun. I thought, you know, she could teach you a few things for your honeymoon."

"You really think I'd do a striptease with a *chador*?"

She shrugs. "Who knows? You'd kind of think that's part of their attraction, you know? Like tearing the wrapping paper off a Christmas present or something."

"That's a very interesting perspective, Eva," I say, "but I just don't think that's the case."

"Really?" she asks in her cute little Eva-oops way.

"Really," I say back, mimicking her.

"Sorry, Janie," she says with a sigh. "I guess you can go."

The stripper raises her eyebrows at me like *I* am the one who has offended *her*. I give her an apologetic smile. I am not about to judge her morals. If I've learned nothing else in my time here, I've learned this: In America, sex is everywhere and sex is good. For everyone but me, anyway.

Eva opens the door for her stripper friend.

"Excuse me, miss?" Agata suddenly calls to her.

Janie the Stripper turns back.

"Do you-a know how to do zat tvirl-arounda-ze-pole thing?" Agata asks. "You know, pole dancing?"

"Of course," Janie says easily.

"Yes! Great idea!" Eva decides, and turns to me. "Can Janie give us pole-dancing lessons?"

"Please?" Agata pleads.

I hold up both hands in surrender. "That's fine with me. You all go right on ahead. Only, please take off the chador. I'll just get myself another drink."

While I pour myself another Cosmopolitan, Eva pulls a mop and broom and vacuum cleaner hose attachment from her closet. Nadia and I hold hands on the couch as we watch the less inhibited members of our party learn some new moves. Eva struts her stuff with a finesse that makes me suspect she's done this before, but it is Agata I watch. She is clumsy and not at all graceful. The walk-arounds and deep bends look silly coming from a short, pudgy woman my grandmother's age. But her self-confidence is irresistibly sexy.

It is time for presents. Agata places a chair in the center of the living room and instructs me to sit in it to open my gifts.

I pretend to be embarrassed by the rubbing oil that makes one's skin tingle in sensitive areas. I pretend to be amazed by the edible underwear. But in reality, since I know they will be shoved into a drawer, forever unused, they do not embarrass me at all.

And then it's time to open Eva's gift to me. I have no idea what it is when I first open the small, square box, so I look to her for an explanation.

"It's a vibrator," she informs me. "A bunny vibrator like from *Sex and the City*."

"*Sex and the City?*"

"You know, it was only *the most popular show* in America for women under forty."

"I'm afraid we just watch the Persian news from Los Angeles in my house."

Eva crudely demonstrates through her clothes how it is to be positioned and the facial expressions and sounds one is likely to generate while using it.

"They do this on the television show?" I ask incredulously, covering my mouth with my hands and laughing in embarrassed shock. "Can we move on to Nadia's presents, please?"

I get up from the chair of honor and help Nadia settle into it. I bring her gifts over, and Eva watches with feigned interest from the couch as Agata unwraps them for Nadia. Knowing money is tight in her home, we have supplied her with receiving blankets, diapers, a portable play crib, bottles, and bibs, as well as clothing to last until her daughter is eighteen months old. We have even picked out some after-baby new clothing for her, so she can stop wearing that horrid husband's old T-shirts. I can tell from Nadia's expression that it has been a long time since she's been treated so nicely.

"I don't know how I can ever thank you all enough," she says through tears. She cannot wipe them because her one good hand is holding baby clothing. Agata brings over a cloth napkin to wipe Nadia's face.

"We love you," I tell her, and pat her knee. "We wish there was more that we could do for you."

Nadia smiles so bravely for us.

"You forgot about my sister's card," I remind her, and jump to bring over her purse.

"Will you open it for me?" she asks. "I will have trouble doing it with my one hand."

"Of course," I agree gently.

I slit the envelope open and carefully pull out the card. I gasp when I see what is inside.

"What's wrong?" Nadia asks. I look up at her.

"There's, ah, quite a bit of money," I say with a nervous laugh.

"How much?" Eva demands to know.

"A lot."

"It must be a mistake," Nadia says.

"Read the note," Agata suggests.

I unfold the pink linen stationery that contains a note in my sister's handwriting. I take a deep breath and begin reading out loud.

"*Where I am from, there's no such thing as a shelter for battered women.*" I clear my throat as I am reminded of yet another use for veils. They help women to hide their bruises. They enable men to hurt their wives.

"*In Iran, there's no such thing as a second chance. You make your choices, limited though they are, and you live with the consequences forever. I don't know what it's like in Russia where you are from, but here, it's different. Here in America, you get to reinvent yourself as many times as you need to.*"

I pause and look up at Nadia. She sits like a statue and I cannot tell what she thinks of Maryam's note. Agata sits on the floor next to Nadia with her hands clasped so tightly that her knuckles are white. Eva makes big eyes at me and bites her bottom lip. I try to keep my voice steady.

"I have a friend who is driving to the San Francisco Bay area tomorrow. She has room in her car for you, as well as an extra bedroom in her house out there. She says you are welcome to stay with her for as long as you need to. Her name is Nazila; she is a family friend. She will be parked in front of Eva's apartment tomorrow morning at four-thirty A.M. *and she will wait ten minutes for you. You could be across the state line before noon. There would be no way for your husband to find you."*

I again look at Nadia, but she is looking down. At her baby gifts and at her broken arm.

"If you decide to stay, at least please tuck this money away someplace safe where he can't get his hands on it, so it will be there for you when you really need it. With great affection, Maryam."

There is a stunned silence when I finish reading. I let out all my breath and reach to hand the note to Nadia so she can read it for herself.

"She's giving you a thousand dollars," I tell her.

Her eyes immediately well with tears.

"A thousand dollars?" she whispers. "Why would she do this?"

"I will never say another bad word about your sister for as long as I live," Eva declares.

I swallow hard as suddenly I am flooded with memories of my sister and me in Iran that first year after we were back from America. She'd hold me in her lap and sing to me as we watched in the fading twilight as the military tanks rolled past our house. Being so young, I did not understand why I was forbidden from playing outside.

Our world went from blue skies to gray in the span of one year, as we came back to a homeland that seemed to hate us.

We watched helplessly as our parents fell into terrible depressions that to this day have not really lifted. Maryam was the one who pushed the clouds away for me the best she could, with her gentle words and constant touches and her promises of a brighter future when we would all get back to America one day, when we would all be happy together once more.

"My sister cares about you, Nadia," I say with conviction. "She wants to do more than wipe away your tears. In Iran, so often that is all we can do. And it is not enough."

"Nadia, dear." Agata reaches over to her and squeezes her knee encouragingly. "I hope you go."

I brace myself. I think my heart will break all over again if Nadia does not take this chance to start a new life for herself and her baby girl.

"All I've been thinking about is how I can keep my daughter safe," she whispers. "I'd hoped that if I love her enough and kiss her enough, maybe I could somehow protect her from the ugliness of my marriage."

She shakes her head and sounds defeated.

"You aren't even going to be able to *hold* her, with that broken arm," Eva says. "There's no way you can protect her from him."

"I know," Nadia whispers.

"And do you really want her growing up in a world where all she knows is fear?" I ask. "That's what'll happen if you stay. She won't know what it feels like to be safe for even one day."

Nadia takes a deep breath. She looks at me, only at me. "Danny asked me to stay after class the other day."

My heart jumps. I hope his news to her was good.

"He told me that no one will take my baby away from me if I leave my husband." I reach and squeeze her knee. This is good news. "He told me my husband could go to jail for how he has hurt me. He told me I am perfectly legal to stay here without him. I have my green card and there are protections for me."

Her voice has grown bitter, but also stronger.

"Then there is nothing to hold you back," I tell her firmly. "You are so strong and you came all this way for a better life. *And now you can have one.*"

Please, Nadia, take this chance.

Nadia lets out all her breath. The rest of us collectively hold ours. She stares for a long moment at the swarm of presents we have given her.

"These are such beautiful gifts," she murmurs. She sounds dreamy, far away.

I want to take her by the shoulders and shake her. *Come back to this moment. This is the moment that counts.*

"Do you think there will be room in the car for them?" She looks at each of us in turn and smiles back at us as we nod that yes, of course there will be room in the car for her baby things.

"Good," she says. "Because I love them all so much. I love *you* all so much."

"Yay, Nadia!" I yell, and jump up from the couch.

Eva and Agata follow my lead, and soon enough we have surrounded Nadia. We jump and cheer and clap and do a little dance around her chair.

"I wish I could celebrate like you," she tells us, laughing and holding out her broken arm.

"You will someday, because that arm's going to heal just fine," I bend down and remind her quietly. "And someday, Nadia, your heart will not be so sad, either."

She gives me a small smile. "I hope you're right about that."

"I know I am," I say with a confidence I do not truly feel. "Given enough time and distance, the heart will always heal."

I want so badly for this to be true. For her, for me. For my mother, for all women.

30

As I wait for Rose to answer her door the next afternoon, my eyes fall on the running shoes Ike gave me, still resting in the basket Rose so kindly placed outside her door. I have to bite my lip to keep from crying. I am not here to cry over Ike. Today, Rose and I will enjoy our tea date and say our good-byes.

"Tami!" She throws open her door and spreads her arms for a hug.

After we hug, I step back and look at her. "I am getting married tomorrow."

There. I have told her. I have dreaded saying these words to my unmarried Rose.

Her eyebrows rise.

"Are you terribly upset with me?" I say it in a pleading way.

"Not at all!" she declares. "He seems like a delightful young man."

"Who?"

"Ike! That young man who walks you home." Her voice fades as she realizes it is not Ike I am marrying. "Why don't you come in for tea and tell me all about it."

Rose has this way about her that reminds me of my mother. She stands willing to enfold me into her life, to accept me without judgment. Without really even knowing me. *Tell me all your secrets,* she seems to say. *I will like you, anyway.*

I step over her threshold, into La Casa de Rosa, and, as always, I am overcome with its character. It reminds me of Café Poca Cosa, a Mexican restaurant that Maryam and Ardishir took me to shortly after I'd berated Maryam for never cooking anything other than Persian food. It was there I was introduced to cilantro and salsa, two things Masoud has promised me are in Chicago as well. The walls of the restaurant were lime greens and deep purples. Hers are turquoise and magenta, with stenciled flowers arching over the doorways.

While she busies herself preparing our tea, I take a seat at her kitchen table. It is a table for two, with only one place setting.

"Why did you never marry, Rose?"

She sets two saucers and teacups on the table and pours our tea. After she sits, she pushes a small plate of shortbread cookies in my direction. "I would have liked to, I suppose. But the two men I've loved didn't love me back, and the two men who did love me, I didn't really love. After a while, I just came to accept that I was meant to be alone."

"Do you ever get lonely?"

"Sure." She sips her tea and flinches from its heat. "But I know plenty of women who are lonely in their marriages, and to me, that's worse."

I fold my hands into my lap and lean into the table. "I have to get married in order to stay in the United States, you know."

"I expected as much." Her voice is matter-of-fact. Non-judgmental.

"He's gay."

She says nothing.

"He's Persian and he lives in Chicago and I'm not at all sure he's a nice person underneath the surface."

I watch her exhale. Her look is serious.

"Is there no other way?"

I shake my head.

"Tucson is filled with illegal immigrants. Plenty of people live here illegally."

I have read about this in the newspapers. There is a group who hunts them at the border as they cross over to the United States from Mexico.

I shake my head again. "What kind of life would that be? I couldn't get a job. I couldn't go to school. I couldn't travel. And if I got caught, I'd have to leave America forever."

Rose tilts her head. "I'm curious. What does your handsome friend think of your dilemma?"

I stumble. "Ike? He, ah . . . I don't see him anymore."

"I think you should marry Ike." She is so decisive.

"Ike's not ready to be married."

"Are you?"

"Sure." I hear the falseness in my voice.

"But he's not?"

I shake my head.

"Why do you think that is?"

"Because . . ." My voice breaks, and I am forced to pause. "Because I've been told my whole life, *Get ready for marriage, get ready for marriage,* and he's been told, *Go make your dreams come true.*"

She clicks her tongue. *Tsk, tsk, tsk.* "Well, that doesn't sound very fair to me."

I hate it when Americans talk about fairness.

"It's *not* fair, but that's not the point. The point is, it's time for me to be married. It's time for Masoud to be married."

And it's time for Ike to make his dreams come true.

It is the morning of my wedding. Everything is ready. I have picked up all the paperwork I will need from the immigration office. Maryam's wedding dress has been fitted for me. Ardishir has cleared the living room for the traditional ceremony we will have tonight.

My friends from class are all so curious to see what a Persian wedding ceremony is like. And I have left them to wonder, for they will see tonight as my wedding guests.

When my doorbell rings at ten o'clock, I hurry to answer it. I have invited Agata, Eva, Edgard, Josef, and Danny over to make Persian Wishing Soup. Traditionally, a woman who has a wish invites her friends over. Each provides an ingredient and they share the wishing soup. This is supposed to make the woman's wish come true.

For my wishing soup party, I start my own tradition. I do not want this party to be for only me. I want my friends to have their wishes come true, too. So they will toss in their ingredients and it will be *our* soup. Maryam thinks I am crazy to have a party the same morning as my wedding, but this is time just for us. They are all off to Lake Havasu City tomorrow, and I will be in Chicago by the time they return, so this is our farewell luncheon.

Ardishir and Maryam come with me to answer the door. Ardishir practices his videotaping skills, as this will be his job tonight.

"Good morning, good morning!" Josef calls out when I answer the door. He carries with him a beautiful bunch of red roses and a little bag of chopped onion for the soup. I am so happy to welcome him in my home. I introduce him to my sister and brother-in-law.

Agata enters next and hands me two bags. One contains dried apricots sliced into thin strips and the other contains chopped parsley. When I introduce her to my sister, Agata throws her arms around Maryam and lifts her off the ground with the strength of her hug. "So dis is zee voman who has given our Nadia a better life."

Maryam blushes and waves off Agata's compliments. "It's nothing."

"Nothing?" Eva says, barging in and tossing me a bag of chickpeas and a bag of rice. "You Persians need to get over your modesty. You *changed her life* by your kindness and you didn't even know her. You're a hero, in my book."

Ardishir glows from the praise Eva has heaped on his wife. He holds his hand out for Eva to shake and gives her a kiss on both cheeks. "You look lovely as always," he compliments her.

I am suddenly horrified to realize that Danny, our teacher and therefore most honored guest, is still outside the door. Edgard and Carrie are still outside as well. I give them a smile of apology and welcome them all in.

"Thank you so much for coming!" I introduce them to my family.

"Mint leaves and ground cinnamon," Danny says, handing me his plastic bag.

"Turmeric and toasted pine nuts." Edgard hands his ingredients to me.

Agata sees my *sofreh aghd* spread out on the floor. "Is this for tonight?"

"Yes," I tell her. Maryam and I have worked hard to prepare a beautiful *sofreh aghd*. Mine is made of white silk and adorned with many symbolic items.

My class friends cluster around it.

"What's that for?" Carrie asks, pointing at a dish of honey covered with Saran Wrap.

"After the ceremony, Masoud will dip his finger in the honey and I will lick it off. Then we will reverse the gesture. Once we have tasted the honey, we are ensured a sweet and joyous life together."

"I love it!" Carrie tells me. "That's beautiful. Is it a Muslim tradition?"

"A Zoroastrian one," I tell her. "Zoroastrianism came first. Many, many Persian ceremonies and traditions have their roots in Zoroastrianism."

"Ees dat your-a parents?" Agata asks, pointing to a picture of Masoud's parents.

"Those are Masoud's. These are mine." We have placed the photos on either side of the cloth. In the center sits a large mirror, to bring light and brightness to our lives; two candelabras, one on each side of the mirror, to symbolize fire and energy. We have a spice tray to guard against the evil eye; decorated eggs to beckon fertility; and a dish of gold coins to bring us prosperity.

"What's that for?" Eva points to a small plate holding a needle and thread.

"That's my favorite," I tell her. "It's to stitch my mother-in-law's lips together to prevent her from meddling in our marriage. Symbolically, of course."

Maryam thinks I should have left that off the *sofreh aghd* so as not to offend Masoud's mother, but I insisted. It is an old tradition, and who can be offended by tradition? Plus, I mean to send a message: Leave us in peace. I hope Minu includes it on her *sofreh aghd* as well.

Ardishir keeps the camera rolling as I invite everyone to accompany me to the *ashe-paz khaneh*.

"The bathroom?" Eva asks.

Maryam and I giggle. "Why would we prepare our wishing soup in the bathroom?" I ask. "The kitchen," I say in English this time. "Let's all go to the kitchen. I am the *ashe-paz*, which means the cook, or literally, soup preparer. That should tell you how important soup is in our culture."

Everyone washes their hands and helps to make lamb balls by rolling pine nuts, onion, ground cinnamon, salt, and pepper into ground lamb. While they do this, I heat some oil and cook some onion until it is golden. I then stir in the turmeric, rice, and some cinnamon, and after a while I add the apricots, parsley, and soup stock.

"It already smells delicious," Carrie says, peering over my shoulder. She puts her arm around me. "Are you excited for your big day?"

"I am," I tell her. "I only wish I weren't moving so far away from my friends."

She nods. "It's hard, isn't it? Edgard is terribly homesick for his family and friends, too. Even though he knows it's better here."

"It's the contradiction of life," he says. "If I were with them, I would only wish to be far away. Now that I am far away, all I do is wish for one more day surrounded by them."

"The life of an expatriate," Danny agrees.

I love these people. I truly do. They understand me in a way few others can. And they never, ever judge me. Well, except for Eva.

"So just think," she says with her characteristic pluck, "if it wasn't for me, tonight you'd be marrying Haroun."

I flinch at the very mention of his name, which makes the others laugh.

"Stop taping," Maryam urges Ardishir. "The evil eye," she says with a knowing nod to me. Ardishir clicks his tongue at us, but he does stop taping and puts the camera gently down on the kitchen table.

But it is too late. The evil eye is upon us. I know it the moment I hear the doorbell. Maryam and I look at each other in great fear. This can mean nothing but trouble.

It is Haroun at the door.

Or it is Ike.

I have been half expecting Ike to appear ever since things ended so badly between us. I have half hoped there would be some sort of *Bend It Like Beckham* ending, in which Ike would pound upon my door and insist to my sister that he is worthy of me and he wants to marry me immediately to prove his intentions.

But life is so seldom like the movies.

31

At the door is Masoud, the man I am scheduled to marry in a few short hours. He enters with a smile and an enormous batch of tulips, Iran's national flower.

"Is the party starting early? Am I missing my own wedding?" he jokes when he sees me surrounded by my friends at the kitchen table. I hurry over to greet him.

"Thank you so much for the tulips." I take them and sniff deeply. "These are my friends from English class. We're making Persian Wishing Soup."

I introduce Masoud to my friends.

"Ah." He grins and kisses me on the cheek. "And what is your wish, my bride?"

"That our marriage is happy."

"That's an excellent wish." We grin at each other, we co-conspirators.

"Did your parents and uncle get in all right?"

He assures me they are settled nicely at Hacienda del Sol and are resting up for what promises to be a late night.

"I don't want to keep you from your friends, and I certainly don't want to keep you from eating that soup and having your wish granted, but I wonder if I might speak to you for a moment in private?"

"Of course."

I lead Masoud through the French doors that lead to the patio rose garden and fountain in the backyard and squint as I make my way into the sunshine. I take a chair at the wrought-iron table set, and Masoud sits across from me. I must hold my hand above my eyes to shield them from the morning glare. My heart thumps against my chest like it's trying to escape.

He smiles to put me at ease. "Is my bride excited for the big night?"

"Very much so." What I am most excited for is Monday morning when the courthouse opens, so we can register the marriage license. "And my husband, is he excited as well?"

"He is," Masoud assures me. He has a lovely smile.

He takes a slightly deeper-than-normal breath. "There are some things we perhaps should have talked about before now, that in the excitement of our meeting Wednesday I did not think to bring up."

"O-kay." I say it slowly, not panicking because everything he has said so far indicates the wedding is still on, still on, still on. *I am not panicking.*

Liar, my conscience taunts.

"We talked about me paying a dowry to your brother-in-law in case the marriage does not work out."

I nod.

"I had the money electronically transferred to him on Friday."

"Yes, I know. Thank you very much." Ardishir opened an account, and the money will sit there in case I ever need it. My Nadia money, I've come to think of it.

"In America, people don't often pay dowries," he informs me.

"You don't want it back, do you?" That would be so low-class.

"No, no," he assures me. "That is for you, to protect you. It is a good tradition. Yet with so many marriages unfortunately ending in divorce, Americans do something that I think is quite reasonable, and I'm sure you will as well."

I wait to hear what it is I am supposed to find reasonable.

"Has anyone told you about prenuptial agreements?"

I shake my head. My hand is so tired from shading my eyes that I let it fall to my lap. I shift in my chair so my back is to the sun. There, that is much better. Now I can think.

Pre means "before." A nuptial is a wedding.

"A before-wedding agreement?"

"Exactly," he agrees, and pulls out a piece of paper from his shirt pocket. He unfolds it and glances over it but holds it in such a way so I cannot see the words.

"I would like to speak plainly to you. May I?" He gives me a friendly smile.

"Please." I want to snarl at him. I do not appreciate these complications at all.

"You know that I have made some money over the course of my career."

I nod. I don't know specific numbers, but Eva looked up what homes in his neighborhood sell for and the number is in the seven-figure range.

"If our marriage were, unfortunately, to end in divorce, I would not want what I have earned prior to the marriage to be at risk of a loss. I'm sure you can see my point here."

I raise my eyebrows and wait to hear him out. We talked about this the first day we met, and I told him I have no problem with such an agreement.

"I mean, I've been working for fifteen years to establish myself and I made all those business decisions alone and took all those risks alone, and I don't want to lose the rewards from my efforts if, say, for instance, you would choose to seek a divorce as soon as your green card arrives in the mail. Forgive my bluntness." He says this humbly, almost apologetically.

I can feel a deep, guilty blush explode on my face. It is a thought I have not permitted myself to consider consciously. Yet Eva's words pop into mind: *Marry the guy. You won't have to sleep with him. And if you hate him, just ditch him as soon as you're legal.*

"It certainly is not my intention," I assure Masoud. "When one marries, they should marry for life."

"Of course, of course," he agrees. "And yet, I am not comfortable taking this on as a matter of trust."

"That's fine," I say briskly. "I will sign the agreement."

He brightens at my words. "Excellent."

I reach out for the paper. "Do you have a pen?"

He holds the paper close to himself. "There are a couple other small points still to cover as well."

He reaches across the table and takes my hand. It is all I can do not to pull it back. A girl should not spend her wedding day discussing legal matters.

"What are these small points, Masoud?"

"I want for us to have a baby right away."

I exhale slowly, trying to hide my anger. "That's fine."

It is not fine. It is petty and controlling, but there is nothing I can do about it at this late date.

"You're sure?" He gives me a hopeful look.

"That's fine, Masoud."

"Because it is something my parents are very much looking forward to, their only son having a child of his own."

"I said that's fine. We can do that medical procedure anytime."

"Excellent! Then you won't mind this next clause of the agreement."

"You are writing in a contract that we must have a baby right away?"

I like him so much less than I did ten minutes ago.

"The contract states that we will wait to file your immigration papers until after our child is born."

"WHAT?!"

"It is necessary for the same reason the monetary agreement is necessary, to make sure this marriage produces what I expect." Masoud speaks so calmly. This really is a business transaction for him. "You know my motives for getting married. My parents are elderly and infirm. They want very much to see their only son get married and have a baby before they pass on. Your motives in this arrangement are to secure for yourself a green card so you can stay in America forever. This ensures that we both get what we want."

Tears well up in my eyes, and I angrily wipe them. I pull my hand away and glare at him.

Masoud sits back, calm like a businessman. "Signing this doesn't mean we aren't going to have a good relationship. We will have fun and be good friends and have a child together, just as we planned. I really mean this. I want to marry you. I think you're a great girl. I thought we were only formalizing what we already agreed to. But we shouldn't get married if you feel so strongly about not signing this agreement."

Bile rises in my throat. "You know I have no choice. I have to be on an airplane back to Iran on Thursday if we don't get married."

"It may feel as if you have no choice, but you do, Tami. You always have a choice."

"Give me the agreement," I say with venom.

"Are you sure?"

I reach for it. Masoud bites his lower lip and hands it over. He watches as I read through it, ready to hand me a pen when I finish.

"Can you understand it all? It's in English because that is how business is conducted here."

"What is this last part?"

"What last part?"

"The part about custody of children in the case of divorce."

"Oh," he says easily, giving me a half smile. "That part says that in case of a divorce from a marriage that produces children, we shall follow Iranian law for custody purposes."

"Is this a joke? This is a joke, right?"

"No, it's not a joke."

In Iran, the father gets full custody of any sons when they reach the age of two. He gets full custody of any daughters when they reach the age of seven, and I would not even get any visitation privileges. If we were to divorce, I would be dead to my children.

I throw the agreement on the table. "I will *never* agree to this."

"Tami," Masoud tries to reason with me, "I don't want to get divorced. That is not my intention. You have said it is not your intention, either. So this is our guarantee that we *won't* get divorced. Because now we have too much to lose."

"You mean I *have too much to lose,"* I snap at him. "I don't see how you will lose anything, except me, which doesn't seem to be your concern."

"Tami," he admonishes me. "Of course I care for you. As my wife, you will be my best friend. I will always take care of you."

"Do you think I can't read?" I demand. "You say one thing and your contract says another. You get everything you want! You will get married and have children and make your parents proud. They will die happy. Then you can divorce me anytime you want and keep full custody of the children, and I will be left with nothing. Nothing!"

"I would never do that," he promises.

"Then put *that* in the agreement, Masoud."

He pales. "It is not necessary."

"To me it is. Make it say, *Masoud will not initiate divorce proceedings. Masoud will not take the children away from their mother."*

He shakes his head, no. "If you were in Iran, we wouldn't even be having this discussion. I would be the only one who could initiate divorce and I would get custody. Period."

"We're not *in* Iran, Masoud. This is why I *left* Iran. Because of men like *you."*

He doesn't like this, being told he's like the others, like the ones who make such a beautiful country such an intolerable place to live. He narrows his eyes and puts his elbows on the table. He folds his hands and rests his chin on them. "This is nonnegotiable, Tami."

I sit back and stare at him.

"This cannot be happening," I say, stunned. "I just really can't believe this is happening."

He gives me a small smile and raises one shoulder in a shrug. "Sometimes there's a price to pay for freedom."

My eyes sink closed. I lean my head back to feel the sun's

warmth and let out all my breath. All this way I have trav-
eled, all these compromises I have had to make, been willing
to make, and it comes to this. This man wants me to bear his
children and then put them in his arms and walk away.

*Sometimes you need to hold them close, and sometimes you
must let them go.*

I sit up and open my eyes. Around me, I see the cloudless
skies, the clear air, and the buffer of the Catalina Mountains to
the north. A jackrabbit scurries from one hole he's dug under
the wall to another by the agave cactus. Birds sing their songs
of freedom from the palo verde trees around us. The bougain-
villea blooms explosively and the air is scented with the blos-
soms of the honeysuckle. It is so beautiful here. So very, very
beautiful. It is a wonderful country in which to be born. And
American citizenship, it is a wonderful gift to give a child.

Sometimes you need to hold them close.

And sometimes you must let them go.

I lick my lips and then rub them together. I turn my attention to Masoud. The look in his eyes is not entirely unkind.
There is some sense of understanding there, too.

I sigh wearily. "I thought you were coming to me with
good thoughts, good words, and good deeds."

"I have to look out for my best interests here."

I sigh again.

It is the sigh of someone who is very sad. It is the sigh of
someone who has no hope anymore for a happy ending.

"You're very fortunate to be in a position where you can
look out for your own best interests. I am not so fortunate. I
need to look out for the best interests of the children I hope to
have one day."

I give Masoud a rueful half smile as I stand and pass the
prenuptial agreement back across the table.

"And I just don't want them to have a father like you."

32

Things go from horrible to unbearable in a matter of minutes. Masoud begins to holler at me and wave his contract in my face, insisting that I have misunderstood his intentions, that I should sign it and it is no big deal. Ardishir rushes out of the house and shoves Masoud back. A good, old-fashioned Persian shouting match ensues. And I hurry inside, now desperate to get away from the man I intended to marry in a few short hours.

There is dead silence from my classmates when I come back to them and their many pairs of pitying eyes, which confirm what I already know: I've lost my quest to stay in America. Come Thursday, I must go back to Iran.

Agata stands and rushes to hug me. "Honey, you can marry Josef. Right, Josef? You vill marry Tami so dat she can stay, von't you?"

Josef stands up straight and thrusts out his chest. "Good girl, Tami," he declares. "I will marry our good girl."

My tears burst forth at their kindness. He is more than worthy, but I cannot marry Josef. I crumple into Agata's fleshy arms and let her guide me to a chair next to Eva. I bury my head in my hands and try to accept what just occurred.

I have to go back to Iran.

I hear the deliberate *clink, clink, clink* of a soup ladle stirring the pot of Persian Wishing Soup. I look up and emit a bitter laugh as I see Maryam standing there by the stove, stirring and stirring, mocking the fact that there is no need. The soup can be poured down the drain. I have no wishes left; none of mine are to come true.

"The bride has gone to pick flowers, Maryam," I say bitterly.

She looks only at the swirling of the soup, not at her little sister who is so desperately in need of comfort.

"Maryam?"

I see her cheek muscles tighten, but still she does not look my way.

"Don't you want to say I should have listened to you? That I should have followed your plan and married Haroun?"

Her head shakes involuntarily, like she is thinking something she'd rather not say. Like she is suppressing a great anger.

"Say it, Maryam," I demand. "You knew best. Like always. And I should have listened to you. And I deserve to go back because of how stupidly I behaved."

She stops stirring and taps the ladle against the soup pot. She turns to me. "Is that really what you think I want to say to you right now?"

This is such classic Maryam. "*Yes.*"

"I would never bring up such things right now." *Even though they're true*, her tone implies.

"That's so good of you," I spit out at her. "You're so perfect."

"What are you mad at me for?" she yells. "What did I do? Tell me, Tami, exactly where I went wrong, because when I look at this, I can't see what more I could have done to help you out. *You blew it.* You're as stupid as *Maman Joon.*"

I gasp.

"You never wanted to marry anybody! He knew it! That's why this happened. He didn't trust you. You were too busy running around having fun when you should have been demonstrating your sincerity to your future husband that you weren't going to leave him at the first chance you had for your little coffee-shop boyfriend!"

"I didn't see Ike even once since I met Masoud!"

"That's not the point! Your heart was never in it."

"How would you know?" I scream in Farsi. "You give up the right to think you know me when you leave home and stay away for *fifteen years*, Maryam! What kind of sister does that? Tell me. What kind of sister, what kind of daughter, does that to her family?"

Maryam's face crumples. She opens her mouth to defend herself but no words come out. Eva grips my arm. I turn to her. "*What?*"

"Calm down," she cautions. "Don't take your anger out on your sister."

"Whose side are you on here?"

"Yours, Tami. But what happened has nothing to do with your sister, and you know it. Just be quiet for a little while."

"Aaaargh! *You're* the one who always talks too much, Eva. *You're* the one who needs to be quiet once in a while."

I look around at them all, ready to take on anyone who dares cross me.

"Should we go?" Danny asks suddenly. "Maybe we should go."

"Yes," Edgard quickly agrees. "We should go."

"Damn right we should," Eva mutters.

My classmates give their hurried good-byes and are out the door in less than a minute. Eva, the last to leave, slams the door behind her.

I peek out the back window. Masoud is gone. Ardishir sits alone at the table, his head sunk in his hands. Maryam continues to stand there staring at me.

"You better go check on your husband," I tell her. "It looks like he needs you."

"You need me more," she says quietly.

"No," I tell her plainly. "I don't need you. There's nothing you can do for me anymore."

33

I kick my bedroom door closed behind me and look around for something else to kick. I see my suitcase propped against the dresser, so I go over and kick it and then I kick it again. I was already packed for my new life in Chicago.

And now I have to go back to Iran.

I have to go back to Iran.

My *hejab* is buried at the bottom of my suitcase, underneath my beautiful purchases from Victoria's Secret. I was so sure I would never have to wear it again.

I unzip my suitcase, pull it out, and drape it over my head. I stare at myself in the mirror. There I am again, me with a veil, looking more like *Maman Joon* than I ever have.

This thought nauseates me. I yank the *hejab* off and drop it to the ground and for the next hour I lie on my bed and stare at the ceiling. I do not send mean thoughts Masoud's way; it seems there is no point. It was not meant to be, that is all. There is some reason I am needed back in Iran. Perhaps my parents will require my assistance in ways they do not yet know. It is good for older people to have at least one child remain with them, to care for them as they age.

You're lying to yourself, Tami. They don't need you and you let them down. You failed them.

Maryam was right. I did waste too much time with Ike. Eva and I should have placed ads earlier on Persian singles websites, and I should have spent those hours after class calling each prospect on the telephone. I had three months. I could have met so very many men in this way. I could have even gone to an Internet café in Tehran and placed my ad before leaving. I should have insisted to Haroun that we marry immediately, even without Ardishir's permission. Failing that, I should have married Masoud the same day I met him. We should have come back to my sister's house already married, before he had time to decide he needed a contract from me.

I think these thoughts over and over, around and around, for hours, until finally there is a tapping on my door.

"Come in."

It is Ardishir. He looks devastated. I sit up in bed and he comes to sit next to me. "God, Tami, I am so sorry."

"It's okay," I tell him. "I'll be all right back home. I miss my parents."

He shakes his head. "I called Haroun just now," he says after a long moment, then purses his lips. "I thought maybe, you know . . ."

"He said no, right?"

"He said no."

I nod. "It's okay," I whisper.

"It's not."

"Well, there's nothing we can do about it. Maybe my father will be able to get another visa for me next year or the following year and I can try again."

Ardishir gives me a sad smile. "You're too good for this. You should not have to jump through all these hoops in order to stay here. America would be lucky to have you."

I let out my breath. I would be lucky to have America. I *was* lucky to have it for the short time I did.

"I have a favor to ask of you, Ardishir."

"Sure, anything."

I reach over to my suitcase, pull out the camera he gave me and my photo album, and I hand them to him.

"Will you keep these for me?"

"I, ah . . ." He purses his lips and I can tell he is trying not to cry.

"Please," I say. "It's best I leave them behind. They'll never make it through the airport. And I can't stand the thought of their dirty hands on them, pawing through them and . . ."

I stop. I can so clearly see how it will unfold if I take these pictures. I would pull on my veil as we enter Iranian airspace. I would step off the plane onto Iranian soil—the soil of my homeland—into the chaos of Mehrabad Airport. My parents will wait anxiously for me, but they will have a long wait, for because my passport has an American stamp in it, I will doubtlessly be searched and harassed. I will be pulled aside into a windowless room and forced to defend my photographs. They will call me a whore and a *badjen* and tell me I should be ashamed of myself for having loose morals. I will sit there, veiled and silent and docile and in fear. I will let them say these horrible things in the hopeless hope that they will give me back my pictures. I would rather die than endure watching them tear my pictures into pieces with their hateful, dirty hands.

I hold up a photo of Eva in a miniskirt and thigh-high leather boots. Ardishir smiles. I hold up one of Agata pole dancing. He laughs. "You see why I can't take these back with me."

Ardishir reaches out and cups my cheek in his hand. "You're sure, *Tami Joon?*"

My tears start falling at his touch. I bite my lip and nod.

"Okay." He drops his hand and slowly goes through my photo album. "You've really got talent. I hope you know that."

I say nothing. Talent means nothing in Iran. Creative expression can kill you.

When Ardishir gets to the last page in the album, he finds the long-ago photo of *Maman Joon* holding me at the ocean that day. He pulls it out from its place and tries to hand it to me. "You need to keep this one at least."

"I don't want it," I choke out. "I don't think I can stand looking at it anymore."

He again tries to hand it to me. "You need to keep it. Maryam has told me how much it means to you."

"Why is she so mad at Maman? I don't think she has any right to be mad at her."

Ardishir shrugs. "You can't help how you feel, can you? If you're mad, you're mad."

"But why?"

Ardishir stares at the photograph for a long moment.

"Please, Ardishir. Tell me."

His eyes are black when he looks at me. "Your mother is the one who decided the family should return to Iran. It was right after Khomeini arrived back from exile. She thought things would be so much better in Iran. You know, that women would get to keep all the freedoms they'd been granted under the Shah, only there would be none of the Shah's corruption. And they'd all get to help create this just society."

"Lots of people thought that," I counter, stunned though I am. I'd always thought it was my father's decision. I'd always thought they went back for only a visit, and got stuck. "It's not fair for Maryam to be mad at her for this."

"Everyone told your mother not to return. Her parents, her grandmother. Even your father was very wary. But she insisted. And then . . . well, you know the rest, I'm sure."

"I don't think I do."

Ardishir gets up from the bed and walks to the window. Facing away from me, he says, "You know your mother was arrested, right?"

I gasp. I cover my mouth with my hand and shudder at the thought of my poor mother being hauled off to jail. Tears fill my eyes as I shake my head. "No," I whisper. "I didn't know this."

"They'd only been back two weeks when Khomeini mandated that women had to wear the veil again. She was arrested at a protest. She wasn't an organizer or anything, she just was in attendance and happened to be one of the ones they hauled off. She spent something like five months in jail. Maryam doesn't know what happened to your mother in jail. It's something no one talks about. But all the fight left her. All her confidence. Maryam said she's never been the same since."

I reach for the photograph. I stare and stare at *Maman Joon*. At her long free-flowing hair. Her muscled legs. At her certainty that she could comfort me in the way I needed. She lost all that, and so much more, because of one bad decision.

"I remember running around our house in Iran, wearing my mother's *hejab*. She got so mad at me. She chased me around, yelled at me, grabbed it back. But I thought it was so exotic." My voice breaks. "Isn't that all that every little girl wants? To be just like her mother?"

I look into her confident eyes. *What did they do to you? Did they rape you? Humiliate you? Force you to renounce your beliefs? You must have wondered if what had happened was even real or if you were going crazy. So soon back from America, you must have lain on a mattress in a sunless prison cell, with cockroaches crawling through your hair, and you could still smell the salt of the ocean, couldn't you? You could still remember the breeze in your long black hair. You must still have remembered what it was like to watch your two daughters run open-armed into the waves. Did you remember lifting me up that day, Maman? Did I get knocked down by a wave and become afraid? Did you yank me out of the water and tuck me into you, into the person I knew best, the person with whom I always felt most safe? Did you think of that day at the beach, Maman Joon, when you were locked in that prison cell?*

Yes, my mother made a choice. And yes, it completely altered the course of her life in a horrible way. Once upon a time, the world *was* hers for the taking; the proof is in this photograph. And she would have wanted that for me and for Maryam. If she had any inkling of what was to come, I know with all my heart that she would not have made the choice she did.

I forgive her. Unlike Maryam, I forgive our mother.

I raise the picture to my lips and I gently kiss the image of my mother. Ardishir is right. I must keep this precious photograph forever. It is uniquely important to me.

But the others—well, I know just the person to give them to.

"Will you do me a favor?" I ask Ardishir.

"Of course. Anything."

I reach into my suitcase and pull out an envelope that contains all my negatives. I hand them over.

"I have a friend named Ike," I tell him in a raspy voice.

"And after I'm gone, I'd like you to give these to him. Maryam will know where to find him."

Ardishir nods at me. His eyes are wise and sad. Clearly, he has heard about Ike.

"He's opening a coffee shop soon, my friend is, and he told me once...that he'd display my work...and I thought maybe..."

I cannot go on. I collapse into Ardishir and sob. "Oh, Ardishir, I've ruined everything, haven't I?"

34

It is early the next morning. Maryam has broken the news to my parents. Ardishir has booked my return flight to Iran. And, with their kind urging that I should collect some last-minute memories, I find myself with my classmates in a rented minivan on the way to Lake Havasu City.

It is a long seven-hour ride. Edgard, our driver, pushes the button on the van's CD player to play Woody Guthrie's track number four, "This Land Is Your Land." It is fun the first time, and we sing along the second and third times as well, but after that we groan in protest and he ignores us and plays it perhaps literally one hundred times. Agata and Josef bicker. And Eva tells me every dirty joke she knows and explains each to me in excruciating detail.

But once we arrive, the fun begins. We park the minivan near the London Bridge and have a Strongbow cider beer in one of the English pubs in the fake-London tourist village. I look forward to telling my girlfriends in Iran that I not only visited America but a little bit of England, too. A replica, anyway.

Josef has rented for us a thirty-six-foot houseboat that comes with its own captain. It's amazing. Here we are in the middle of the Mohave Desert and there is this huge blue-green lake nestled in the canyons. It's a man-made lake, and I think this says so much about the American spirit. Give them a desert, they turn it into a lake.

We tour the boat, touching everything. None of us has experienced such luxury before—there is even a Jacuzzi on deck! This boat has three stories and three bedrooms and is bigger than my home in Iran. Josef points out all the amenities, but he doesn't need to worry about *me* overlooking anything. I have left Ardishir's camera at home, but I tuck everything into my heart, to draw on later. I know this trip will be over all too soon.

After we inspect the houseboat, we head upstairs to the sunshine. We line up side by side at the front of the boat as the captain takes our picture before setting off to find us a private cove to anchor for the evening. I smile at Eva beside me. I close my eyes and lift my face to the sun. I fill my lungs with this fresh air and I luxuriate in the moment. I reach for Eva's hand and she squeezes mine.

"Come on," she announces to everyone. "Let's drink some more beer." We pass the afternoon playing blackjack and throwing fishing lines into the water. Edgard and Josef catch three fish each, which the captain agrees to grill for our dinner. The others change into their bathing suits and go swimming off the side of the boat once we arrive at our private cove. I do not join them, for I don't know how to float. At least, I don't think I do. I may have learned as a child in

America, but I would have forgotten as a girl in Iran. And so I cling to the side and shout encouragement to my friends. The sunlight glistens on the waves.

When they tire of swimming, Agata and Josef disappear for a period of time. They come back up to the deck wearing thick terry-cloth robes. Later, Edgard and Carrie disappear for a time.

"They're going to have sex, you know," Eva leans over in her deck chair to inform me.

She is so predictable. "Good for them, Eva."

"Hey, let's have our next beer in the hot tub," she suggests. "It's getting chilly up here."

"I don't think so."

"Have you ever taken a hot tub before?"

I laugh. "You know I haven't."

"Then come on. You've got a lot of firsts and lasts yet to do before you go back."

"I have nothing to wear."

"I brought an extra suit for you."

We descend to the bedroom we are sharing. She ruffles through her bag and tosses me a swimsuit.

"Here, it'll match your cowboy hat."

I gasp and cover my mouth with my hands. It's a pink bikini.

"What's wrong?"

I stare at her in wonder. "Did I tell you about my mother? About how she wore a pink bikini like this when she lived in America?"

Eva shakes her head slowly, realizing that for some reason, this is a big deal for me.

"Eva, my mother wore a pink bikini!"

"And . . . ?" She looks at me like, *Yeah, so what?*

"I should have married Masoud," I say miserably, and sink onto my bed.

Eva shakes her head in disagreement. "He's an *asshole*. You did the right thing. I'm just sorry I even got involved. If it wasn't for me running that stupid personals ad, you'd be married to Haroun by now."

I have to laugh. "Who would have thought Haroun would turn out to be the keeper?"

We share a laugh at his expense. But it is short-lived. I pick up Eva's pink bikini and smooth it out on my leg. It's tiny. Tinier even than the underwear I have on.

"You know why I quit teaching in Iran?"

Eva shakes her head.

Tears well just thinking about it. "I couldn't do those ceremonies anymore. I got sick for days every time I had to help a girl get ready."

"What ceremonies?"

"When a girl turns nine, our school officials hold a ceremony for her. It was my job to prepare her. I had to dress these girls in a white *hejab* that covered their whole bodies."

Eva swigs her beer. "There's nothing to cover at the age of nine!"

"I was to tell them to listen carefully to the religious men who would speak to them in the ceremony, who would tell them that from this day on, they cannot run about freely. They cannot laugh too loudly; they are not allowed to play with boys anymore except for their brothers. They must cover themselves anytime they go out in public, anytime they will be around men."

My voice drops to a whisper. "I *hated* it. Every time I wrapped those white *hejab* around them, I felt like I was smothering whatever it was that was special about them, whatever hopes and dreams they had."

"Maybe you were just telling them to tuck their dreams away somewhere safe, for when the day came that they could live the life they choose."

I hand the pink bikini back to Eva. There is no way I can wear it.

"That day will never come," I say bitterly. "Not for them and not for me."

The next day, Agata and Josef announce they want to leave Lake Havasu City and make the two-hour drive to Las Vegas and get married, with us as their witnesses. They tell us they have already booked our hotel rooms at The Venetian.

"Now-a you can tell-a everyone zat you visited America, England, *and* Italy!" Agata tells me, as if she were doing this all for me.

"I have to get back," I tell her regretfully. Las Vegas is in the other direction from Tucson.

"We can get back tomorrow, can't we?" Edgard asks hopefully. He turns to me with a pleading look. "I've been wanting to go to Las Vegas ever since I got to America, Tami."

"Let me ask my sister."

"Don't ask her," Eva instructs. "Just call her once we're there."

I really want to go. I really want to see Las Vegas, the City of Sin, with Eva, who has tried so hard to corrupt me.

"Maryam's working today," I tell her. "Maybe I could leave a message for her at home."

Eva grins. "Maybe you could."

I tell Maryam in the message that there has been a slight

change of plans, and I am sorry but I am going with my friends to The Venetian in Las Vegas and I will not be home until Wednesday night. I hang up the phone and smile broadly at Eva.

She winks at me.

And off we go.

For all of us, this is our first time in Las Vegas. I am sure we look like the new-to-America tourists that we are. Collectively, we view the extravagance of Las Vegas with a mix of delight and disgust. Agata informs us that the energy required to run the Dancing Fountains at Bellagio for one hour could feed a family of six in Poland for a month. Edgard tells us that the tips collected in one hour by a gondolier at The Venetian could vaccinate an entire village in Peru.

I walk arm in arm with Eva. The minutes are ticking by. I feel an intense need to keep her close, to touch her and bask in her laughter. I am certain I will never meet anyone like Eva ever again.

Ahead of us walk Josef and Agata, also arm in arm. Suddenly they stop and Agata points to a wedding chapel up the block.

"Zis ees eet!" Agata declares.

Danny wrinkles his nose. "An Elvis Presley wedding?"

"*Love me tender, love me sweet,*" Josef croons to Agata. He sings very off-key.

They take each other for a-better and-a zee worse, in seeckness and in-a zee health, for as long as zee both-a shall live. We clap as Elvis pronounces them husband and wife and we cheer as they kiss and walk down the little aisle out of the chapel to the tune of "Burning Love." *A hunk, a hunk of burning love.*

While they are off consummating their marriage in the next room over, the four of us break out the champagne and hold our own little party while we wait for them to join us for a celebration dinner.

Eva knows how to keep a party fun. She turns on the country-music video channel and teaches me some more line dancing. Edgard and Carrie practice their two-step. The four of us have great fun toppling into one another often as we try to dance between the beds and the television. I relish the unrestrained laughter of my friends, and I want very much to keep it going, to hold this day in my heart forever.

So when Eva urges Carrie and me to learn her new poledancing moves, for once I am willing. For once, I will not be the spoilsport. We have no poles, of course, so we only pretend we do. Feeling fuzzy from my drinks, I tip to the side three times in a row as I try the bend-and-thrust and fall against Carrie each time. Finally, she and I fall to the floor, howling in laughter while Eva pole dances by herself. Edgard sits on a chair at the desk and covers his eyes in mock horror.

I am in the middle of a gulp of champagne when there is a knock on the door. Eva slinks her way over, dancing suggestively the whole way. As she opens the door, she yells, "I hope you did a pole dance for your new husband, or you're going to have to do it right here, right now, in front of all of us."

The rest of us laugh at her. But then I see her laughter turn to confusion, and when I look past her, I see the reason why.

It is not Agata and Josef who are at the door.

It is Ike.

Finally, finally, there is a knock at the door and it is Ike.

35

It is Ike, and I have been drinking, which causes me to think that nonsensical things make perfect sense. That is the only reason I can imagine why it suddenly seems smart to throw my champagne glass at the table five feet away, to dive across the bed and to roll off it onto the floor by the window and try to hide from him.

This might have worked if it was pitch black in the room and if he hadn't already seen me. But it's not and he has and so this is a really stupid thing to do.

"What exactly do you think you're doing?" He stands in the narrow aisle between the bed and the window, looking down at me in disbelief.

"A clever trick?" I offer.

He shakes his head and smiles at me.

"I'm going back to Iran on Thursday," I tell him.

"So I heard." His eyes are burning blue.

"This is my going-away party. We were pole dancing. Right, Eva?" I pop my head up so I can see over the bed, and find everyone looking at me like I'm crazy.

"Focus, Tami," Eva orders me. "Ike came all this way to see you. Maybe he has something to say."

"Oh!" I exclaim, and turn to him. "Did you come here to see me?"

"You're drunk, aren't you?"

I consider this. "I might be." I think a little longer. "Yes," I decide. "I'm almost certain that I am. Would you like a drink, Ike?"

"Oh, my God." He laughs. "You're trashed."

"I am not trash!" I say indignantly.

"You have *no* tolerance."

"I am very tolerant!"

He turns to Eva. "How much did she drink?"

Eva shrugs. "Not much. We only had two bottles between the four of us, and the second one's still half full. She's just a lightweight."

Ike looks back to me with an amused expression. He holds out his hand. "Up you go, Drunk Girl."

I reach for him and yank playfully, just hard enough that he loses his balance and falls on top of me. We are wedged into a very tight space and I have never had a man on top of me like this and all I can do is laugh and laugh. Ike pushes himself up so he can look at me. His face is inches from mine.

"You're not going to make this easy, are you?" he asks.

I giggle. "You have big nostrils."

"Jesus Christ." He springs back up and crosses to the other side of the room. All of a sudden, the strangeness of the situation hits me and I try to shake the fuzziness from my brain.

I get up from the floor, stand up straight, and smooth my

skirt and sweater. I look at Ike and the others while I pat down my hair. Everyone looks so serious.

"What are you doing here?" I finally ask him.

He tilts his head and looks at Eva. Eva's eyes twinkle back at him.

"Eva, did you arrange this?"

She shakes her head, not taking her eyes off Ike.

Ike turns to me. "Maryam came to see me at Starbucks."

My heartbeat quickens to the point that I feel I might pass out. I am instantly sober.

Ike motions me over with his pointing finger. "Come here, Persian Girl."

I shake my head and look at the others. Carrie sits on Edgard's lap. Eva leans against the dresser with her arms crossed. She makes big eyes at me and gestures with her head toward Ike. *Get over there,* she is telling me.

I swallow hard and reluctantly start over to him. He meets me halfway, takes my hand, and leads me to the bed. We sit side by side, our legs touching. It is all so very awkward. He holds my hand tightly, like he never wants to let me go.

All I can do is fight back tears as I imagine what Maryam must have told him and how mad it must have made him to learn I lied to him the entire time.

But he's here. He can't be too mad. This thought alone keeps me from crying in shame.

After a long moment, he exhales loudly. His face is so pale, his eyes so frightened. This is a look I have never seen from him before.

"I'm so sorry I didn't tell you what was going on," I say quietly.

He nods and takes a deep breath. Then he shifts on the bed so he faces me directly. It is like the others are no longer there. His eyes search mine, searching for I don't know what.

"You should have told me," he chokes out.

"I didn't know how." I swallow hard.

His eyes moisten. "This last week has been the worst week of my life."

"Mine, too," I whisper.

Ike reaches his hand to my chin and pinches it lightly. "Tami, don't you know I'd do anything for you?"

My heart lurches.

We are interrupted by a knock at the door. Eva rushes to get it and shushes Agata, who bursts into the room with Josef, ready to go for the dinner party we have planned. Agata's eyes fall on Ike.

"Oh," she murmurs, and pulls Josef against the wall so Ike and I can continue.

"That's Agata and Josef," I inform Ike. "They just got married."

"Congratulations," he tells them curtly, and turns back to me. "So let's talk about us."

I gulp a huge breath of air. Ike grips my hand and shakes his head. "I've never felt about anyone else the way I feel about you, Tami. I know we haven't known each other long, but it doesn't matter. I've never felt this way about anyone before. I love you. Totally and completely, I love you."

Tears fill my eyes. He reaches for both my hands, and holds them so gently. He strokes his thumb across the back of my hand just like my father did when I was a child.

"I've never felt this way, either." I can hear the ache in my voice. When you love someone, there is suddenly so much more to lose.

Ike lets go of my hands and stands, but only for a moment. When he drops to one knee and reaches for them again, my heart thunders.

I have seen this in the movies.

I know what comes next.

"I think maybe fate brought us together." His sweet voice shakes. "I think all the stars were aligned in exactly the right way, you know? I mean, consider all the bad that had to happen in order for you to end up here, in Tucson, Arizona."

I reach for his hand, bring it to my lips, and kiss it. My beautiful philosopher-poet Ike. He is trying so hard.

"We're in Las Vegas, Ike," I correct him, and ruffle his hair playfully.

He cracks up with laughter and his nervousness leaves him. I look to the others, who are laughing as well. And all of a sudden, I know for certain: *I am going to have laugh lines someday, too.*

I look back at Ike. "I love you," I tell him. "I love you, I love you, I love you."

He smiles and firms his grip on my hands. "Tami, I have something very important to ask you. Are you ready?" His face turns serious.

"Wait." I pull him up off his knees so we stand eye to eye.

"Tami Soroush, will you marry me?"

His words are so simple, so earnest. We stand together as equals and he has asked me to marry him. I break into a broad smile. What a question my dear Ike has asked. Could he even imagine my answer would be no?

Over Ike's shoulder, I look at my friends. Eva holds her hands over her mouth, waiting to scream in joy when I say yes. Carrie and Edgard clutch each other, tears of happiness running freely down their faces. My gaze rests on Agata and Josef, two people who have found true love again so late in life. Two people who know better than most that amid all of the horror of life, that amid all its pain, there can also be incredible beauty. They know better than most that love is not something to walk away from.

I turn back to Ike and crinkle my eyes into the sweetest smile I can.

"You were the first American man I spoke to, did you know that?"

He shakes his head, *No.*

"You were! And I was so scared. I had to summon all my courage that day to ask for something so simple as a glass of water."

He grins. "And I made you take that horrible iced tea you hated so much."

I laugh at the embarrassing memory. But only briefly, for never has a moment been so important in my life.

"And now here you are, asking me to marry you. You are so brave."

He squeezes my hands. I squeeze back.

"I don't think it was a coincidence that we met, either, Ike. I think I was supposed to meet you. Beautiful you." I reach to stroke his cheek, touch his lips. I continue, softly, "You have such wonderful dreams and plans, and you're working so hard to make them come true. I think I was supposed to meet you first so that you could remind me what it is to dream. And what a wonderful gift that is to give a person. *Thank you.*"

These last words come out in a choked whisper. For I was shrouded in white when I turned nine, too, just like those sweet girls I taught. And the dreams I smothered that day *must* be tucked somewhere deep inside. *They must be.* It is up to me to find them again.

"I want to marry you, Ike. I do, with all my heart. I want to stay in America and help you and support you as you make your dreams come true."

His eyes well with tears. And I know he will wait for me as long as it takes.

"But I have dreams, too."

He nods. "And I'll make yours come true, Tami. I promise."

He takes my breath away, Ike does.

But I have to make my own dreams come true.

"Ike," I begin, but have to pause. There is a lump in my throat that my words cannot force their way through. I am dangerously close to becoming hysterically weepy.

Seeing this, Ike steps toward me, tries to pull me to him for comfort. But it is not comfort I need. It is courage. I must ask for what I want in life, or I'm never going to get it.

"One of my dreams," I begin again, and again I have to pause. *Breathe.*

"One of my dreams..."

"Say it!" Eva demands from the side of the room. "Just say it, already!"

I glare at her. I open my mouth to scold her for her rudeness, but then I realize that my anger toward her has given me the resolve I need. I turn back to Ike.

"One of my dreams is to live alone. All by myself." I redden. "I know this may not seem like such a big dream, and maybe it is only a silly little dream, but there it is. I want to live alone."

I have confused him.

"You don't want to get married?" he asks.

"I want for us not to jump into everything so fast." It is all suddenly very clear to me. "I want for us to date. Really, truly date. Go to dinner. See a movie. Maybe even dinner *and* a movie."

He laughs. He remembers that day on Rose's porch just like I do. And I think he gets it then. We have not even been on one official date and he has asked me to marry him, yet this is America, where dating comes first and then comes love and *then* comes marriage. And *then* come the babies in the baby carriage.

"I want to hold your hand and walk down the street with you and not be afraid of showing the world how I feel. I want to treasure every moment of falling in love. I want to learn how to kiss you without fear."

He leans toward me. "I think you kiss pretty well already," he whispers in my ear.

I kiss his cheek and step back.

"I want to make my own money and not have to ask anyone's permission to go on trips with my friends. I want to maybe buy my own red scooter. And I want to live with you someday, when we're ready. When *I'm* ready."

I give him the biggest, bravest smile I have. "That is what I want."

"You drive a hard bargain, Persian Girl." His eyes have a look of tearful pride. "I don't think I've ever heard you say *I want* before."

Oh, my heart, my heart. It has leapt right out of my body and into his. I cannot remember a time I said the words *I want* out loud.

"When the only answer a little girl ever receives is no, from her parents or her teachers or her world, at some point she stops asking for what she wants. She begins to expect nothing, so as not to be disappointed when that's exactly what she gets." I exhale, shaken by my own realization. "But," I tell him, "as it turns out, I do have wants."

He smiles at me.

I grin back. "I have a lot of wants."

"Good."

I feel the sparkle in my eyes. "The bride wants to pick some flowers."

There. I have made my declaration to the world.

"Then go," my beautiful Ike encourages me. "Go pick your flowers."

I break into a broad smile. I grip his hands and look into his ocean eyes, and I already know, before even asking, that his reply to me is going to be *yes*.

"Will you marry me, Ike? Under these conditions? Will you, please?"

And even though I already know his answer, it is very sweet to hear the words.

"*Yes,*" he tells me. "Absolutely, I'll marry you."

The instant he says it, my friends burst into cheers and squeals and yells of congratulations.

"I love you," I tell him firmly as I throw my arms around him. "I love you so much."

We hold each other for a long time. When Ike finally steps back, he takes my face in his hands and kisses me gently on my lips. And I think perhaps it is the sweetest kiss the world has ever known.

The best part of what comes next: When we get married by the Elvis impersonator later that evening, *I do not wear a veil.*

Epilogue

It is eight months later.

I have flown on an airplane to visit Nadia in San Francisco. Ike would have liked to come, but his coffee shop is scheduled to open next week and he cannot spare the time.

It is windy today, but I don't mind. I love the feel of the ocean breeze dancing its way through my hair. I am at the ocean with Nadia and her beautiful baby girl. She gurgles and squeals with delight at the world around her. I have never seen a baby so happy. Nadia has named her daughter Maryam, after my sister. My sister is also pregnant now, and she is also having a girl. I made Maryam promise that she will name her baby Hope. For above all else, a Persian girl must have hope.

I am here at the ocean because I have a promise to fulfill for my father, who most likely will never again set foot on this stretch of sand, at this beach he and my mother loved so much.

I hold in my hands the little blue perfume bottle he gave me for my fifth birthday, the one I was disappointed to discover contained not perfume, but rather grains of sand he collected from these very shores. I was so young then. I did not understand what a precious gift it was.

Slowly, deliberately, not rushing this moment, I unscrew the lid of the perfume bottle. After I give it a few shakes, the sand tumbles out, easily catching in the breeze and gently finding its way back to the shore it was taken from so many years ago.

I look out over the ocean with far eyes, and I see my house in Iran. I am outside, looking toward the living room window. My parents stand inside, facing out. They hardly ever go outside anymore. My father has his arm around my mother, and she leans her head on his shoulder. I see that they are sad and happy at the same time, for although it caused them great pain, they made the right choice. They held my sister and me close for as long as they could. And then, when we were ready, they let us go.

Thank you, Baba Joon. *Thank you*, Maman Joon.

Thank you so very much for giving me this chance to be happy.

I whisper this into the wind, confident my words will find their way home.

About the Author

LAURA FITZGERALD is married to an Iranian-American and divides her time between Arizona and Wisconsin. For more of her writing, visit www.laura fitzgerald.com.